"I simply never had your opportunities… or your courage." He leaned forward a little, and Brendan reciprocated, and their lips met.

Brendan pulled back abruptly. "No. No, sir, I must not, you have been too kind—"

It might have been the brandy, the high emotional fervor of the evening, or the loneliness that had been Carlisle's constant companion for the past decade. Perhaps it was all three. "If you don't wish this, then go. But I'm fifteen years your senior, and you need not fear for me."

Brendan pulled him close as a drowning man might. They clung to one another, embracing so fervently that the chairs they sat upon began to creak.

"Not here." Carlisle managed to resist the intense attraction. "We must go upstairs. If you wish—"

Brendan stared at him as though mesmerized, his pupils huge and dark. "Since the moment I first saw you."

Somehow they managed to remove to Brendan's bedroom without waking any servants. A small part of Carlisle's mind was warning that this was a terrible mistake and he must stop immediately, but he could not heed it. For the first time in ten years he felt alive again, consumed with affection and desire for this beautiful young man.

He locked the door after they entered; ⌐⌐⌐⌐ ⌐⌐d the bolt home for safety's sake. "I'll not ask aga  ʹtain, but if you should change your mind—"

Brendan spun and threw himself agains⌐ ʹping both arms around him. "Please," he said h stop asking me to run away. Send me off if you wi ⌐ther be dead than endure your indecision."

M/M Romances from Running Press

TRANSGRESSIONS, by Erastes

FALSE COLORS, by Alex Beecroft

TANGLED WEB, by Lee Rowan

LOVERS' KNOT, by Donald L. Hardy

Available now
Wherever books are sold

TANGLED WEB

An M/M Romance
BY LEE ROWAN

RUNNING PRESS
PHILADELPHIA • LONDON

9 8 7 6 5 4 3 2 1
Digit on the right indicates the number of this printing

Library of Congress Control Number: 2009927579

ISBN 978-0-7624-3684-2

Cover design by Bill Jones
Cover illustration by Larry Rostant
Interior design by Jan Greenberg
Typography: Amigo and New Caledonia

Running Press Book Publishers
2300 Chestnut Street
Philadelphia, PA 19103-4371

Visit us on the web!
www.runningpress.com

DEDICATION

As always—PS I love you

In memory of Waya, who mas my sunshine

◖ CHAPTER 1 ◗

London, 1816

He must be insane!

Brendan Townsend cursed his own stupidity in accepting Antony Hillyard's invitation to the private gentleman's club, The Arbor. He hadn't understood what was so hilarious about the name until they were within its luxurious walls, and Tony explained that the name was short for *Arbor Vitae*— and not the classical "tree of life," but thieves' cant for the erect male member.

Which was precisely what Tony was displaying now. He'd had too much to drink, which Brendan might have expected and probably should have discouraged, but as Tony's guest here, he really had no right to tell him what to do and small hope that he'd have been able to stop him in any case. Along with plenty of his father's money, Tony had a total lack of common sense, and Brendan had known that before he'd agreed to come here.

So all he could really do now was thank God that the members of the Arbor, as well as their guests, were able to enter through a private door and to don black velvet masks before being allowed to meet anyone else in the place. Safely anonymous, they were admitted to the private rooms upstairs… to watch the show.

Tony had said "Oh, you *must* see the show, Bren. I promise, you've never seen the like."

He never would have believed Tony could accomplish understatement, but when the masked fellow at the front of the room had flipped back his cloak and revealed nothing beneath but an abundance of body hair, Brendan had been not only startled, but forced to confess the truth of the promise. He'd certainly never seen anything like that happen in polite company. Or anywhere else.

When the performer started fondling himself, Brendan had been repelled and begun edging back toward a quiet corner. But Tony, ever the attention seeker, had applauded the exhibitionist's efforts. His approval had been rewarded with an invitation to join in the fun, and to Brendan's utter mortification, Tony had done just that. Like a schoolboy promised a treat, he'd skipped up to the area set off as a stage. The naked fellow had seized him in an intimate embrace and immediately started unbuttoning his trousers.

"That's the boy, all balls and no brain. Let's have a seat now, shall we?" He dropped into a chair, pulling a laughing Tony down into his lap.

Brendan retreated immediately, getting as far away from the stage as he could, fetching up in a curtained nook where the shadows were deep and reassuring. But what was he supposed to do now? There was Tony, his host, the only son of a well-to-do merchant, lounging in a stranger's naked lap with his pantaloons puddled around his ankles and his cock being expertly manipulated by a total stranger.

"Ah, there's a brave lad, look at 'im," the showman crooned. "More meat and potatoes than many a man ever sees on his plate, wouldn't you say so, gentlemen? And proud of 'em, he is, aren't you, boy?"

Tony grinned vapidly. He was drunk. Drunk, and stupid with drink. Watching his friend writhe around, Brendan slouched down in his chair and thanked Heaven that every eye on the house was focused elsewhere.

The show didn't last long—Tony never did when he was in his

cups. He shouted, pumped wildly against the hand that encircled his cock, and shot his load toward a piece of furniture that had a piece of muslin tossed over it—no doubt that he'd been aimed in that direction.

Brendan glanced around. He must be the only man in the room who was not enjoying the performance. Some of the men—respectable, well-to-do English gentlemen, from the look of their clothing—were practically falling out of their chairs as Tony lolled, limp and spent, in the stranger's arms.

After a moment the performer patted him on the cheek, shoved him to his feet, and directed him through a doorway to one side of the stage as the audience applauded enthusiastically. One older gentleman went so far as to catch at Tony's hand on his way out, and say something that Brendan could not hear but could imagine. The man was old enough to be his father, for pity's sake; he looked very much like—

Dear God!

Brendan felt the blood drain from his face. *I could be wrong, I could be mistaken…* no, he was not mistaken, and he had better make himself invisible.

The alcove he was in had a curtain that could be drawn across it; there for the convenience of members and guests, Tony had said, and now Brendan had a notion of what that meant. He drew the curtain shut and positioned himself where he could view the room without being seen.

At first he'd been afraid Tony would march right back to him; as it happened, he disappeared into what was probably some sort of area for performers to tidy themselves up. With the show over, the audience began to disperse, and the gentleman Brendan had recognized headed off to the adjacent card room where refreshments were being dispensed.

Brendan waited. And waited. After a barely-endurable stretch of what felt like hours, Tony came prancing out, very pleased with himself and ready to join the party once more. He surveyed the room as though he'd expected the audience to wait for an encore.

His patience stretched beyond its limits, Brendan shoved the curtain aside and seized his friend's arm. "We're going home."

"Home? But the party's just begun!"

"The party is over," Brendan said shortly. "You can stay if you like, but I'm going right now, and you're so damned drunk you need a keeper."

"But—you saw, that older gent invited me upstairs!"

Gritted teeth. "Yes, I saw, and that's why I must go before he returns. I am leaving. Now. *I cannot be seen here!*" He pushed open the hall door, nodded to the gatekeeper, went down a steep stairway toward the private exit Tony had shown him earlier. He dropped his mask in the box on a table beside the doorway; it was obvious from the other masks already inside that it was put there for that purpose.

Tony trailed along as the passageway led them out into a narrow lane between two buildings. There were several doors along the lane, mainly businesses that had closed for the evening; Brendan decided it would be wise to take the longer way, which would bring them out on a street that was not the one from which they'd entered. He kept his wits about him and his stick at hand, but they were in luck and encountered no trouble.

After several minutes in the cool night air, Brendan's head began to clear and he realized that Tony was talking to him. Or, rather, babbling: "If you must drag me out of a fine party, you might at least talk to me, Bren. I thought you'd enjoy the show!"

"Then you were mistaken. I'd never have set foot in the place if you'd told me you were planning to *be* the show. How could you be so imprudent?"

"Imprudent? Bren—"

"I will not speak of this matter in the open street. We were both mistaken—you, in your notion of my tastes, and I in your judgement."

And that was the root of this, wasn't it? He had entered into a highly dangerous relationship with Tony, never realizing that his college roommate had such a tendency to reckless living. College discipline must have exerted more restraint than Brendan had realized. He'd only been sharing Tony's lodgings in London for a few weeks, but he was already coming to realize that their friendship was not what he had believed it to be.

It wasn't until they were back in their room at the top of the lodging house, a room chosen for its solid construction and quiet, that he found himself able to answer Tony's question. He'd probably have to answer it again tomorrow, since Tony was so soused right now he might not even remember the evening's events in the morning. Brendan tossed his hat on the rack, hung his coat on a peg, and said, "Very well. I'll tell you why we left, and why I am not going back there ever again. That gentleman who solicited your company, after a performance any whore would be proud of? *That was my godfather!*"

Brendan wouldn't have thought it was possible, but Tony actually sobered at the news. He dropped onto the chair beside their bed and said, "Oh."

"Indeed. 'Oh.' So I'm afraid I shan't be able to accept your *generous* hospitality at that foul pit you call a club, and if you have any sense you'll resign your membership. If you have plans to move into Society, you will not improve your chances by trying to creep in through the gutter."

Tony blinked foolishly. "Oh. Then I sub—suppose you don't want to hear what the manager offered me—us."

"I suppose you're right, but speak if you must." Brendan undressed and quickly slid into his nightshirt; he was in no mood for any rambunction tonight.

"He told me it was a *stunning* performance and invited me to come back again—and you, as well!"

A chill touched Brendan's heart and found its way into his voice. "I *beg* your pardon?"

"He asked if you were my guest. I said yes, we were friends. He said—" Tony's brows drew together in muddled concentration. "He said '*intimate* friends?' so I said that—"

"You *what?*" He seized Tony's shoulders and shook him. "You fool! How very tactful of you, to share my exceedingly personal information with a stranger!"

"But he's not a stranger, Bren, he's the proprietor—"

Distaste made him release his grip. "He's a stranger to me, Mr. Hillyard, and I hope he remains so. Have you forgotten that what you and I have done together in private could get us hanged? If you cannot exercise the merest discretion, I dare not continue to associate with you."

Tony's handsome features blurred into a sulk. "I did not tell him your name or pedigree. Really, Mr. Townsend, if I'd known you to be such a prig I'd never have invited you to join me."

They glared at each other for a moment, and finally Brendan, recognizing that he wasn't going to get any sense out of Tony until he'd had a chance to sleep off the drink, forced a laugh. "Ah, I suppose there's no harm done. But I really must not go back there, Tony. If Uncle Cedric knew I'd seen him there—"

"Well, he was there himself, was he not?" Tony began undressing, letting his clothes lie where they fell. "A member of the club. He has just as much reason as we do to keep mum."

"He does, to be sure, but you must remember that he's older than either of us, richer than both your father and mine put together, and he's a damned old hypocrite besides. You should hear him holding forth in other venues—on the evils of sodomy!"

Tony gave an unpleasant laugh. "Oh, that sort?"

"Very much that sort. Tony, he'd see us both hang—and I mean that literally—before admitting he'd been in that club. He's never seen us together, so far as I know, and as long as you politely decline his invitation—"

"Oh, must I?" Tony leaned forward, and said, on a gust of spiritous breath, "He seems a most *vigorous* gentleman."

"If you do—if he sees your face, unmasked—I swear I shall sever our association on the spot."

Looking around the room—his room—Tony asked sarcastically, "And where would you go, Mr. Townsend? Home to rusticate?"

"If necessary." He'd been happy enough to take Tony up on his offer of shared lodgings. As a youngest son of a none-too-wealthy family, there was never an excess of funds for hotels when his family had a perfectly fine town house in London. But Brendan was beginning to realize that the opportunity to spread his wings a bit had some unforeseen drawbacks. "I am serious, Tony."

"You always are." He dropped onto the bed and flopped back, spreading his arms in a way that pulled his nightshirt tight against his well-knit frame. As a general thing, Brendan would find that pose enticing, but not tonight. "Someday," Tony announced, "I shall teach you to frivol."

"Not likely, if tonight's performance was how you define the word. Whoring around in public is not my style. But I may teach you some small measure of discretion—if I'm not already too late."

He cleaned his teeth and climbed into bed on the side opposite Tony, shoving away a clumsy attempt to embrace. "You've had enough for one night, I think."

"True enough, Bren, but you haven't—"

"I haven't the—" He almost said "stomach for it," but caught himself. This was not the time to start a fight. "Haven't the strength. Seeing my godfather in there simply unmanned me."

"He'd never have known you—the mask, remember?"

"I recognized him, mask or no mask. And I hope to God he never sees us together in public. He may be a hypocrite, but he's no fool, and I promise—he would recognize you."

"Not in a thousand years. Don't fret, I shan't pursue the acquaintance if it bothers you. Never thought you'd be so chicken-livered, though."

Brendan ignored him, and in a few moments Tony began to snore. Weary, but still unnerved by the narrow escape, Brendan pulled the blanket up to his ears. He ordered his body to relax, but his mind would not be still.

Uncle Cedric, of all people! Brendan could still remember the

day—he could not have been more than eight or nine years old—
that he realized he was not quite like the other boys. It had been
the occasion of some older cousin's marriage, one of Cedric's
sons. The family had trooped out of church after the wedding, to
wave goodbye as the bridal couple drove away in their carriage.

Brendan had asked, in all innocence, why Cousin Gilbert had
to marry a girl, since girls were good for nothing but sewing and
couldn't even ride very well. That had given all the adults a fine
laugh, and Uncle Cedric, the old fraud, had said in a patronizing
tone that irritated even then, "Oh, when you're older you'll
change your mind about girls. I suspect by the time you're sixteen
you'll understand well enough."

But here he was, twenty-two years of age, and he had somehow never arrived at that understanding. He still felt, as he always had, that women were so vastly different from men that
there could be no true attraction between them. He was fond of
his mother and had a great deal of affection for his sister and even
his nieces, but the notion of going to bed with a woman left him
unmoved.

One thing he had learned, though, and learned young. He
had observed that men could admire the abilities of other men,
especially if they were good at manly pursuits—riding, hunting,
swordsmanship and the like—but if they noticed a man's looks,
"Young Smythe is growing up handsomely," they must immediately add some remark about how popular that man would be
with the ladies. If a man had breeches that fit exceptionally well,
emphasizing his thighs and calling attention to tight, strong buttocks, it was appropriate to inquire the name of his tailor; if one's
eyes were drawn to a handsome face, one might ask its owner
what he called the style of his cravat. A man's looks could be ap-
preciated, but there was a subtle difference in the way such admiration was expressed, very different from the way one would
compliment a lady.

By the time Brendan turned sixteen and his father had The
Talk with him, he'd already learned to mask his impulses. If a

handsome gentleman caught his attention, he would let his admiring gaze slide over the man and come to rest on the nearest female form. When his father had escorted him to an irregular establishment and left him to the tender mercies of an experienced and really quite pleasant lady, he'd emerged the next morning with several guineas' worth of restful slumber and the lady's invitation to return some time in the future when he was not too nervous to enjoy himself.

He'd never gone back, of course. There'd have been no point. He didn't grudge her the money, though; at least she hadn't laughed at him. She had even consoled him by sharing a small secret: he was not the first young man who had failed to live up to his father's expectation. "It's the nerves, dearie. Happens to all gentlemen sometimes, don't fret yourself."

It had been easy to deceive his father the next day, pitifully easy. All Brendan had needed to do was allow his parent to believe that things had gone as expected, accept his new status as a man of experience, and promise to be discreet in his future sowing of wild oats.

Life had become easier when Brendan went up to Oxford. Contact with the gentler sex was rare and strictly regulated, so he was seldom required to feign an interest he did not feel. His first year was spent either reading history—the subject he was supposed to be studying—or filling an empty seat in lectures on art or the natural sciences, which he found far more interesting.

If he'd had his way, he would have stayed at home in his father's stables, working with the hunters and other horses, learning what he most wished to know under the tutelage of their head groom, Spencer. But the paternal foot was put down at that. No Townsend was going to be a glorified groom. Horses were all very well, but they were a diversion, not one's life. He would get an education first and consider gentlemanly amusements in the future, when and if he could afford them.

If Sir James Townsend, Viscount Martindale, had any notion of what his son would be learning in the hours after classes, he might have thought twice, because in his second year, Brendan found himself sharing rooms with Antony Hillyard. And by the end of term, he was also sharing his body.

It had all been so much simpler then. And exciting. Tony was a handsome young man, with broad shoulders and a narrow waist, hair the color of wheat-straw, and sparkling blue eyes. His father was a commoner, but he had a respectable self-made fortune, enough to send his heir to school with the sons of the ruling class. Tony's manners were a trifle less refined than they might have been, but he was never short of pocket money. He also had a knack for secreting the odd bottle of sherry or gin amongst his personal effects, and was quite generous with it.

As the weeks passed, Sunday evenings became the time that Brendan and Tony would draw their chairs closer to the fire, the bottle on a low table between them, and enjoy the last few hours before the start of another week. Sometimes they read, sometimes they played cards, but most of the time they simply chatted and enjoyed one another's company.

The drink had been Brendan's downfall. As the level in the bottle grew lower, so did his discretion. One evening, when Brendan was pleasantly foxed and contemplating the play of light on Tony's hair, the lovely balance of his lips and chin, he was startled when the object of his attention turned suddenly and smiled in a knowing way.

"I have noticed you looking at me, Mr. Townsend."

Taken aback, Brendan floundered. "I—I beg your pardon, I meant nothing by it."

"That's a pity. I hoped you did, for I've been looking back." And it didn't stop with looking; Tony had leaned across and given Brendan a light kiss, the barest touch of lips. If he'd been sober, Brendan would have stopped then and there, but it felt so very good that he leaned in for more, his usual reticence discarded.

He had no idea what he was doing, but Tony had experience enough for both of them. Before he knew what was happening,

Brendan found himself embraced and unbuttoned, caught some-where between mortification and ecstasy. Everything that hadn't worked with a hired doxy was suddenly functioning perfectly. He didn't stop, then, to wonder where Tony had learned to do such things; the only thing he regretted was the speed at which it was all over.

From that moment, Brendan's education after lights-out outpaced his daytime schedule. He made sure his studies did not suffer; Tony would tease him for being a stick-in-the-mud in that regard, but Brendan was able to exert some benevolent influence himself, and keep his companion at his studies far longer than Tony would have otherwise had patience for the task. It was no chore. For the first time in his life, Brendan un-derstood what all the fuss was about. It was no wonder men did mad things for love, took foolish risks. To be held by a lover, to lose oneself in passion—it made every day something new and wonderful.

Living day by day, they had never given serious thought to the future. Brendan had expected to turn his hand to some useful task on the family estates, perhaps helping his brother James, who was gradually assuming some of the management in prepa-ration for the day when he would one day inherit. James was the best of brothers, but he had no understanding of horses, and that was one area, perhaps the only one, where Brendan knew his ex-pertise was superior.

But the day that James might need his assistance was a long way off—very long, God willing; Brendan's father was still in ex-cellent health for a man halfway through his sixties. When Tony had taken a room in London to have a place away from his own father's vigilant eye, Brendan had accepted his invitation to come along. With James as heir to the family estate and his other brother Andrew in His Majesty's Navy, Brendan was in the am-biguous position of a young man with no heavy demands placed upon him, but no clearly defined role in life.

Tony seemed to envy that, in a good-natured way. "You're a

lucky old thing, Bren," he said, not long before they'd left Oxford. "Money enough to live on, older brothers to carry on the family line—you're free to do as you please."

"If I'd money enough to do as I please, I'd call myself lucky," Brendan had retorted. "My grandmother left me a competence, but it's not enough to do what I wish. I could not afford to set up my own household, even if I wished to marry. From where I stand, you're the one who seems to have all he could desire."

"I? Not likely! My course is set. I'm to spend half of every day with my father, learning all he knows. I shall acquire an encyclopedic knowledge of everything from the cargos of the ships he owns to the names of every rat aboard them. And if I'm a very good boy," he said with his typical exaggeration, "he'll find me some ugly maiden with a pretty title so we will be sure my sons get into the stud-book."

"Don't you want to marry?"

"Not I. I'd rather be a wastrel black sheep, traveling the world without a care or a connection. But I'll never be free so long as my father's alive—and he'll see me tied down to wife and family before he goes, you may be sure of that."

His bitterness made Brendan uneasy. What a wretched thing it must be, to have such animosity for one's own father. "He can't force you to marry, can he?"

"Oh, he certainly can. And he will, too, you just wait and see. My dear papa always gets what he wants—just ask him."

Brendan pulled his mind back to the present, wishing he could quiet his thoughts and get some sleep. Why had he remembered that conversation now? Natural enough, perhaps. They'd had variations of it so many times. But after this evening's near-disaster, Brendan knew he would have to quit this irresponsible dallying, move into the family's house here in town, and consider his own future.

And it would have to be a future without Tony.

When they had first begun their pleasant games, Brendan had fancied himself in love and imagined wild, unlikely schemes in which they ran away together. He knew now that this would never happen. The young man he'd shared intimacy with had turned out to be, in the cold light of day, nothing more than a resentful, irresponsible boy. Far from loving him, Brendan was beginning to realize he didn't even like Tony very much. Not anymore.

He was oddly relieved. Not that he regretted a moment of the affair; at the advanced age of two-and-twenty, it would have been a shame not to have at least experienced physical passion, even if it was the sort that would have horrified his father. Sodomy… Brendan shied away from the term, even though he knew it was what the law called the act. The law also called it a capital offense. Discretion was literally a matter of life and death, and Tony's increasing recklessness was bound to lead them into trouble. At best it would be a horrible scandal, and at worst it could get them both hanged.

And that would certainly ruin all those plans Tony's father has laid for him, wouldn't it?

Brendan's eyes opened wide, sleep temporarily banished. Could Tony be that foolish, that reckless, that resentful—that fatally *stupid*—to risk his own life just to prove to his father that he would not be mastered?

Yes, he could.

Time to leave, before things get any worse.

◖◕ CHAPTER 2 ◔◗

Brendan's resolution wavered the following morning. He awoke to
the snug comfort of Tony's arm across his body, and Tony's warmth
curled against his back. As his body began to awaken, it reacted to
that closeness, his cock stirring a bit in anticipation.

It was only as he came fully awake that he remembered his intentions of the night before, and the sensual appeal withered. A
part of him would have shrugged off the night-fears, but in the
light of cold morning he knew they were more real than this physical closeness.

Tony groaned. "Damnation, Bren, what was I drinking last
night?"

"Brandy, mainly. And too much of it." Brendan slid from beneath the covers, wrapping himself in a dressing gown. "I've
never seen you so bottle-headed and still on your feet."

His companion dragged the blankets up over his face with a
groan. "I've a head the size of a coachwheel, and all you can do
is lecture me. What did I do?"

Brendan found his watch, realized the housemaid would be
bringing up hot water in only a few minutes, and began hunting
for clean clothing. "Do you mean to tell me you don't remember
what you did?"

"I just said as much, didn't I!"

Had Tony always whined so? "Very well," Brendan said, setting out his brush and razor. "What *do* you remember?"

"We went to the Arbor, I had a lovely time, then you dragged me away and commenced scolding like a fishwife."

"A lovely time?" He remembered what he'd done, Brendan was sure of it. But to go through it all once more... No. "That's not what I should call it. You behaved disgracefully, you were propositioned by a gentleman who is a relative of mine—I believe he took you for an employee of the club. And if you remember anything at all, you must remember I advised you to resign your membership or forfeit our friendship."

"You cannot mean that." The blanket lowered to reveal a pair of bloodshot, accusing eyes. "Brendan, you are a beast!"

"Indeed, I am not. I am showing far more forbearance than you deserve." Ah, the knock at the door. Brendan accepted the pitcher of hot water, confirmed that he would be at the breakfast table in fifteen minutes, and warned the chambermaid that Mr. Hillyard was not feeling well. The maid, a girl of twelve or thirteen, took that news with a knowing look and took her leave, as well.

"I'm off to Sunday services," Brendan said, trying to speak between attempts to scrape the stubble from his face. "You may as well stay in bed until your disposition improves—there's fresh water here, and by the time you bestir yourself I imagine it will be cool enough to drink."

Tony only growled and burrowed deeper into the blankets. His lack of concern about the previous night's misadventure allowed Brendan to depart with an untroubled conscience. He consumed a light breakfast of hot chocolate and bread-and-butter with jam before bidding their landlady farewell with an air of virtuous sanctity.

He did feel a bit of a hypocrite, given where he had been the night before. But church on Sunday was something he'd been doing since childhood; it was, for lack of any deep conviction either for or against religion, a commendable social activity, and most of all, the walk to church would give him the chance to spend some time alone and think the situation through.

The morning was fine, still a bit cool for April, but early daffodils made a brave show in garden boxes and the air was crisp and clear. If only he could somehow persuade it to waft through his brain as well as his lungs!

He should have told Tony that he intended to leave for good. He had deliberately avoided telling him anything, and that lie by omission went against the grain. But Brendan saw no other way, not at present. That news must wait until the very last moment, since it would cause injured feelings at best and at worst an ugly scene.

In any event, it could not truly be said that he was moving out, since he had never officially moved in. He kept only a few clothes at the rooming house, a pair of riding boots, and his toilet articles; for discretion's sake, he had never stayed more than two or three nights in a row. He was a guest, not a regular lodger; his meals were paid for by the day, so all he needed to do was pack up, go back to his family's town home, and cease visiting Tony's place.

Easy enough—but it was a coward's way out, and it would leave poor old Tony at the mercy of his own foolishness. Still—what else was there to do? If he stayed, Tony would make an effort to drag him back to the Arbor, and when his wish was denied, Tony was sure to create an unpleasant scene.

Brendan could not, must not, go back. That was indisputable fact. Equally indisputable was the way Tony craved attention. Foolish or not, whether or not Brendan was with him, Tony would be back there, and likely onstage, and eventually in Uncle Cedric's bed. And when Tony was drunk, he babbled.

And then what?

Brendan shied away from the thought, but immediately forced his mind back to it. *Think this through. What is likely to happen?*

Well, at worst, Uncle Cedric might make inquiries, discover that his nephew had indeed roomed with Tony at University, and conclude that the claim might be true.

Would he pursue the matter further? Why should he? What benefit would that gain him? He would hardly want to stir up a family scandal, not with his own disgraceful secret the key to his knowledge. Even if he suspected that Tony was telling the truth, he would probably order him to keep his mouth shut if he valued his health. He might question Brendan about it privately, but even that would make him vulnerable to being questioned in return.

By the time he was climbing the church steps, Brendan had managed to convince himself that the most sensible course of action would be to remove to the family home, allow Tony to follow his own course to perdition, and staunchly deny any accusations, if it ever came to that. He hated the very idea of such deception, he did not believe he had much talent for lying...but there was no proof of any misbehavior on his own part. Damn, it, he had *not* misbehaved, at least not ever in public. If Tony had a particle of sense, he would realize that wild talk would only harm himself.

If Tony had a particle of sense...That was the question, wasn't it?

Enough. He could fret himself into a state, and what good would it do? He needed a change; his thinking had gone stagnant. He'd been spending too much time indoors. He'd been spending too much time in bed. It was time to put aside his youthful indiscretions—everyone had them, even if his was more indiscreet than usual—and give serious thought to his future. After church, he would pop back to the rooming house, put on his riding togs, and revert to his natural state—horseback. A trot around the park would get his mind moving again, and he hadn't had poor Galahad out for exercise in two days. Neglecting his own body was one thing, but neglecting his horse was inexcusable.

He'd arrived only just in time for service; the strains of the organ had begun. Brendan found a place in an anonymous pew near the door and settled into the familiar ritual. The scent of candle-wax, the soft colors of light through stained-glass windows, the hushed echoes from the high, vaulted roof above ... Strange, since he had no strong feeling for religion, how much he enjoyed the calm, stately grace of churches and cathedrals.

From where he sat, he could see the family pew and observe that his eldest brother, James, was in attendance with as many of his nearest and dearest as could be trusted to sit through a sermon without fussing. Imogen and young Jamie, ten and eight years old, were well-behaved youngsters, but Alan was only four and inclined to break into song at inappropriate moments. He was probably at home in the nursery, and just as well.

Brendan was happy to see his relatives here, more so than he'd expected to be, and made a point of meeting them at the door. "The prodigal returned," he said, when James looked up and noticed him standing nearby.

"Indeed, and not a moment too soon," his brother said sternly, using his additional inch or two of height to achieve a magisterial air.

They walked out into the sunshine. "How so?" Brendan asked.

"I have been commissioned to summon you to duty." James maintained his solemnity for only a moment, then the smile he'd been suppressing broke through. "Via a letter from our mother. She and Elspeth are arriving from Bath this afternoon, and you are expected to escort your sister to Almack's on Wednesday evening."

"I see." The children were obviously waiting for attention, so Brendan took a moment to express his admiration for Imogen's new bonnet and return Jamie's handshake. He offered his young niece his arm, and they strolled through the chatting crowd to where the family carriage waited at the curb. "Almack's. Of course."

Almack's fashionable establishment, repressively respectable and exclusive to the point of absurdity, was *the* place for a young lady of quality to meet eligible gentlemen. Like most such gentlemen, Brendan found the place tedious. It served only lemonade and dry cake, small incentive to lure a man into a roomful of anxious, competitive misses hoping to be invited to dance. Still, Elspeth was a lovely young woman, hair dark as a raven's wing, with expressive brown eyes and a fine complexion. She would do the family proud in any setting. Now that she was out in Society she would be obliged to attend those affairs—and, knowing her ebullient nature, she would be eager to step out onto the dance floor.

"Certainly, I will do my duty," he said, "if Mama can wangle a voucher so we mere mortals may be permitted to purchase tickets. Elspeth is surely eligible, but I'm not much of a catch for those thoroughbred maidens."

James rolled his eyes. "You'll do well enough if you can refrain from referring to the ladies as though they were horses. Ellie has passed muster, and Lucy was allowed to transfer her voucher. As for you... if rumor is correct, this Season has an unusually high proportion of newly-launched ladies to suitable gentlemen, which may explain how Mama was able to obtain admission for you. White cravat and knee-breeches, of course. Norwood will see to it you don't disgrace us."

Norwood was James' valet, and dictated Brendan's attire when he was in residence at the family home. "I shall be as neat and discreet as Brummel himself," Brendan promised. "How has Ellie fared thus far? Any disreputable knaves to be driven off?"

"She has *two* very proper admirers." Anne, James' wife, was really the font of knowledge on the subject of Elspeth's progress. "Harry Edrington, the Earl of Edrington's younger brother, is the suitor I favor. The other is a handsome but rather intense divinity student who came to dinner with the Bishop last month."

"My dear," James put in, helping his wife up into the carriage, "that is a very incomplete description. Young Nigel is Bishop Fenwick's nephew, after all."

She arranged her skirts around her and made sure the children were settled as James and Brendan seated themselves opposite and the coachman set the horses in motion. "Yes, that's true. But they are nothing alike. The Bishop is a merry gentleman, quite good-humored. His nephew seems almost grim in comparison."

"My impression was that he is focused on his studies," James put in.

Anne's expression spoke volumes. "Very true, my love. His dedication is commendable, but he would be more attractive if he could find it in him to *rejoice* in the Lord. I have the impression

Mr. Fenwick has formed a very serious attachment for Elspeth, with no encouragement on her part."

That sort of gentleman did not sound like a good match for his high-spirited, cheerful sister. "Is she seriously attached to him?" Brendan asked.

Anne laughed merrily. "Oh, no. Ellie is enjoying the admiration, of course, but she told me that she has no wish to be a clergyman's wife with a whole parish to care for besides her own establishment. And your mama says that if anyone goes into the Church, it will most likely be yourself."

Brendan winced. His mother had once caught him making a sketch of a memorial in St. Paul's cathedral and mistaken her youngest son's affinity for religious structures for an interest in theology itself. He had not welcomed her suggestion that he look toward a career in the Church. "I most often go into the church to admire its architecture. I have no wish—" He stopped, noticing young Jamie watching him, listening intently. "It's the physical beauty that draws me, I'm afraid, not spiritual zeal. I have not been blessed with a calling to the ministry."

The presence of the children kept him from adding that he saw no qualities in the Church of England that were sufficiently superior to any other religion to cause him to embrace it as a lifelong career. And he could hardly explain that his sexual peculiarity was prohibited by that Church and all Christian religions.

If the Church of England had the same sort of rules as the Church of Rome, he could almost see some use in it—an edict to refrain from taking a wife would neatly mask his lack of interest in such a course. But England's church put no such unnatural strictures on its clergy, and if he were to enter the Church, Brendan knew what would happen. A young, unmarried clergyman with even passable looks was a natural magnet for high-minded young ladies, and the job carried with it the expectation that he'd seek a wife and helpmeet. No, the welcoming arms of the Church were hardly a haven for a man of skeptical principles who wanted to avoid entanglements with the fair sex.

"Have you considered the study of architecture?" James suggested. "I know Robert Smirke slightly; he was recently made Chief Architect for the Office of Works, and he would be the man to ask for direction if you have an interest in the profession."

"I should look into it," Brendan said. "I really must decide what to do with myself. Even if I were well-breeched enough for the idle life, I haven't the inclination."

"Well, you needn't decide this afternoon." James gave him an understanding smile. "I expect I should have been hard put to make such a decision at your age. Being firstborn made the decision for me, you might say. Never fear. You'll always have a home with us, at any rate, and even if Father means to keep you from spending all your time with the horses, I should welcome your help."

"You will be staying with us, I hope?" Anne added.

"Yes, of course, if you'll have me. I had thought that the life of a gay dog out on the town would be diverting, but truth be told, I find it rather dreary. I fear I'm a dull stick."

James shook his head. "You are an unusually sensible young man. I had no idea you'd come to that conclusion so quickly, but I confess it's a relief to hear you say it. There are too many pitfalls in this city, just waiting for young men who haven't any sense."

Brother, you have no idea how right you are! Brendan quickly steered the conversation away from that dangerous topic. "I'm not sure it's sense so much as a low tolerance for spirits and a dislike for games of chance. In any case, I imagine our mother will have plenty of errands for me. There is no escort so useful or uncomplaining as a son."

"It's only fair you take your turn with Elspeth," James said. "I had the honor of being general dogsbody when Mama launched Lucy, even though we all knew she and Richard had set their minds to each other before she ever put her hair up."

"It should not be too terrible a hardship," Anne assured him. "Your mother and I will accompany Elspeth to many of the events, and she often shares a carriage with her friends and their own mothers. You will be conscripted for one or two affairs a week, at most."

"You need the experience," James said. "Every man should be required to dance attendance on a sister—it lets him know what he is in for once he acquires a wife." The smile that passed between him and Anne made it clear that his words were only teasing.

Brendan felt a deep pang of envy. What a wonderful thing it would be to have a wife, a helpmeet, a companion. But he knew himself too well to think that his fondness for his sisters could ever metamorphose into the tenderness his brother clearly felt for Anne, and he had seen too many unhappy marriages to want the form without the substance. He would never have a wife. He would never have anyone.

He was in the bosom of his family… and he had never felt so alone.

ᝰᙉ CHAPTER 3 ᙈᝰ

After a more substantial second breakfast with his family, Brendan excused himself to go retrieve his belongings, borrowing the carriage to simplify matters. He left the carriage just outside the house, and was pleased to find Tony absent. With no more than a twinge of guilt for the relief he felt at being able to avoid a scene, he wasted no time in bundling his clothing back into his suit-cases, and setting them beside the door. He could carry them downstairs himself, and save a little time.

Should he leave a note? Courtesy demanded it, but given Tony's tempestuous nature Brendan was reluctant to commit anything to paper, where it might be misinterpreted. It took him longer to decide what to say than it did to write the message, borrowing a sheet of Tony's writing paper as well as his pen and ink-bottle.

"Dear Tony:

Many thanks for your gracious hospitality. I am sorry to have missed you, but my mother has summoned me to attend to family duties, and I cannot be certain when my time will once more be my own. I expect we shall see one another before long; I do not believe I shall be sent out of town during the Season, much as I might wish it. Best regards…"

That should do the job. Simple, noncommittal, and devoid of any suggestion of irregular attachment or impropriety. He sealed the sheet with a wafer, melted a bit of wax on it, and pressed it shut. Done!

He did not precisely hurry down the stair and out the door, but he did not dally.

Galahad was an excessively happy horse. His delight in being released from the confines of his stall expressed itself in far more prancing and head-tossing than Brendan would expect as his usually even-tempered mount was led out of the stable and into the sunshine. It wasn't fair to blame the horse, though. Everyone knew chestnuts were a bit high-strung, and that had been clear from the moment Brendan set eyes on him. But when Galahad was treated well and properly exercised, that reservoir of energy made him a delight to ride, sensitive and responsive to his master's every wish.

"He's right glad to see you, sir," said the stable-boy. "I had him out for a walk yesterday, but he's never so bright as when he sees you a-coming."

"Is that so?" Brendan took the lead, handing the boy a coin. "I should have been here sooner, then. This lad needs to stretch his legs."

"Yes, sir. Thankee, sir." He touched his cap and nearly offered a leg up, then remembered that was unnecessary with this rider, and vanished back into the livery stable.

"So you missed me, did you?" Brendan patted Galahad's sleek neck. "I missed you, too, old boy. I should've been spending more time with you than the company I've kept of late." He swung up into the saddle and turned his horse's head toward Hyde Park.

Galahad was more rambunctious than usual, but the sheer joy of being on horseback, out in the beautiful afternoon, soothed Brendan's own anxiety, and before long the improvement in his mood reflected itself in his mount's behavior. Just as well, too; a full-out gallop would have calmed them both, but only a witless fool would try a stunt like that here. That would only get him banned from the park for his trouble. He entered at the Marble Arch gate and directed Galahad from a walk to a trot until he was warmed up, then let him glide into his smooth, rocking-horse canter. This was heaven—no quarrels, no threat of temperaments or sulking, just a sweet happiness in the sunshine and the wind of their passage.

Brendan noticed a few of his family's acquaintances as he rode around the Row, but they were absorbed in their own socializing. If they saw him, they left him to his exercise, and he was just as pleased with the solitude. Halfway through his third circuit, however, he found himself coming up behind a carriage that seemed familiar. As he guided Galahad to one side in order to pass without alarming the horses, he realized with a shock that Tony and his father were two of the passengers.

Tony glanced up and blinked in surprise, then immediately looked away. In a flash of hooves Brendan was past the carriage, Galahad's long strides opening the distance from the vehicle. Brendan was left with a quick, sharp impression of the other two passengers. Two ladies, one young, the other somewhat older, and old George Hillyard had seemed to be engaged in conversation with them.

Tony had looked somewhat sullen, as he usually did when in his father's company, and Brendan could imagine why. That young lady must be the prospective bride Tony had mentioned. Brendan did not recognize her, but that meant little, as he would not have met her socially; she would certainly be older than his sister Elspeth but younger than Anne's set. Besides, if her parents were desperate enough to be considering Tony as a match, she would have some fatal flaw that would exclude her from those young ladies Brendan's own mother would have introduced him to as suitable.

The girl was not a beauty from the quick glimpse he'd had, though one could not fairly call her unsightly. Her looks had not been enhanced by a discontented expression that was regrettably similar to Tony's. Some girl of better breeding than dowry, willing or instructed to lower her sights to a husband whose money came from trade. *That* courtship would not be conducted at Almack's; Brendan remembered Tony being vindictively pleased when his father's attempts to procure a voucher for his heir had been unsuccessful.

Brendan felt a pang of sympathy for the girl, whoever she was. What a sorry situation—a suitor who would rather debauch himself with strange men than tie himself to a wife, and a young woman who had no choice but to marry beneath her station or face some even more unhappy alternative.

As the Hyde Park Corner gate loomed closer, Brendan brought Galahad down to a walk and turned him toward the exit. It was not the gate nearest the stable, but that was perfectly all right; neither of them had had enough exercise, and taking the long way around would extend the ride without the risk of Mr. Hillyard recognizing his son's noble friend and calling him over to introduce him to the ladies. A month ago, Brendan knew, he would have avoided the encounter out of jealousy—he would not have wanted to see his lover with anyone else, man or woman. But Tony's shameless promiscuity at the Arbor had cured him of that; at this moment, he all he could feel toward either of them was pity.

Once Galahad was stabled, Brendan walked around from the mews to the family's house in Brook Street. He'd barely changed into proper attire when he heard light footsteps hurry down the hall, and found himself enveloped in a warm hug from his younger sister. He gave her a kiss on the forehead. "Hello, my dear! How was your trip? Where's our mother?"

"The trip was lovely, but Mama has been so busy in Bath that she quite wore herself out. She's taking a little rest in her room. Come, I was just about to have a cup of tea in the drawing room. You must tell me about your Town adventures. Have you been to the gambling hells?"

He laughed at her enthusiasm as she settled herself and poured them each a cup of tea. "A few, and I must say that they were really rather boring—harmless enough for an hour or two, but no more. I would rather spend an evening with a good book."

"How is your friend from Oxford, Mr. Hillyard?"

"Oh, he is well." Brendan felt himself slip into his habitual state of caution, weighing every word to yield truth, but never in full measure. "He's being set to learn his father's business, so I thought it best to leave him to it. We had our little holiday, but we both need to stop wasting time with foolishness and games of chance."

He looked her over critically; her pale green gown was one he had seen many times, but her demeanor had altered ever so slightly since the last time they'd met. She was changing, too, from the lively playmate of his childhood into a poised young lady. "And how is your own game progressing, my dear? James tells me you already have a pair of admirers looking daggers at one another."

"You are too bad, Brendan! James told you no such thing." She sipped her tea, eyes dancing. "They are both perfect gentlemen, and I am having a grand time. When Lucy was doing her first Season I felt I would never get out of the nursery and be able to put my hair up and sit at the big table with the rest of you."

"Your patience has been rewarded. You have arrived, and you look very grown-up and elegant. Who'd have thought either of us would be so presentable, after all the time we spent spoiling our clean clothes in the nursery?"

"You do look most impressive," Elspeth admitted. "Handsomer than James, I think, but I would never tell him so."

He grinned. "You are exceedingly perceptive, Ellie, but pray let us keep that between ourselves. Have either of your admirers spoken to Father yet?"

"No… and I don't mind, truly. I am enjoying myself so, I would prefer not to receive a formal offer too soon. But I do like the Honorable Harry. I think we might suit very well. Do you know him?"

"Edrington? I think we have met once or twice," Brendan said. "He finished at Oxford the year I began; I would not say I know him well."

"I thought not. I would very much like for you to meet him at Almack's, and tell me what you think."

"I should be happy to. But if James and Anne approve, he must be unexceptionable, and surely my opinion is not as important as Father's?"

"Of course Papa will have the final word. But I think you know me better, in all truth. Papa will ask questions about Mr Edrington's income, and his relations—all important matters, I am sure, but not the things I most need to know. You would be the better judge of that. Will he suit not only me, but the rest of the family?"

"If you love him, Ellie, I'm sure the rest of the family will do our best to make him welcome."

She selected a biscuit from the plate, and nibbled at it thoughtfully. "I do hope you like him, Brendan. I am quite dazzled. We dance well together—he is not too tall for me—and he has lovely manners. Quite handsome, as well. And… Brendan, he has asked me whether I would mind if he spoke to Papa."

"Is that not the wrong way round? I thought he was supposed to ask Papa first."

"And you are my *elder* brother!" she said, laughing. "Brendan, when you find yourself in that position, remember that the *proper* thing to do is to speak to a lady's father. The *sensible* thing to do is to ask the lady first. Not to make an offer of marriage, but to find out whether she would be willing to receive an offer."

It occurred to Brendan that men and women operated by two different sets of rules, and men were floundering in the dark. "I suppose that is sensible," he said cautiously, not wanting to appear any more ignorant than he already felt.

"Of course it is! Considerate, too. Only think how foolish we would both have felt if I had taken him in dislike!"

"Then you gave your consent to Edrington asking if Father would give *his* consent?"

"Oh, yes." Elspeth seemed reluctant to speak further, but Brendan knew her well enough to be sure he had only to wait patiently. Finally she said, "I do like him, very much. But there are so many things men know about each other that a girl would discover only after it is too late."

That was a shot too near the gold. Brendan thought instantly of Tony and Miss Unknown in the park. "What do you mean, Ellie? Has he said or done anything to make you uneasy?"

"Oh, no, nothing. His manner is all that is pleasing, it is only…" Elspeth bit her lip. "One of my friends who married a few months ago—I cannot tell you her name—discovered that the gentleman who was so well-behaved and courteous in public drinks terribly at home. His whole household lives in terror of his temper… and she is married to him now, and trapped. I do hope Harry is a true gentleman, but how ever would I learn something like that?"

"Ask our redoubtable Norwood to talk to some of Edrington's servants," Brendan said promptly. "I learned that in Oxford. The servants know everything."

"Oh, I could not!"

"No, of course not; a young lady is not supposed to know about such things. But I can, and I will, if Edrington offers and you are inclined to accept his suit." He patted her hand. "Fear not, little sister, I'll see that you are kept safe from any lurking Bluebeard, no matter how well he may dance."

She bounced from her chair and hugged him. "You are the best brother! And what of your own game? Has any lady yet caught your fancy?"

Brendan hoped his smile looked as carefree as her own. "No, not as yet. You know very well that I cannot think about settling down until I decide what I mean to do with myself, Ellie. It's as well that my heart seems to be immune. And no matter what Mama may expect, I have no more desire to be a churchmouse than you do."

"Really?"

"Yes, I have heard all about Mr. Fenwick."

Elspeth covered her mouth to hide a smile. "Oh, dear. Yes, Mr. Fenwick is a good man, I am sure, but he is so dreadfully somber. We should make one another quite unhappy, whatever he may believe. I have decided to introduce him to my friend

Millicent Peabody. She thinks him quite handsome, and her father is a Vicar, of a very good family. Millicent also has a serious, reverent outlook on life. She has cross-stitched several of the Proverbs, and they hang on the walls of her father's study."

Brendan would never have rolled his eyes if their mother had been present, but he felt free to do so now. "I hate to speak ill of your friend, but she sounds a bore."

"You would find her so, I'm sure, and I am seldom able to spend much time with her without being driven to distraction. But she is exactly what Mr. Fenwick needs in a wife. Millicent would be *excessively* happy organizing a parish and scheduling christenings."

Brendan thought the prospect appalling. "How do you propose to transfer Mr. Fenwick's affections from yourself to Millicent?"

"I mean to ask Anne's advice. Mama has advised me not to meddle, but it would be an act of Christian kindness to put them in one another's way."

He grinned. "And an act of kindness to yourself to remove yourself from Fenwick's!"

"Yes, indeed!" Elspeth admitted. "Virtue is its own reward, they say."

Brendan laughed aloud. Almack's would be dull as dust, no doubt, but his sister was never so. He could do much worse than to devote the next few months to helping her sort the wheat from the chaff.

❧ CHAPTER 4 ❧

The next week passed in such a blessedly ordinary whirl of social activity that Brendan began to feel as though the disquieting incident at The Arbor had been some sort of unpleasant dream. He found himself content to be settled in the normal routine of his family home, with Elspeth's social success the focus of everyone's attention and the only crisis he had to deal with the uproar that occurred when Imogen borrowed her aunt's pearl-and-silver bracelet without permission and forgot where she had put it. But even that was not an unmixed blessing; the resulting scramble put Elspeth into such a state of exasperation that she forgot to be anxious about her debut at Almack's.

Brendan duly escorted his sister, made his manners to the esteemed ladies who ruled Almack's, met the Honourable Harry, and liked him at first sight. Edrington was a young man of medium height and forthright address, and Brendan had to admit that if his sister's suitor had not been obviously smitten with Elspeth, he'd have wished him inclined in another direction. Harry's coloring was similar to Tony Hillyard's—light hair and blue eyes—but there was a spark of energy and intelligence about Edrington that Tony lacked completely.

"Well?" Elspeth asked, as Edrington set off, unnecessarily, to fetch her a glass of lemonade. "What do you think?"

"I remember him now," Brendan said. "I was not as keen on sports as many of my peers, but that gentleman was said to be his college's finest bat at cricket."

"That's—" Elspeth frowned. "I fail to see what difference that makes in his potential as a husband, though I suppose it might be helpful in raising a son. But what do you think of *him*?"

It seemed to Brendan that he could have given no higher praise, but he only said, "He seems a promising specimen. And he's quick off the mark to protect you from thirst—I perceive he's already won through at the refreshment table. See, the conquering hero comes!"

He stayed nearby while Elspeth consumed the offering brought by her devoted Ganymede, and made desultory conversation with them both until the floor was cleared for dancing. He made his own escape to the refreshment table when Edrington led his sister off to take their places in the first country dance.

It was at affairs like this that Brendan was most keenly aware of the difference between his own feelings and those of his contemporaries. The card-players, already settling down at the tables to play whist and basset, the music-lovers who were there mainly to dance, the peacocks displaying their finery to the young ladies… it seemed that everyone else in the place was there to see and be seen, the ladies flirting with their fans and the gentlemen bestowing their lordly attention.

Brendan checked his own self-pity and reminded himself that he was not here for his own amusement, but for the protection and encouragement of his little sister. He might as well resign himself to his fate and try to bring a bit of happiness to some of the young ladies who were a little too plump or too plain of face, and not receiving the attention being paid to the belles of the ball. He was, after all, probably not the only person here who would prefer to be at home with a good book.

He sighed, and marched off to do his duty.

The week passed quickly, and the following Tuesday found Elspeth anticipating her second Wednesday evening at Almack's with far less fluttering than the first. Brendan offered to take her for a turn around the Park, but she cried off, all her attention focused on choosing her costume for the next evening.

The role of older brother was proving much less onerous than Brendan had anticipated. At home to receive callers or out on feminine errands of their own, Elspeth and his mother were kind enough not to demand a gentleman as escort every day; he even suspected they preferred to be on their own, free to dawdle in the shops. As a result, he found himself with plenty of time to give Galahad a daily hour of exercise that did them both a great deal of good.

He dismounted at the stable yard and, with a final pat, handed Galahad's reins over to the boy on duty, the only question on his mind whether to walk home or stroll about for awhile. When he turned to the street, however, he found himself face to face with Tony Hillyard, who said, without so much as a word of greeting, "Have you been avoiding me?"

The accusation was so abrupt that Brendan had no immediate answer. Then he said, "Your manner last week, when I passed you in the Park, suggested you would prefer I did just that. How is the young lady?"

"To hell with the young lady!"

"That sentiment is hardly flattering to either of you," Brendan said. He did not wish to continue the conversation in the presence of the hostler idling beside the stable door, so he turned and started off up the street, with Tony falling into step beside him as he made his way down the bustling avenue. "What brings you looking for me, Tony? I was not avoiding you, precisely, but I have been occupied with my family, as I mentioned in my note."

"Your family is well, I hope?" Tony asked, apparently recalling the niceties of polite speech.

"Very well, thank you." He knew better than to ask after Tony's father. "And how have you been?"

"Bedevilled. Caught between my father and a blackmailer. Brendan, you must help me."

Brendan's heart leapt into his throat. "A *blackmailer?* How— No, we must not speak of this in the street. Do you have your carriage nearby?"

"No. I've left the rooming house and taken a room at the York—we can talk there. I'm at my wits' end!"

Brendan saw no way out. "Very well, I'll come with you."

Tony hailed a hackney, and once they were seated within, Brendan asked, "Why did you leave Mrs. French's?"

"I gave that as my residence when I registered at the club. Not that the change will do me much good—the cur knows how to reach my father—but at least he can't lay hands on me quite as easily."

Brendan nodded and fell silent. He could hardly caution Tony against careless speech in public and keep chattering in the cab-driver's hearing. But the drive was brief, and in too short a time Brendan found himself following Tony up to his room.

The door was scarcely closed and locked behind them when Tony threw himself into Brendan's arms. "God, Bren, I've missed you… how could you be so cruel?"

Brendan's head told him this was a very stupid thing to do. His heart had mixed feelings—irritation at Tony's presumption, pity for his anxiety, and some lingering affection. But his body, particularly his cock, thought that this was the best thing that had happened in nearly two weeks. He was hard before he knew it, and Tony's body pressing him against the wall didn't make self-control any easier. "Tony, if you're to be married, we should not—"

"I haven't proposed, Bren. I'm not engaged. And even if I were…" His lips, warm and insistent, covered Brendan's; then he moved his attention to Brendan's neck, always a vulnerable spot. "Bren, you were right. I was a damned fool to ever go to the Arbor, and I must have been mad to let that molly get his paws in my breeches. I'm sorry, truly I am. Won't you let me apologize?"

It was a poor excuse and Brendan could guess that Tony's main purpose was to have it off with someone he knew would not betray him…but it had been a long dry spell, and damned if it wouldn't feel good to just let Tony slide his hand down and un-button—*yes!*

Brendan thrust forward as his flap fell open, and reached around to clutch at Tony's warm, firm buttocks as the crafty little devil thrust against him. Nothing too intimate, he'd never risk that again, but dear lord, why was it that something so universally condemned could feel so perfectly wonderful? He stopped considering the matter in any coherent way as his body demanded what it had been missing, and in a few brief moments he was brought to climax by Tony's hot seed spurting against his belly. He stayed there, leaning against the wall, pinned by Tony's weight, until they both had time to catch their breath.

At last Tony stepped back, grinning, and Brendan straightened, taking a step away from the wall. He felt thrown off-balance by the sudden, almost impersonal intimacy, resented Tony for springing it on him, and was furious with himself for allowing it to happen. "Your hospitality is a little abrupt, Mr. Hillyard," he said, taking refuge in formality as he tidied himself with his handkerchief. "I thought you wanted to talk."

"Are you complaining?" Tony asked, his self-satisfied smirk fading.

"Perhaps I should be. If that was your only purpose in bringing me here, I think I had better take my leave."

"Oh, Bren…" Tony took two steps across the smallish room and flung himself on the bed. "I said I was sorry, I admitted you were right—what more do you require?"

This room was not as spacious or comfortable as his previous lodging, but it seemed clean enough. No doubt Tony had hired it at short notice. Brendan chose one of two straight-backed chairs beside a table near the window. "I don't mean to be brusque, but I want you to tell me what you were going on about—what's this drama about blackmail?"

"It's no drama." Tony threw an arm across his face. "It's real, and I don't know what to do about it. Remember I told you about Dobson—"

"Sorry, who?"

"Dobson—Dick Dobson. Calls himself Dickey Dee, so his real name doesn't get about." He bounced to his feet, pacing restlessly.

"I don't know either name," Brendan said, "or what he has to do with you."

"He's the owner of the Arbor, Brendan. He's been threatening me, and I'm at my wits' end. I don't know what to do."

That was obvious. Brendan found a brandy flask where he expected it to be, in Tony's valise, and poured a tot into the cap. "Drink this, sit down, and tell me everything. Start from the beginning."

Tony threw back the drink as though it were water, and sat on the other chair. "The beginning… That was the night you went to the club with me."

"When you…" Brendan wasn't sure how he should put it.

"When I got stinking drunk and made a fool of myself, yes. You told me so. I must have been insane."

Rather than agree with this accurate but unflattering assessment, Brendan said, "You told me he asked you to repeat the performance."

"Yes. He asked. But he's stopped asking, Bren. Now he's *ordering* me to perform at the club."

"Ordering you? Whatever for?" No, surely even Tony could not have been so stupid! "You didn't agree, did you?"

"Of course not! After you left, I thought it over, and I realized you were right." He uttered the words with obvious reluctance. "And I stayed away for a week or two, but things have been so damned boring since you left…" He put a hand on the tabletop, as though reaching out, but Brendan made no move to meet him halfway. "I went back this past Friday night. Just for some company."

Brendan nodded, but could still find nothing to say.

Tony licked his lips. "Dee called me to his office. He made me an offer. I could take my pick of one of the men from the molly house on the corner—he owns that too, did you know? Calls them his 'downstairs gents.'"

"What about them?"

"That show we saw… he'd been inviting one or two of the mollies up to the Arbor to show off the way that one fellow was doing when we were there. They pick up a little money for the show, perhaps an engagement for the evening. What Dee wanted was to have me perform onstage. With one of those men. Or with you."

"*What?*"

"Or he'll tell my father." Tony poured himself another drink.

"Oh, dear God." Brendan nearly reached for the bottle himself, but decided against it. One of them had to keep a clear head. "What basis does he have for such a threat? You didn't sign any sort of agreement, did you?"

"Give me credit for some sense, would you? Of course not!"

"Then—did you tell him my name?"

"No, I did not—and I shan't, and even if I did he couldn't prove it was you. But he has my name and residence on the membership register."

"Did you actually sign the thing?"

"Yes, but it only says, 'Membership Register.' It doesn't even give the club's name."

"Then that's nothing. He would never dare use it. Who would he report you to? The law? He's keeping a disorderly establishment, he's in more danger than you."

"Bren, he threatened to show it to my father!"

Brendan could barely contain his irritation. "It's an empty threat. What would he stand to gain by doing that? Your father would call him out—or beat him senseless," he added, realizing that Tony's father was not likely to employ a gentleman's option.

Tony was shaking his head worriedly. "It's not an empty threat. He could see that I was afraid he'd talk. Bren, you have to help me. I told him I would do it once, if he'd tear that page from the register and burn it, and he agreed. But he said I'd have to do it with you."

"*No.* Absolutely not."

"Brendan!"

"Tony!" He took a deep breath, calmed himself, and refrained from mimicking his friend's whining tone any further. "Stop and think, please. You did something foolish, but you know it was foolish, and you know it would be a worse mistake to do it again. If he can make you do what he wants by holding that paper over your head, how can you think he would ever consent to give it up?"

"He said—"

"A man who would stoop to that kind of low dealing would say anything. You must realize that it would be the most serious kind of mistake to have anything further to do with him, or with that place. As for dragging me down to that hellhole, no. Absolutely not."

"I thought you would help me!"

"Then you weren't thinking very clearly, were you? There is no way I would be caught dead on that stage. I told you that once, and I'm telling you again. If you have a grain of sense, you'll realize that this is Danegeld. Once you pay it, you're trapped into paying again and again. He'll not be satisfied with one performance. Why should he be?"

"What can I do?"

"Stay away from the place. What do you expect me to do, suggest you set fire to it? The way those buildings are connected and the abysmal luck you've had of late, you would probably murder everyone but Dobson himself, and no one deserves that. Or you might just report him to the police, anonymously. It's illegal to keep a molly house, after all."

Tony brightened. "Do you think that would serve?"

After a moment's consideration, Brendan shook his head. "No. The problem's the same— you can't do that without harming everyone else, including my godfather. And if you did turn him in, the fellow would certainly guess you had informed on him, and name you just out of spite."

"He would," Tony agreed. "And that's just what he'll do it if I refuse."

"Tony, that's absurd! It would make no sense—can you imagine he would be stupid enough to incriminate himself on such a serious charge, just to spite you?"

"Yes, I see that, but you're talking about the authorities. I'm not so worried about them as I am about my father."

Brendan did not believe that Dobson had anything to gain by such an act, but he knew there was no way he was going to convince Tony. "Very well. Let me see what I can do. Put him off for a week or two. Tell him you are considering his offer."

"But I need help right now!"

"I can't give it right now," Brendan said flatly. "Tony, I must have time to think, and to ask my brother's advice. I'll keep your name out of it, never fear, but I know that when he was in the Army, he and his friends got into all manner of scrapes."

"Nothing like this!"

"I certainly hope not, but I am at a loss to answer you and it may be that James would have some helpful suggestions. It's the best I can do." He rose, making sure his clothes were back in their proper order. "I must go now."

Tony looked crestfallen, but realized he'd get no better answer. "Oh, well. I suppose I can avoid that part of town for a few days."

"If you can, you should get out of town altogether, go off to some quiet place in the country."

"No, I could never do that. Not without telling my father why I was leaving." He poured himself another drink, and looked up hopefully. "I don't suppose you'd like to spend the night?"

Brendan bit back a retort. "No, thank you. I'm mending my ways, and you might want to consider doing the same."

Tony looked up, his expression crafty. "I'll tell Dee that I'm working on you… trying to talk you into coming back to the club."

"Don't." Startled by the hardness of his own voice, Brendan saw the shock on Tony's face, too, and decided to press on for emphasis. "I mean what I say, Tony. Make no mistake—I am deeply offended by your deceit. You lured me into that club under false pretenses. 'A club with good food and interesting entertainment,' you said! *Interesting!'* You knew I would never have gone if you'd told me what kind of place it was!"

"Of course you wouldn't. You're so worried about the proprieties—"

"Yes, I am! And it seems I have reason to be. Have you no sense at all?"

"Of course I have! Damn it, you carry on as though I'd given him your name and address." He pouted. "And what if I did, hey? What would you do?"

He was spoiling for a fight—a sordid squabble, so they might kiss and make up. But Brendan wasn't about to oblige him, on either account. "I would do nothing," he said. "Nothing at all. If I told the truth—the whole truth—about my visit to his club, you and he would both be hanged. If you do not have the sense to realize that, I am certain he does. If he were foolish enough to come looking for me, I would tell him I had not the slightest notion why you took me there. But he would not dare bring that kind of accusation into my father's house."

Tony took another swallow from his flask. "He might… if I brought him."

Brendan stared at the once-loved face, distorted by anger, fear, and drink. He would not have thought Tony would ever stoop so low—but he'd learned a lot about Tony's potential, hadn't he? Forced to the wall, he replied, "Then I would call you a liar. And I'd call you out. That is how a gentleman deals with an unspeakable insult."

Tony's face crumpled. "Gentleman? You bastard! I'm just trade, is that it?" His voice took on a mincing tone. "'The stink of the shop,' isn't that what you lordly *gentlemen* say? My father's money isn't like yours, he earned it with his own hard work, not off someone else's back."

"This has nothing to do with your father." Brendan wanted to shout it, but he kept himself under control. Like it or not, he *was* a gentleman, born and bred, and he was not about to allow this situation turn into a brawl.

"It has everything to do with him." Tony was starting to go to pieces, and Brendan had no idea what to do. "Everything. Might as well blow my brains out. I'll do it, too!" he threatened. "See if I don't! What else can I do?"

Brendan closed his eyes briefly. He wasn't about to accept Tony's harebrained, disgusting proposition, but he didn't want blood on his hands—even if he knew it wasn't really his responsibility. "No," he said. "Give me a week. I think you're a fool to worry about Dobson, but there must be a way to spike his guns. I'll be in touch. Just—whatever you do, for pity's sake stay away from The Arbor!"

Brendan left the hotel feeling soiled. How had something that had once seemed so deeply moving, so delightful, deteriorated into something so demeaning? How, *how* could Tony be so incredibly stupid?

Well, maybe it was not stupidity so much as ignorance. Tony's father had taught him to get what he wanted with money, wheedling, or threats. Tony probably did not truly understand that Brendan's family, or any upper-class family, would close ranks against an unsupported accusation of something so outrageous, especially from someone of Tony's class. If he were to show up at the Townsend home with the keeper of a mollyhouse in tow and the admission that he had lured Brendan to a genuine den of iniquity… he would be turned back out on the street with the threat of a court action for slander. Surely, if he were thinking rationally, he would know that his threats were not only empty, but self-destructive.

What if he was genuinely self-destructive, though? What desperate measures might he be driven to by his panic?

And who was there to go to for advice? James had met Tony once, and had asked Brendan if he wanted their father to intercede with the college to replace his wealthy but trade-tainted roommate with someone of their own class. At the time, of course, that was the last thing he'd wanted, so he'd fobbed his brother off with some nonsense about broadening his experience of the world. He didn't think James could possibly have guessed the real situation. It was a pity they'd met, since Brendan had few intimate friends and no matter how delicately he phrased his explanation of the problem, James might well deduce who was in trouble.

It would have to be James. This was certainly not something Brendan could take to their father, even if the Viscount weren't up to his ears in spring planning and planting at Martindale. Their father had an estate manager, of course, but he took a real interest in the management of his properties, and at this time of year he would invariably be out in the fields and orchards, seeing to it that all was going as it should.

Besides, his advice would be the same as it was when his own sons got into scrapes: Tony must apply to his father for influence or money to smooth his way out of trouble and accept the scolding that would go with it, or gird his loins and face the music himself. Which was impossible. Tony was as likely to deal with his own problems as Galahad was likely to begin playing a harpsichord. Neither had the capacity.

Brendan turned his footsteps homeward. He needed to think things through. One good thing about James—he could be trusted to keep a secret, and he was probably so busy with his own affairs that he would not exercise undue curiosity about his younger brother's concerns. How could James imagine his quiet, sensible younger brother might possibly get himself into serious difficulty?

By the time he arrived at home, Brendan had a general notion of how to present the situation, but he had also come to the conclusion that home was the worst possible place to bring it up. After dinner, he drew James aside, mentioned that he had something to discuss, and asked his brother if they might meet in private somewhere. James suggested White's, and the following afternoon Brendan met him at the club for a drink.

The very atmosphere of the place was soothing, with its high ceilings and murmured conversations. Comfortable chairs, a table in a quiet corner, a pristine white tablecloth and polished glasses… everything contributed to an air of dignity and security. This was so far removed from Tony's grubby dilemma they might as well have been on the moon.

James requested a bottle of madiera. "You're very mysterious with all this, little brother," he said as the waiter departed. "It isn't anything in the petticoat-line, is it? Or have you begun to have serious thoughts about a lady?"

"I wish it were that simple," Brendan said. "I have a friend…" Seeing the sudden look of dread on his brother's face, Brendan stopped himself and laughed. "I know, you must be thinking 'what has he got himself into, that he can't even own up to it?' But honestly, I am asking on behalf of a friend. He is at his wits' end and hasn't another soul in the world he can confide in, but I haven't the experience to know how to advise him."

"The usual formula is to claim the problem is that of a friend," James said. "I admit, those four words are the last any responsible man wants to hear within the family."

Brendan had to smile. "James, I may be naïve, but I would never have landed myself in such a pea-brained predicament."

James relaxed a bit. "I had to wonder. You've always had an old head on those young shoulders, but I do still remember the scrapes you got up to with Ellie when you were both in the nursery. What's the problem, then?"

Now that he had permission to unburden himself, Brendan realized he could not—at least, not fully—but the return of the waiter with their wine gave him a moment to collect his thoughts.

"My friend did something … indiscreet," he said, turning the stem of his glass and watching the light reflect through the shimmering liquid. "Very indiscreet, the more so because he did it in front of a number of people. It's not as bad as it sounds, in a way; the witnesses would never take any action themselves because they were engaged in equally improper behavior. But another party, who had no direct involvement, is attempting to blackmail my friend into doing something even more unsavory by threatening to inform his family of what he has already done."

James frowned and took a sip of his wine. "You really should consider entering politics," he said. "You've just managed to tell me everything without actually telling me anything."

"I am sorry," Brendan shrugged helplessly. "If it were my own problem—but there, I'm back to the beginning. I should never have done anything so stupid. He was drunk."

"And you've never been drunk? After three years at Oxford? The place must have become a positive monastery since my days in those hallowed halls."

"Of course I have, and I've never noticed any monks, but surely there's a difference between pleasantly muddled and too foxed to remember what one did at the time."

"There is, little brother, and I'm pleased you are aware of it." James held up a hand as Brendan started to protest. "No, no, you're old enough to know, of course. But this friend of yours— I take it he cannot simply go to his family himself—tell the truth and shame the devil?"

"No, not possibly." Brendan considered old Hillyard—a Tartar if he'd ever seen one. "He's like a horse with its spirit broken, that will shy at a fence because there's no heart left in him. His father beat him when he was a boy. May still do, he's frightened enough. And not just the odd caning, James. I've seen the scars." The sweet taste of madiera could not dispel the ugliness of the words. "The old man might even do murder."

James' face reflected his distaste. He was firm with his children, but had rather strong opinions on grown men who would beat women or children. "This unsavory activity your friend took part in—was it illegal?"

"Well, yes, though as far as I know no one was likely to be injured by it. And the worst of it is, he's likely to cave in and do worse if something's not done to prevent it. What makes it difficult is that this deed is not something he can do alone, which is how he happened to come to me for help. Why he ever thought I would agree—"

"You've refused, I hope!"

"Of course. But he is in a terrible fix. I doubt there's anyone else he might approach for help in getting out of it, and I haven't the faintest idea how to proceed—short of telling him to get out of London altogether, which he can't do because of family obligations."

"That's... an interesting situation, I must say. May I assume this trouble is not something he could buy his way out of?"

"I hadn't thought of that." Brendan considered the possibility, then shook his head. "No. I suppose it might be possible, but he hasn't any money of his own, at least not the sort of sum that might loosen this scoundrel's grip."

"That might not be wise in any case," James said. "I shouldn't have suggested it. If he could buy back evidence, compromising letters or some such thing, that might be worth doing. But is there such evidence?"

"What do you mean?"

"Legal proof that your friend did whatever it was the villain's threatening to use against him. You said the witnesses wouldn't testify?"

"Of course not, they'd—" He caught himself. "James, it's a peculiar situation. To the best of my knowledge, the only evidence is his signature on a registry, but that really says nothing of the activity in which he was involved. As far as I know there's no evidence whatsoever."

"Then what is he afraid of?"

"His father. That's what it comes down to. I've met the old man, and I think he'd be entirely willing to believe the accusation. One look at his son's face and he'd know it was true."

James studied the half-glass of madiera before him. "So the real problem is that your friend hasn't the nerve to tell his black-mailer to go to the devil, lie to his father with a straight face, and settle his own affairs."

"Yes," Brendan admitted. "That's it precisely." He was fairly sure what James' next question would be. But he was mistaken.

"Brendan, are you telling me the whole truth when you say you are not involved in this mysterious illegal behavior?"

"Yes." Well, that was technically true. He'd done nothing but avoid notice at The Arbor. "I can't believe he did such a stupid thing, and if I'd had the slightest inkling of what he intended—"

"Then why are you trying to settle this for him? It's admirable to be concerned for a friend's welfare, little brother, but why not let him stand on his own two feet?"

"Because I know he cannot. And he asked me for help." He'd asked for a lot more than help, and James was right—but Brendan knew that if he simply turned his back on Tony, he would carry the guilt for the rest of his life. "Tell me, James—your tiger, Achilles. You don't need a tiger. I know you once said it was a silly affectation to have a boy riding around in your phaeton merely to blow a horn at a crossroads, and he's really too young for the job. Why did you hire that little ragamuffin?"

James scowled. "It's not the same sort of thing at all, you Jesuit. Achilles is ten years old and if someone hadn't done something, he'd have starved in the gutter. He was stealing oats out of my stable, for the love of heaven—he'd nothing else to eat!"

Brendan nodded. "So you had to do something, or stand by and witness a tragedy. And you did the only decent thing you could do."

"Touché." James touched his forehead with one finger in a mock salute. "But I still cannot see what there is for you to do. If your friend has no spine, you can hardly nail one on from the outside."

"I know that. I am sorely disappointed in his character, if you want the truth. But I feel I must help. He is in such a state that he's threatened to take his own life, and I fear he means it."

"That's a pretty threat, isn't it? Makes him a bit of a black-mailer himself, from the sound of it."

Brendan's heart sank. "I know. You have the truth of it. But… James, can you say his lack of character releases me from my promise to help? I wish it did—but if the Watch were to fish his body out of the Thames I'd still carry the guilt of knowing that I might have prevented it."

James shook his head and glanced about the room as if wishing for distraction. "Well, with our sister being courted by a man of the cloth, I can hardly scold you for being your brother's keeper, but it's damned inconvenient. You couldn't talk to Father, either. You simply could *not* talk to Father. He'd be convinced you were in some dire trouble, and send you on a Continental tour."

"That might be interesting," Brendan agreed, "but not helpful."

James fiddled with his glass. "It is too bad he never took much interest in you. I work with him so closely, and I've only just realized how little you two have to do with one another."

Brendan shrugged. "I have no complaints. Father's two great passions are Mama and the estate, and he's done well by all his children. I must be a terrible puzzle to him, but when I look at my unfortunate friend's predicament, I know how lucky I am."

"You're a better friend than he deserves."

"I wish I were a more resourceful one."

They stared gloomily at one another. Finally James said, "I think you must talk to the Major."

"The Major?"

"Carlisle. My commanding officer, in the Peninsular Wars. He has been to our house, but that must have been when you were up at Oxford. He was the sort of leader any man would've died for—no nonsense, no coddling, but if one of us had a problem, we knew that if the Major couldn't resolve it, things were beyond hope. I can give you an introduction, if you like."

Brendan found himself surprised to realize that it might be easier to discuss this whole affair with a stranger than to sift and sort the facts to avoid scandalizing his brother. "He is discreet?"

"The soul of discretion. In fact…" James looked uncomfortable. "I'd rather not go into detail, but if not for him,

I'd have been in some very hot water over a little matter of a Commodore's wife."

"James!"

His highly respectable brother's expression was so pained Brendan almost wanted to laugh. "She wasn't as careful as—no, I'll say no more. But I warn you, never dally with a woman whose husband has been too long at sea." He laughed at Brendan's startled expression. "For someone who has no interest in the Church, brother, you are too easily shocked. This was before I married, of course, and I was always careful to use French Letters. I'm sure Father gave you the same advice."

"Yes…" Brendan had the odd feeling that by getting into this predicament, even secondhand, he had, in his brother's eyes, somehow crossed some obscure Rubicon of misbehaving manhood. Or was James so accustomed in his role of father to his own brood that he was trying to be sure his little brother was being given proper guidance? "Thus far I've found it easier to simply avoid entanglements."

"That's difficult to do in the Service. Still, I'm sure it's far better to wait for the right girl, if you have the fortitude." James brought out his pocket-book and extracted a bit of paper and pencil. "Let me give you Major Carlisle's direction. I saw him at Angelo's fencing club a few days ago, and I'll put his club down here, too, in case he's gone out of town. He's as horse-mad as you are, spends more time out at his estate than anywhere else." He scribbled the name and addresses down and gave Brendan the note. "I'll send him a letter this afternoon begging his assistance for my unworldly younger brother."

"Thank you, James. I'm sure you're right, and I'm being foolish…."

"At least you're looking after a friend, and not in the basket yourself. I do hope you give Carlisle more details than you gave me, or he'll have a devil of a time giving you any more advice than I could!"

Brendan waited for two nerve-wracking days to be certain that

James' letter had reached Major Carlisle. When he finally screwed up his courage to present himself, he had rehearsed what he had to say so many times that he was afraid he'd be talking in his sleep.

He took a hackney to Carlisle's home; he had no wish to leave his horse or James' carriage standing outside while he conducted confidential business. Suffused with a lack of confidence and an ever-mounting anxiety, he found himself presenting his card to a noncommittal butler and standing in a handsome vestibule just off the foyer, admiring the black-and-white floor tiles and carved wooden pillars at either side of the doorway.

"Mr. Townsend?" A deep, well-modulated voice brought him around, and he found his mind protesting, *no, not fair!* even as he extended a hand to clasp the one extended to him by Major Philip Carlisle.

Major Carlisle's lean, handsome face, bronze-gold hair, and steady hazel eyes created such an overwhelming impression of male beauty that Brendan was ready to fall to his knees before Carlisle's high-top boots, and weep. The most dazzling man he'd ever seen—a man who suddenly made him believe in the phrase, *love at first sight*—and he was here to seek his help in dealing with a situation so disgraceful that he was not sure he could explain it. It was cruel of the Fates to have dealt him this blow.

"Major," he said, pushing his disordered thoughts aside. "I-I do apologize for intruding. My brother suggested I consult you, but if this time is inconvenient—"

"Well, it is, I'm afraid," Carlisle said regretfully. "I must leave town for a day or two, but I remember your brother with much gratitude—he pushed me out of the way of a bullet, once—and I am entirely willing to be of service, if I can."

Of course—preparation for travel would explain the way he was dressed, the trim buckskin breeches and riding boots. Abashed, Brendan apologized, and added, "I should take my leave, sir, and return when you are not pressed for time."

"Oh, not at all. It's my valet who's hard at work; I have little to do while he packs my case. If you will explain your difficulty, I shall endeavor to give you what advice I may. Come, let me offer you some refreshment."

Brendan followed him down the hallway, much the same way one of James' spaniels would have trailed behind him. He hoped he could explain the problem without shocking or angering the Major, or sounding like an utter idiot for getting himself into this stupid situation.

CHAPTER 5

Philip Carlisle found himself nonplussed, an unusual circumstance. James Townsend's letter had been so vague as to be nearly useless. That was unexpected. From their time in the service, he knew James Townsend to be a man who could both think and write clearly, so the source of confusion must have been the younger brother, Brendan.

If that letter had been the only one to arrive in the morning post, he'd have tackled it without reservation—but another letter had arrived at the same time, one that left no doubt that there was a serious issue requiring his intervention. What he needed to do was obvious—put off young Mr. Townsend's visit to a later date, and leave town with all possible haste. He led his visitor to his study, intending to explain that he had urgent business and make an appointment for the following week.

But something in the young man's desperation touched his rescuer's instincts. Brendan Townsend had not gone very far into his explanation before Carlisle realized why James had been so vague in his letter. Either he knew such things must not be set down in black and white, or he had been left in blissful ignorance of how serious the problem really was... and Carlisle suspected the latter.

He wasn't certain he wanted to deal with this matter at all. He was not unaware of the existence of such establishments, but to find a respectable youngster such as this wandering into one was more than he'd expected. A fine-looking lad, too, much more handsome than his older brother. Had his friend—not much of a friend, in Carlisle's estimate—been trying to seduce him? Or was it even worse than that?

"I'm not certain I understand," he said, when Townsend's exposition stumbled to an awkward halt. "This innkeeper, or whatever he calls himself—is he attempting to blackmail you?"

"Oh, no, sir!" There was no artifice in that denial. "No, I—I don't mean to sound like a prig, but I should never have put myself into such a compromising position. If I'd had any notion what sort of place it was, I'd never have gone within a mile of it. I could not even bring myself to describe it to my brother!"

Relieved, Carlisle asked, "Then how does it concern you?"

"Well…" Townsend toyed with the glass on the table before him, but he did not empty it, as Carlisle knew a man in desperate trouble might do. "I *was* there, you see. I knew that my friend was in his cups, but I did nothing to stop him—and before you say it, I also realize that he was so very bosky I might not have been able to do anything more than create a scene. That was part of the reason I did not try—but now I wish that I had."

Carlisle nodded. This had a familiar sound—the sensible but overly amiable youth drawn into a bad situation by a poor choice of companions. *I should have turned Roman and become a priest,* Carlisle thought. *I seem to spend half my time listening to confessions.* "So you are not directly involved in this shambles."

"No, sir. I was there because I had no idea what sort of place it was—my friend admitted afterward that he knew I would not have gone if he'd been honest about where we were going."

"What does your friend wish you to do, then? Pull his chestnuts out of the fire, after he lied to you?"

"That's what it amounts to. From what he has told me, this innkeeper has no credible hold over him. It's the threat of scandal that worries him… and the fear of what his father may do."

"A fine time for him to worry about the risk of scandal."

Carlisle shook his head. "So long as there are no witnesses, the customer of an irregular establishment is never at as great a risk as the proprietor. One may leave, the other cannot. Do you think the fellow would make good on his threat?"

"I have no idea. I've never met him."

"And a second, more obvious question—why is he doing this? With no proof of his claim and no witnesses who'd ever come forward, the man is bound to be bluffing."

"I am afraid my answer is the same. I can only speculate. When I was there, the members of the club seemed quite... taken with my friend's performance. He's a handsome young man, and one of the patrons—a very well-dressed older gentleman—seemed anxious to make a closer acquaintance. It may be..." The young man broke off, in obvious embarrassment.

What an utterly wretched situation. "Do you suspect the innkeeper is acting as a procurer?"

"I should hate to think so." He hesitated. "I suppose that may be possible. But if that were the case, why should he not simply relay the gentleman's invitation? I've never met this Dobson, nor do I want to, and my experience of such matters is—" the youngster broke off with a nervous laugh. "I was about to say, regrettably limited, but I've no experience of it at all and I can hardly regret that."

Carlisle frowned. "Investigation must be the first step, then. Until you know something of your opponent, you have no way of guessing his reaction."

Brendan Townsend spread his hands, palms up. "Sir, I know I must sound incredibly naïve, but that is where I come to a dead end. I have no idea how to set about such inquiries, and the matter is such an unpleasant one that I fear my clumsy efforts would attract the very attention I seek to avoid."

"I see." Carlisle glanced at the clock on the mantle. If he were to leave in an hour, two at most, he would be able to reach Twin Oaks this evening and meet with Livingstone early in the morning. "Well, Mr. Townsend, I would be willing to help you with this dilemma, but I have a previous claim on my time. If you are at liberty to accompany me, we might discuss your problem en route, and it may be possible that you can assist me in some way. What do you know of smuggling?"

Townsend blinked in obvious bewilderment. "In the sense of general knowledge, sir, or practical application?" he asked cautiously.

Carlisle saw that his line of reasoning had veered off rather abruptly, and laughed at the delicacy of the young man's question. "I am not suggesting you join the Free Traders, sir! I breed horses on a small holding out in Kent, and an old friend of mine is the local magistrate. As you might expect, since the place lies near to roads that run between the sea and London, there is a certain amount of smuggling, and, as you might also expect, much of that activity goes unpunished."

"I have a brother in the Navy," Townsend said. "He says that in some coastal towns, that's almost the whole of local industry."

"Your brother has it right," Carlisle said. "Well, as a magistrate, my friend is not at all pleased with the situation, but he has no Bow Street Runners to stop it. He tolerates what he must—but one thing he will not tolerate is murder. A young man has been severely beaten, and that is all I know of the situation at the moment. I was asked to come down and see if I can be of assistance."

"Can the magistrate not bring in the military?"

"He has done the next-best thing; he wrote to me." Carlisle suddenly realized how vain that must sound, and explained, "I have some experience with these matters. There is an army base at Chatham, not far away, so help can be summoned quickly at need. But he knows that if he brings in the military in force, he'll never know the truth. Even if the locals may not approve of what happened, they'll close ranks to protect their own. Since I am a local man, he hopes that I may be able to get a line on who is responsible. I must attend to this as quickly as possible, and I fear this matter outweighs your friend's difficulty. The man who was attacked lies near death. If he does not recover, I will be hunting a murderer, so if you choose to accompany me, you should know there is a certain amount of danger."

"I'm a fair shot," Brendan Townsend said diffidently. "I'm afraid I don't have my brother's military experience, though— I've never fired at a man."

Carlisle was impressed by the young man's honesty as well as his readiness to step up to the challenge. "Never mind that," he said. "You'll find the ability appears miraculously, when the other fellow is shooting at you. Can you be ready to leave within the hour?"

"So long as my sister does not require an escort tonight or to-morrow, yes. But I may be forced to return to London before your business is finished."

Carlisle rose, and offered his hand. "I'll have my coachman drive you home," he said. "We shall leave as soon as you return. If you cannot get away, send word back with him, and I'll be in touch as soon as I come back to town."

Brendan settled back against the squabs in Carlisle's well-up-holstered chaise, his thoughts spinning. It would not do to be so excited at the thought of spending several hours in a closed carriage with Philip Carlisle.

What a splendid gentleman! The calm, assured manner, the air of easy competence, the willingness to help someone he'd never met before… the warm, firm handshake, kind eyes, and a chest that Brendan wanted only to throw himself upon, be enfolded by those strong arms and feel safe against all the world's uncertainties… *Look at yourself, you dunderhead. You're smitten, and if you had any sense at all you would cry off before you make matters any worse.*

He bit his lip. The older man was tremendously attractive, but Brendan had not missed Carlisle's slight frown when he explained just what sort of establishment the Arbor was, nor the look of distaste when he revealed what Tony had done there.

Major Philip Carlisle was clearly no sodomite, and even if he was willing to consider helping disentangle Tony from his plight, he was obviously repelled by the situation.

As Brendan was, himself. Perhaps it was some hidden effeminacy that made him squeamish of sex with a stranger, but he saw very little connection between what he had wanted, the love he had hoped would develop from the intimately affectionate friendship he'd had with Tony, and the crude physical experience at the club.

Or, he suddenly realized, the crude physical experience in Tony's hotel room a few days earlier. He could have stopped that in a moment, shoved Tony away. Why had he not done so? Perhaps he had simply become accustomed to sexual satisfaction—so too did a drunkard become accustomed to inebriation. That was hardly an excuse. He should be thankful that his experiment in sodomy had reached such an unsatisfactory conclusion, and give it up as a bad effort. Did he really want to spend the rest of his life in brief, meaningless affairs with men like Tony or that low-life molly in the Arbor, and end like Uncle Cedric, sneaking around to paw at men young enough to be his son? God forbid! It would be better to die than to live that way.

He had to pull himself together and exercise a little self-discipline. Perhaps Tony's demand for help was a blessing in disguise. He could find a way to free Tony from the threat of blackmail, and free himself as well. Major Carlisle… was obviously a man of normal inclinations and considerable virtue, and it would simply not do to harbor disgraceful desires for him.

If he minded his manners and didn't make a complete fool of himself, perhaps he could even earn Carlisle's friendship. He might be of some assistance in the smuggling affair—he might not be experienced, but an able-bodied assistant would surely have some value.

Lost in his ruminations, Brendan was surprised when the carriage came to a stop outside his family home. He thanked the driver and hurried in, only to find everyone in the family out on their own errands and the usually ubiquitous Norwood, for a wonder, occupied with some task in the butler's pantry.

A quick consultation with his diary assured him that the next two days were his own, so he threw a couple of shirts and neck-cloths into a bag, added a pair of shoes and some smallclothes, then took the time to pen a quick note to his mother and Elspeth, assuring them that he would be in town long before the next event at Almack's.

As he was pulling on his riding boots, he wondered whether he should leave a note for James as well. Better to do so. Since his brother had known of his appointment with Major Carlisle, he wrote only, "Major C called out of town, am accompanying him and should return by Sunday." James might wish for more information, but if the note were to fall into the hands of any of the ladies of the household, there could be no possible cause for concern. James knew how to contact Carlisle, at any rate, in case of an emergency.

Halfway down the stair, Brendan realized he would need a warmer outer garment if he meant to go jaunting out into the country, and risked a quick return to his room for his riding coat. Even with this delay, he was pleased to return to the Major's town house well within the prescribed hour.

When he saw a light carriage pulling up before the front door with a pair of matched bays in harness, his attention was once more distracted from his problems. What beauties! Not only were they a true match in color, they were within a hairsbreadth in height and conformation as well, and moved like one soul in two bodies. They came to a stop just before the front steps, standing with their heads high, alert but not fidgeting, awaiting the next command.

"Major Carlisle's cattle?" Brendan asked the groom holding the reins.

"Aye. Bred 'em himself. Romulus and Remus."

"Classic indeed." Brendan circled them, his case in hand, lost in admiration. If this was the sort of horse Carlisle was breeding, he hoped their sojourn in the countryside would allow time for a visit to the stables.

"I see you've met the lads," Carlisle asked, coming down his front steps. "What do you think of them?"

"A proper pair of high-steppers," Brendan said admiringly. "They make me wish I were rich, so that if you decided to part with them, I might make an offer."

"I should have to be in desperate straits to part with these two." Carlisle patted the nearest horse reassuringly, giving the harness and fittings a quick inspection and apparently finding it all to his liking. "I must warn you, Mr. Townsend—I have a small eccentricity when it comes to travel. I prefer to drive myself whenever possible, and the day looks to be holding fair. Would you mind riding outside?"

"Not in the slightest!"

Carlisle's eccentricity apparently did not extend to leaving the coachman at home, so he was given the privilege of riding inside while the two gentlemen climbed up to the driver's box. The Major snapped his whip and the team moved smoothly into motion, joining the flow of traffic through the busy London streets. Brendan recognized that the job of driving a team in these circumstances required a certain amount of concentration, and made no attempt to converse.

Once they had cleared the city congestion, Carlisle relaxed slightly. "We shall be on the road the rest of the day," he said. "I don't demand you martyr yourself to my whims, though; I expect I'll call Edward up to take my place when we stop to rest the horses, but if you'd rather be out of the wind at any point, just let me know."

"Thank you, but I would not trade this for the world." Brendan suddenly realized he did not know how long the trip would be, or even where they were going. "Will these two be able to take us all the way there, without changing them for another team?"

Carlisle nodded. "Yes, of course, touch wood. They can do up to fifty miles in easy stages, but my place is a shade under thirty-five miles away, and I'd not push them further."

Brendan was impressed. "What stages, sir? How do you ration their fodder?"

Carlisle cast him a sidelong glance. "A horseman, are you?"

"Merely a student of the art, sir."

"Aren't we all?" Carlisle said with a smile. "I'll make a stop after ten miles, give them a drop of water and a bit of hay, nothing that will lie too heavy on their bellies. By the time they're ready for a longer meal, and a rest, so will we be. I don't like to leave them on the road unless I must, but there's a reliable hostler at the Knight's Inn, about halfway home. He'll give them a rubdown and a bait of corn while we have a leisurely meal, and they get corn again after six or eight more miles. After that, they know they have their own stalls and warm mash waiting—you'll see how they fly."

"My father's head groom does something similar," Brendan said. "My father is not as punctilious, but he and my brother tend to leave the horses to Spencer's care—that's our groom. I'm the odd one in the family—I'd as soon live over the stable."

Still smiling, Carlisle said, "I'm glad you caught me before I left town. Even without this situation arising, I'd have been on the road in a day or two. My prize mare is due to foal soon, and I mean to be there for the event, if I can. Silly, I know; my own groom, Matthews, knows more about horses than I ever will, but I do like to be on hand to lend moral support."

"I should do the same," Brendan admitted. "Perhaps it's due to being herd creatures, but the beasts do seem to take heart from having a trusted owner nearby."

"Indeed. They'll gallop into hell for you if you give them your confidence." Carlisle's expression shadowed for a moment. "That was why I finally had to leave the cavalry. War is hell on men, but at least we go into it knowing what to expect. Our horses trust us, and we use them like machines."

"So James said—he called it a waste, but it's worse than that."

"Indeed."

They rode on in silence for a little while, and then Carlisle said, "We've time enough to converse, now, and a clear road. Shall we return to your problem?"

Brendan sighed. "I suppose we must, though if you preferred to go on talking horses, I could not find it in me to object." He watched the team's shoulders moving steadily, in order to avoid looking at the man beside him, and forced himself to say what had been on his mind since he first saw Carlisle's face. "There is one thing I must ask you, sir, and I should have thought of it from the start. I realize that the activities of that club are not only…distasteful, but quite illegal, and so is neglecting to bring it to the attention of the authorities. I am still not certain I should have imposed upon you for your assistance. If you would prefer to reconsider your decision to help me—"

"Not at all." Carlisle guided the team to one side of the road as a post-chaise approached from the opposite direction. When it had passed, he said, "Mr. Townsend, the club you describe is not a place that I would ever choose to visit for my own entertainment. Nonetheless, I have served with many different sorts of men… and one or two were that sort, and I have to say that they were just as brave in the field and far less trouble on furlough than most of their skirt-chasing colleagues. Whatever the law may say on the matter, I don't feel I have a right to sit in judgement."

Brendan had not realized how tense he was until Carlisle's words soothed his fear. "Thank you, sir. What do you think we can do?"

"The first thing I wish to do, when we return to London, is to contact a gentleman I know who will be able to find out who owns the buildings in that district, and see if we can discover whether the fellow who's running the establishment is actually the owner."

"And then?"

"Then… If he's but a hired manager, the owner should be informed of his misbehavior—preferably by your friend, since he is the one who's been threatened. If Dobson does own the place, we must question your friend as to details, and lay our plan accordingly. One way or another, this fine specimen must be made to understand that he is not going to have his way."

The rest of the trip went as Carlisle had described. They maintained a reasonable pace of perhaps six or seven miles an hour, and his host seemed content to let the conversation return to more pleasant subjects, pointing out landmarks here and there. Brendan was happy enough to relax, observing Carlisle's effortless handling of the ribbons—he was clearly one of those men who could sense a horse's every mood through the reins—and enjoying the bright spring sunshine. The coming green of a new season combined with the confidence he was beginning to place in his new acquaintance to lift his spirits out of the depths to which they'd sunk in the past couple of days. Perhaps there really was a way out of this unsavory muddle into which he had blindly allowed Tony to drag him.

It remained to be seen, however, whether he would be able to avoid disgracing himself in the eyes of the handsome, self-assured gentleman beside him. The instant attraction he had felt at their first meeting had not diminished one iota. Hopeless, to be sure, and probably better so. His first attempt at the love surpassing that of women had landed him in a pickle, and he was not about to make that mistake again.

He did wish that he might stop wanting to try.

"My lord, I regret to say I cannot fulfill your requirements." Dickie Dee was exerting every bit of self-control he possessed to maintain the obsequious tone appropriate to his lowly station. It was a struggle, since the pompous fool before him, whatever his social rank, was nothing more than a filthy, bum-fucking sodomite. But His Lordship was willing to pay for the privileges of membership, and, Dobson reminded himself, it would not do to offend a customer.

"What do you mean? I've seen that lad here half a dozen times, and there was nothing shy about him. If it's money he wants—"

"I am afraid that is not the issue, my lord. It appears the young gentleman,"—he said it in a way that let His Lordship know that a man who'd behave that way was nothing of the sort—"realized that he acted outside the bounds of discretion, and has decided to mend his ways."

His visitor answered with a snort of laughter. "What rubbish. What utter rubbish! A young buck who drops his drawers for any yahoo isn't going to mend his ways, and we both know it."

Dobson shrugged. "The Arbor is a private club, my lord. I have no authority over its members. As you yourself observed, he has been quite regular in his attendance at our little gatherings. I'm sure that if you are patient, he will return."

He could not see all of his visitor's face—as always, he had donned his mask before entering the club—but he could see the cunning grin. "Come now… I know you have his name and direction. I'd pay handsomely for that, and no one need ever be the wiser."

Dobson let himself appear to consider the offer. Ah, this was rich—to watch this powerful bastard haggle for what he wanted, to stand before his desk hat in hand, humbled. After a suitable moment, he shook his head, feigning regret. "But, my lord, that is one thing I cannot possibly give you. I am no procurer! If I were to sell his information to you, what surety would you have that I might not offer your own name to another? This is a sacred trust, sir!" *And more to the point, a very profitable one.*

"Damn your sacred trust!" The gentleman stood glaring for a moment, then brought his fist down on the desk. "You must convince him."

"I shall do what I can, my lord. I can do no more." Dobson maintained a façade of virtuous blandness, staring back until the visitor stormed from the room. Then he let out a tremendous breath and sat back in his comfortably upholstered chair, his eye catching the portrait on the wall opposite.

"Uncle Godfrey, you filthy old sinner," he said aloud. Though he should not blaspheme the old man. It was Godfrey Dobson who had, over the course of several years, turned a run-down tavern into an inconspicuous, highly profitable molly house. Upon his death, the establishment had fallen into the hands of his nephew and only living relative, and Dobson had taken to it like a duck to water. He had been more than a little appalled to learn that his reclusive uncle had apparently been a sodomite himself—he could not doubt the enthusiastic eulogies when the Cock and Bottle had been re-opened after a brief period of mourning and legal matters—but he had resigned himself to making quite a good living from immoral sources. After all, if he did not provide drinks to the bastards, and a place to rut, someone else undoubtedly would.

And it was his own ingenuity that had brought The Arbor into existence. The Cock and Bottle was a molly house, nothing more or less, and it had survived for some time by a policy of admission by recommendation only, and judicious bribing of the Watch. But Dobson had not misjudged the desire of the socially superior for the opportunity to look down on the riffraff. A few hints to the more prosperous-looking patrons, an offer to some of the better-mannered commoners of an easy job with the opportunity to meet well-heeled gentlemen, and The Arbor had been launched with no fanfare whatever to a most appreciative clientele.

Dobson congratulated himself again on his initiative. The businesses were paying well, even if he had to rub shoulders with some of the lowest scum in High Society, and he was sharp enough to know that such a lucrative endeavor could not last forever. But the beauty of it was that it did not have to. Between the prices he was able to charge for drink and private rooms, and the membership fees, he should be able to retire in five years.

Or possibly even sooner, if he could lever that sulky Hillyard brat into indulging his childish desire to show off. Or, if he could not, he might at least squeeze a pretty penny out of Hillyard Senior in exchange for banning his wayward son and keeping quiet about it. What a pair. The old man an arrogant nouveau-riche, the young man a drunken sodomite.

"What is the world coming to?" Dobson asked Uncle Godfrey's portrait. "Perdition, nothing but perdition."

And what a fortunate thing for him that perdition was so profitable.

∽ CHAPTER 6 ∾

Philip Carlisle was up at dawn the next morning, his usual habit when he was in the country. Throwing on the clothes he kept for messy stable activities, he passed through the kitchen to drink a hasty cup of tea and collect a couple of scones, which he ate on his way to the stable to see La Reine. His servants, accustomed to this excessively casual behavior, merely nodded tolerantly and prepared themselves to give proper service to Mr. Carlisle's young guest. Surely the son of a viscount would stay in bed until a respectable hour, and stay where he belonged until he was awakened.

Unaware of his servants' regret for his lack of consequence, Carlisle dusted the crumbs from his fingers and slipped into the stable. Most of the horses had been turned out into the field so the stable-boys could begin the daily task of cleaning their stalls, but he could see Queenie's lovely sorrel head peering inquisitively out of the foaling box, her blonde mane draped coquettishly over one eye.

"How are you, my dear?" he asked, laughing aloud when her ears pricked at the sound of his voice. "Still waiting your time?"

"It'll be soon, Major," said the horse in a strangely unfeminine voice—and then Matthews' grizzled head appeared over the stall door. He went on, "The little darlin's bagged up, and just look at 'er. She knows something's about to happen. This week, my word on it—or I'll be standin' drinks at the Owl."

"That would be a first, would it not?" Carlisle asked.

His groom grinned. "Not the first time I've been wrong, sir—just the first time I'd bet on it."

Carlisle opened the box and stepped inside, stroking the side of Queenie's satiny neck as she gave him a companionable nudge. He could see some of the changes Matthews spoke of—the mare's sides were bulging considerably more than they had been when he'd last seen her two weeks earlier, and he could detect a difference in her stance. She sidled, leaning against him just a bit, and that surprised him.

"Aye, she's been a little clingy-like, Major," Matthews said, watching them. "Got a touch o' nerves, don't know what's to expect. I've been sleepin' here the past two nights."

Carlisle noticed the hammock, folded up and hung from a hook beside the door. "Good job. You have the boys ready to help?"

"They're ready, but this bein' her first time, I figured you'd take that watch."

"Indeed I will, but I'm not too proud to ask for an extra hand. Do you mean to turn her out?"

"Aye, sir, a beautiful day like this. Only I thought you'd want to see her first."

"You know me too well." He stepped back as Matthews swung the door wide, and Queenie followed along behind as they walked toward the big door that opened into the paddock. "I wish I could stay, but I'm off to see Sir Thomas Livingstone."

Matthews gave him an inquiring glance, but said nothing.

"It seems the free-trade boys have been playing a bit rough while I was away," Carlisle said.

"Aye, Major, they have at that. I've done as you say—kept my head down, kept an eye on the boys—but there's something strange afoot."

"In what way?"

"Most times they have trouble, it's from the outside—Preventives, or a Navy blockade. You know."

Carlisle nodded. If a local turned up with a black eye or other infirmity, he often came by it dishonestly.

"This time... there's nobody about who shouldn't be. Old Ezra and his boys, Tom and Roger, seem to be in the middle of it—or they was, til Tom got laid out."

They'd reached the door by now, and the two men stood aside while Queenie proceeded out into the paddock, her pale mane rippling as she lifted her head into the breeze. "You've no hint of who might have done that, have you?" Carlisle asked.

"No, sir, nor do I want to," Matthews said frankly. "But there's some as say it was done with a view to takin' over from Ezra. A pity it wasn't Roger they went for; for all he's but a lad, he's forever starting fights and acting the fool. Tom's a sensible lad—or he was, if I heard right. Slipped away yesterday without waking up, they say."

"Yes, so I understand. It's a shame. Sensible in what way?"

"Agin' murder. There's some of these boys get pot-valiant, they're ready to take on all the King's horses and the men as well, kill anyone as tried to get in their way. Tom, he'd calm 'em down, remind 'em the surest way to bring on the soldiers was to start leavin' corpses around."

"True enough." Carlisle allowed himself a last look at Queenie and the other horses enjoying a quiet graze, then reminded himself that it was duty first. "I had better go see Sir Thomas," he said. "Young Townsend will likely be down here before I return. See what you think of him. He's James Townsend's younger brother."

"Aye, Major. Good lad?"

"He seems to be. I let him take the reins for a spell and could not have asked for better; if he had the ambition, he'd soon be known as a top-sawyer. The boy's got a good feel for the horses, and no inclination for useless flash. And I think if he'd had his way he'd have been down here last night, never mind it was past dark when we got here."

"If he wants to ride?"

"Whiskey or Sailor, I think. He might be able to handle Nightshade, but I'd want to be there if he tried." The big stallion, black as night and sire to Queenie's unborn foal, could be a handful even for Carlisle himself. "And now I must be off, or I'll be here all day. Have one of the boys hitch Reverie to the dog-cart, if you would. I'll drive myself."

Matthews touched his cap and returned to the stable as Carlisle hurried back to the house. He'd have just time enough to dress properly and get himself over to the magistrate's, three miles distant. Thanks to Matthews' gossip, he probably had as much information now as Livingstone himself did.

As serious as this business was, Carlisle found it difficult to maintain the proper frame of mind to contemplate murder. The morning was glorious, the sun well up but the spring air still comfortably cool, and his lovely mare was about to give birth to a foal. By the time he presented himself at the door of Greenways, the magistrate's rambling country house, he had just barely managed to subdue his high spirits.

Farnam, Livingstone's butler, welcomed Carlisle in his usual stone-faced manner, and had barely started down the hall when Sir Thomas Livingstone entered from another room. "Major Carlisle. Thank you for coming. I know you're an early riser, but would you care to join me for breakfast?"

"Sir Thomas." Carlisle took Livingstone's extended hand. "Yes, thank you. I had a bite when I first rose, but that seems a long time ago."

Livingstone led him into a sunlit breakfast room, where a footman waited with a silver coffee pot. The man filled their cups, then left. The magistrate added a lump of sugar to his cup, stirred it thoughtfully, and sighed. "Where shall I begin?"

Carlisle thought his old friend, never imposing in stature, seemed even smaller today, and looked every day of his sixty years. "I arrived last night and found your message waiting. It's murder, then?"

"Yes. That's not official, of course; not until the coroner sits on the case. I may see him later today. I sent a rider to London as soon as Jenkins was brought in. It's a pity it was Tom; from what

I gather, there were plenty of others who'd have been better lost."

"Who was he?"

"Tom Jenkins, one of the local lads. He was twenty-four or five, I believe. The elder of Ezra Jenkins' two sons. I don't know if you've ever paid attention, but it's generally known that Ezra is the chief of the free-trade gentlemen in this area."

"Getting on in years, is he?" Carlisle said, thinking of Matthews' assessment of the affair. He was better placed to catch local gossip than Sir Thomas could possibly be—but the magistrate had access to official information.

Livingston nodded. "Yes, that's how I see it, too. Tom was his right hand, and Roger's neither old nor clever enough to take his place."

"Have you any suspects? One of my people says there've been no outsiders around lately; is that correct?"

"Yes, as far as I know. I think it unlikely that he could have been in a fight with Preventives; there were two on patrol in the area the night of the last landing, but I've spoken to them, and they claim they never saw a soul."

Carlisle had heard stories of smugglers' cash being used to buy the silence of patrol officers. "Are they honest?

"It's hard to say, but if they were where they said they were, they'd have been miles away from where he was found. Tom was involved in the trade, of course—they all are—but I say it's a pity because he was one of the more sensible young men who realize that the game is bound to play out. Now that the war's over, there'll be enough soldiers over at Chatham to outnumber the smugglers, and ships to cut them off from their trade. I'd thought Tom might have been amenable to reason, if he'd lived to take over the gang from his father."

"Do you think that's why he was killed?"

Livingston shook his head. "It's difficult to say. I believe there's some sort of division in the ranks at the moment, perhaps a power struggle. I've heard that Jenkins has had words with a fellow named Bowker, but nothing about the cause of the quarrel. If

Bowker set his toughs upon Jenkins' son, it could either be a warning, or revenge."

"That's a nice bundle of speculation, Sir Thomas," Carlisle said mildly. "Is there any particular information you wish me to seek?"

"Why, certainly! Just a collection of nice, tidy, irrefutable evidence that will let me bring Bowker—or whoever is responsible — to trial. I'd particularly like an eyewitness, if you can manage it."

"Oh, and I thought you were going to ask me to do something *difficult*."

Livingstone chuckled. "Carlisle, no matter what I ask you to look for, you can find no more than what's there. But the fact is, *someone* killed him, and Ezra Jenkins has been an influential man around here for a decade or more. Someone's bound to know something."

He seemed about to continue, but the footman returned with a tray: fresh rolls, ham and sausage, scrambled eggs, and a two small loaves of bread. Sir Thomas dismissed the man and they helped themselves to food from the covered dishes, dispensing with business talk for a little while.

Eventually Sir Thomas finished his meal and poured himself another cup of coffee. "I don't expect you to go about making arrests, of course," he said, continuing where he'd left off. "I can call in the Army for that. All I hope for is a good excuse to rid the district of one of its more dangerous ruffians, if he *is* nearby. I suspect he has left the area, transporting that last shipment to the next stop along the line."

"How long would you expect him to be gone?"

"Ordinarily, that would depend on what they brought in, and how they were moving it. If the shipment was broken up and passed along to boats on the Thames, perhaps a few days. If they moved it overland, longer. I don't know what came in, this time. My footman keeps his ears open when he's down in the village, but I've warned him against asking questions, for his own safety.

He has to go among 'em, and I don't want him losing his life from being suspected as an informer."

"I tell my people much the same," Carlisle said, "and what they have heard agrees with what you've told me."

"Another thing—if the parties responsible for the attack on Tom Jenkins know he's died, they may decide to take a holiday, for their health's sake."

That made a great deal of sense. The local folk might protect a man who'd beaten up a rival, but they might draw the line at covering a murder of one of their own. Carlisle almost wished the killer would leave the area and never return. "Perhaps I should not be trying to discover if there are any unfamiliar faces about, but if there's anyone missing." That was something Matthews might know. "Where's the body being kept?"

"At the family home, which happens to be part of the Wise Old Owl."

"Ah, that's right, I'd forgotten Jenkins owns the inn."

"Indeed he does, and I hope the coroner makes all possible speed to hold that inquest. I would not put it past old Ezra to hold the funeral as soon as may be, no matter what the law requires."

"I shall drop by the Owl, then. I suppose I can offer my condolences to the bereaved father, and ask whether he has any notion of who would do such a thing."

"I'd wager any money that he has more than a notion."

"Do you think he'd turn the fellow in—testify against him?"

"No to both." Livingstone took a sip of his coffee. "These gentry won't set foot in a court of law unless they're in fetters. I could sit on minor charges, but of course murder must go to the Assizes. I can't imagine Ezra Jenkins agreeing to testify."

"You think he'd want to settle it himself?"

"Precisely. And that's what truly worries me. If there's one thing this district does not need, it's a gang of heavily armed ruffians engaging in civil war. We've got one man dead, and he's one that would likely be hanged if he were caught in the act. But unless things are settled, and quickly, there will be other lives lost.

Are you willing to help me?"

"I'll do what I can," Carlisle promised, and took his leave.

On the drive home, he found his thoughts straying not to the problem at hand, but to Brendan Townsend's dilemma. He wondered about that young man's rather extraordinary concern for his school friend's welfare. His suspicion was unworthy, and he knew it; it was no business of his why a young gentleman as completely respectable as Brendan Townsend seemed might throw himself headlong into saving a tradesman's son from his own folly—and what incredible folly it was!

Did it matter, after all, what the connection might be between the two? It was clear enough that Townsend had been repelled by the goings-on at that club. If he had committed some unfortunate error in judgement while he was at college, surely the exposure to that disgusting milieu had set him back on the right path.

And it was not Carlisle's affair, in any event. He had known too many evil men who were self-righteous pillars of the community, too many so-called sinners who were Good Samaritans when the chips were down, to put much faith in the self-righteous. It was perhaps superstitious of him to judge someone a good man based on his consideration for his horses, but the young man had put off his own supper to hang around the hostler's yard, making sure Romulus and Remus had warm blankets and bags of oats, and a place to rest that was out of the wind. If he was a sodomite—or had made experiments along those lines—he was a good lad nonetheless.

It was best not to dwell too much on what else he might or might not be. He was James Townsend's brother, and he had set out to foil a blackmailer, a task many older, wiser heads might fear to attempt. Whatever Brendan's motive, that sort of enterprise deserved assistance.

Carlisle caught sight of Brendan as he drove into the stable-yard. The young man had changed his shirt but was wearing the same clothes he'd worn the day before, and was standing at the paddock gate, giving Queenie a companionable scratch behind the ears. The Major handed the cart over to Terence, one of the stable boys, with a notice that he'd need it again in a couple of hours, and joined Brendan at the gate.

"Good morning, sir," Brendan said. "What a little beauty she is! What's her breeding? She's too tall for an Arab, but there's something about her—"

"I don't know anything about her bloodline," Carlisle admitted. "Her dam was in a pen at Tattersall's, bound for the knacker's yard. Some damned fool had run her into the ground and given her no care at all—hooves overgrown, infection under the shoes—I bought the poor old thing with the notion of turning her out to pasture to keep my riding horse company. Matthews ragged me a bit about my charity case, until we discovered she was pregnant."

Brendan laughed. "There's a reward for your kindness."

"Indeed. We dug for coal and found diamonds. We nursed her through that, she gave me the brightest little filly you could hope for—and then just as she appeared to be on the mend, the contrary creature turned up her toes and died. We had to put Queenie here to nurse on a big Shire mare that had just weaned her colt. I don't know who her sire is, but I think her dam had strayed far above her station."

"A midnight assignation in a livery stable?"

It was Carlisle's turn to laugh. "Very likely. You're right, too—she does have a look of Arab in the face and form. Only her height came from her dam, who was just an ordinary, over-worked hack."

Queenie nudged Carlisle's shoulder, and kept doing so until he plucked a bit of clover from outside the fence and offered it to the demanding creature. "She must always receive her trib-ute," he explained, "even if it is something she could easily reach for herself."

Brendan followed his example and smiled as the mare lipped the vegetation from his outstretched hand. "She and Galahad must be cut from the same bolt. If I don't bring him a lump of sugar or some other treat, he acts like a spoilt child."

"I am spoiling her, I know," Carlisle said. "But this is her first foal, so I must be forgiven the indulgence."

"She looks the picture of health, sir—touch wood," Brendan said, tapping the fence rail. "And you must have had a good winter." He waved toward the broad sweep of green in the paddock, and the meadow beyond. "The grass couldn't be better."

Carlisle nodded. "I am hoping we'll have no unpleasant surprises. Have you eaten breakfast?"

"Indeed I have, thank you. It was delicious."

"Very good. I've paid my call on our magistrate, and it seems I need to have a few words with some of the local people, particularly the father of the man who was killed. You are welcome to accompany me, or amuse yourself here. Come, let us return to the house; I must change into some garb suitable for attending a smuggler's wake."

With a last look at Queenie, Brendan fell into step beside Carlisle. "Thank you, sir. I would enjoy seeing more of the countryside, but your groom advised me to be circumspect with people hereabouts; he said the locals are suspicious of strangers."

"That's true enough. It would be best if you not wander off the grounds alone on your visit, lest you be taken for a Preventive spy."

"Preventive?"

"Preventive Waterguard—you'll also hear them called 'riders'— the government agents assigned to locate and disrupt smuggling activity. Any stranger who appears is automatically under suspicion. I am known in the area, and no doubt by now everyone is aware that I have returned. Knowing the power of gossip, I am sure the locals have also heard about you. If you wish to come along, you'll afford them the chance to see you for themselves."

"Then I'll come," Brendan said instantly. "If anyone should ask, we might tell them I'm here on some business about horses. My brother has a black mare and has thought of trying to breed her and raise a match. It's convenient that your stallion would be a perfect stud—in fact, I must remember to mention Nightshade to James when I return to town. And now you can honestly say we've discussed the idea." He seemed about to say something more, but looked away instead.

"What is it?" Carlisle asked.

"When my brother spoke of the smuggling gangs, he said that they would often steal horses at night, to use in moving contraband, and threaten anyone who might object. How do you stop them? I cannot imagine you allow anyone to take your horses for such a purpose."

He seemed so completely convinced of Carlisle's virtue on the issue that the Major felt slightly guilty. "I make my compromises," he said. "Did you notice the two donkeys grazing amongst the herd?"

Brendan nodded.

"Those are my concessions. They are hardier than any horse, and I have them stabled apart from my prime cattle. If they spend an occasional night elsewhere, I overlook it, and the use is paid with a barrel of spirits or some other commodity upon their return."

He saw the look of disappointment on the younger man's face. "Oh, I'm not proud of myself, Mr. Townsend, but your brother is correct—and this arrangement makes life much safer for everyone on this estate. I don't believe the free-traders would attack me, personally, but my people and livestock might suffer. I salve my conscience by turning any ill-gotten gains over to my butler, to distribute among the household as he sees fit."

"But how can you be sure these rogues will use only the donkeys, and leave your horses alone?"

"As for that, I employ the threat of severe bodily harm. I've let it be known that if they touch my horses or my household, I will kill them." He shrugged. "I'm not especially bloodthirsty, but a few of the local fellows served in my regiment; I suspect their tales enlarge upon my exploits. All to the good if it keeps my home safe."

Brendan shook his head. "It seems a strange way to live. Have you ever thought of selling the place and looking elsewhere?"

"If circumstances were not changing, I certainly should consider it, but I'd prefer to stay. My grandfather bought Twin Oaks
before I was born, and I grew up here. It's a prime location, only
a day's drive from London, and perfectly suited to my purposes,
so it's worth holding fast. I believe we are already seeing the beginning of the end of this business."

"How so? Hasn't smuggling gone on here for centuries?"

"Yes, indeed, but—how much has your brother told you about
the free-traders?"

Brendan shrugged. "Little more than I've repeated to you.
He only spoke of it in passing, because he had been part of an action against gold being smuggled into France."

"Well, the power of the gangs has been diminishing, little by
little. Compared to what went on in my grandfather's day, Kent
is considerably safer. My father once said Grandfather got a bar-
gain on this land because he bought it during the years when the
Hawkhurst gang terrorized the coast. They had created what
amounted to a private fiefdom. Magistrates were either suborned
or murdered, men were tortured to death—that sort of behavior
cannot be allowed to stand in a civilized country. Now that the
war has ended, the Preventive Waterguard has been expanded
and the Navy will have ships to spare for blockading smugglers instead of the French. Add to that the army base at Chatham…
soon they will have nowhere to turn."

"My brother James says that the only way to truly stop smuggling is to set import duties at sensible levels, so there's no profit
in the free-trade."

"Your brother is a man of good sense, but I expect it will take
years to convince politicians to take such a rational course. In the
meantime, we must deal with the situation as best we can, and try
to learn which of these fine fellows murdered one of their number—and why."

As they arrived at the steps of the house, Carlisle offered the
services of a footman to act as valet, but Brendan assured him he
could wrestle himself into fresh clothing. Having much the same

attitude, Carlisle retreated to his own chambers and donned a suit of serious black. He met his guest downstairs a few minutes later, and could only approve Brendan's attire: blue coat of superfine and dove-grey pantaloons. He was relieved that the young man was not a dandy; his modest neck-cloth was tied in a simple style and his shirt-points were not much higher than Carlisle's own.

"I must apologize again for bringing you my troubles, sir," Brendan said as they climbed into Carlisle's carriage for their trip to the village. "From the way my brother described you, I thought you a gentleman of leisure. It seems you are rather more than that, and the leisure rather less."

"Leisure is fine in its place," Carlisle said, "but it does not wear well as an occupation. Much as I love my horses, I would be utterly bored if that were all I had to occupy my time."

"You do not hunt?"

"Not often. I hate to see a good horse ridden badly, and the last time I had to watch a horse put down because some young idiot wanted to think himself a neck-or-nothing buck, I swore it *was* the last time. I enjoy the peace of a solitary ride, I manage the land with my bailiff's help, I fence, I sometimes go to Manton's to keep my hand in with a pistol, from time to time I go fishing. But those are pastimes only. I prefer to have something of genuine use to occupy my waking hours."

Brendan nodded. "I feel the same way, sir. When I came down from Oxford, most of my friends were mad for sport or gaming, but those seem rather hollow pursuits. Others have called me dull, but to me they seem mere rattles."

"I've never understood the attracting of gambling," Carlisle said. "Whist is a fine way to pass an evening with friends, but I see no need to be constantly shuffling cards to enjoy their company. What does it benefit a man to sit for hours in a smoky room, observing the permutation of four suits? Money won is always lost again, and the hours of his life are gone for good."

"Sir, you are preaching to the choir," Brendan said with a

smile. "In fact, you have touched on a matter that has filled my mind since I finished my studies. I have no occupation, and it seems to me that I need one."

"It seems to me that you have one, at least for the moment," Carlisle responded dryly. "You are playing knight-errant for your feckless friend. That is not something you can make a career of, however—nor should you, if you will forgive my presumption— but there are worse ways to spend one's time. What did you study at Oxford?"

"History, sir, on the advice of my father. I think he had the intention that I should go into politics or the diplomatic service, but I have no such ambitions. I am not indolent, but I have no gift for persuasion."

Carlisle bit his lip, and refrained from pointing out to the younger man that he had convinced a man he'd never met before to take on a task that he absolutely no interest in performing. "What would you do, if you had the time and funds to indulge your fondest dreams?"

Brendan gestured toward the vista before them, plowed fields stretched across a gently rolling land, with a row of old trees shading the curving road on which they traveled. "This. If your groom had need of an apprentice, I would happily live in an attic room above your stable, keep your stud-books in order, scoop oats into feed-bags, exercise your splendid beasts… but such things are either too low for my noble bloodline—that's my father's view, not my own—or too rich for my purse. If you want an honest answer, that would be my heart's desire. But my mother wants me to preach the Gospel, and James thinks I should study architecture."

"You seem to have a willingness to help your fellow man," Carlisle observed. "Could your mother's wish be a true measure of your talents?"

"No!"

Carlisle raised an eyebrow at his sharp tone, and Brendan added apologetically, "I do love the grandeur of cathedrals, but it is an artistic sensibility, not a spiritual one. It seems to me that a minister of the church must, at the very least, be convinced of doctrinal truth, and I do not have that conviction. I would not be able to preach from the heart; I'd be a whited sepulchre."

"A doubting Thomas, perhaps. You hardly seem old enough to be full of corruption, even if you had the inclination."

"If not, it's only because I haven't had sufficient time. I am no saint, sir… and I don't care deeply enough about religion to preach it without feeling like a hypocrite. Now, my brother's suggestion—to *build* a church? Yes, I might like to attempt such a project. But whatever Power gave me my love for horses neglected to give me any facility for mathematics."

Carlisle chuckled. "A serious oversight, I fear."

"Indeed. I am aware that without maths and engineering, an architect is nothing but a child piling blocks one on another. I'd wind up mashing someone flat with a marble cherub."

"I wish the fellow I had in last year to do some work in my kitchen had been blessed with your ethics," Carlisle said wryly. "My cook and kitchen maid very nearly smothered from the effects of his ill-fitted smokestack."

"It's easy to have ethics if they keep one from tackling a difficult job," the young man said, rather cynically. "No, I expect that I'll wind up at my family's country seat, helping my brother manage the estate. It's a better life than most men have… and every family should have an eccentric uncle, don't you think?"

Carlisle made a noncommittal response. He was puzzled at such diffidence in a gentleman who could not be much above two-and-twenty. At that age he had already been a Captain of Hussars, full of ambition and hopes for the future—but those hopes had been dashed by the time he was thirty. Perhaps young Townsend was wiser to set his sights at a less lofty goal.

"Is this the village?" Brendan asked.

Lifting his eyes beyond the road just ahead of his carriage, Carlisle nodded. "Yes, that's Southfield. There isn't much to it. A church, an inn, a smithy and hostler, a bake-house… Hello, what's this?" A chaise was drawn up to the inn, with a post-boy holding the horses. "It seems the coroner has made good time."

"Shall I stay with the carriage?" Brendan asked as they came to a halt on the side of the street opposite the inn.

"Yes, if you would. I'll only be a moment." He handed the reins to Brendan and leapt gracefully to the dusty road.

CHAPTER 7

Brendan watched Major Carlisle cross the road and disappear into the inn. He thought the village seemed strangely quiet, but that most likely meant everyone was crowded inside to see what was afoot.

He noticed a water pump and bucket just below the signpost, with its slightly lopsided, winking owl, so he drove the horses to a wider spot in the road and brought them around, heading back the way they'd come. That done, he pumped a little water and gave the beasts a drink. It was something to do besides think about his own errors.

He felt like the biggest fool of all time. He should never have intruded his petty troubles on this man. James had meant well, but he'd obviously had no idea that the Major was assisting the magistrate in his district—though this problem was clearly unusual; he could hardly believe that capital crime was an everyday occurrence in a little place like this.

I should have stayed in town. Major Carlisle had to remain here, obviously. If he had time and willingness to help with Tony's problem after the murderer was caught, well and good, but what sort of presumptuous puppy would equate a baseless threat of blackmail to bloody murder? He'd have to see if he might hire a carriage, or even book a seat on a stage-coach. The coaches were uncomfortable, but thirty-five miles would not be too severe an ordeal—the regular changing of horses would mean a fast trip, only five hours or so.

It would be better for him to get back to London anyway—more specifically, to get away from Philip Carlisle. Brendan realized he was developing a severe case of hero-worship, exacerbated by lust. He'd found Carlisle attractive from the start and he had only fallen harder once they'd arrived. The way his eyes softened when he was speaking to his mare, the tone in his voice…

One enormous favor Major Carlisle had already done for him: he had completely finished off the lingering attraction to Tony. That had been a youthful infatuation. This … *This is a full-grown, genuinely idiotic infatuation.* Yes, the man was so nearly perfect he hardly seemed real. Handsome, considerate, brave … and uninterested.

That was almost a relief. The more time Brendan spent with the older man, the more he admired him. He could never have a light, no-strings affair with Carlisle of the sort he'd been having with Tony.

If Carlisle were interested. Which he was not. *So you need to pack your bag, inquire about the stage-coach schedule—*

"Well, that's that," said a voice behind him. Brendan jumped. Carlisle had approached so quietly he had not noticed. "Shall I drive us back, or would you like to take the ribbons?" the Major continued.

"I—Yes, certainly." He got up into the driver's seat as Carlisle climbed aboard on the opposite side.

"We may as well return home," the Major said. "For the moment, there's nothing more I can do here."

"Has the coroner arrived, then?" Brendan asked.

"Yes. His name is George Presgrave, and that is his carriage. He received a letter from Sir Thomas Livingstone the same day I did, and wasted no time. The jury is being selected now; the inquest will be held tomorrow morning. He'll be stopping tonight with Sir Thomas, over at Greenways."

"I have no experience of such things," Brendan said. "Will the inquest take very long?"

"Oh, no, not in this case. There's not much doubt that the verdict will be murder by person or persons unknown—the cause of death was clear and the injuries could not possibly have been accidental or self-inflicted."

"Did you find the men you were seeking?"

"All but one. I had expected to find Ezra Jenkins at home—it's his inn, after all, and his son who was killed—but he was nowhere to be seen. They say he went out an hour ago, and they've no idea when he will return. He is bound to attend the inquest tomorrow to give testimony, so I'll see if I cannot talk to him then."

He looked so strong and resolute that Brendan wanted to either salute or swoon. He did neither. "Major, I have been thinking. My presence here cannot be a help, and is probably a hindrance. Would you advise me of the simplest way to return to London?"

"Your presence is no trouble," Carlisle said. "If you should wish to return—if you have some family obligation—"

"Oh, no. Merely that I do not wish to be in your way."

"Good heavens, why should you think that?" Carlisle turned, obviously surprised. "Mr. Townsend, I have been grateful for the pleasure of your company."

Brendan was equally surprised by his remark. "You are too kind."

"Not at all. You are the first gentleman to look at Queenie, see her obvious quality, and not turn up your nose in disdain when you learned that she has no lineage."

Brendan knew what he meant. His own father had that failing. The Viscount would pay twice as much for a thoroughbred scrub than he would for a much better horse which had no evidence of its pedigree. "Sir, that mare is a diamond of the first water."

"Without a paper to prove it, many would be blind to her virtues."

"The more fools they."

"Indeed, but the world is run by such fools. That was a lesson I learned in the Army, Mr. Townsend. Some men—your brother is one—are everything one might expect from a noble lineage. Others…" He shrugged. "Too much privilege, too little responsibility—whatever the reason, some men may have a high ancestral name and be nothing but a burden in a crisis, while others of humble origin may prove themselves superior. I prefer to judge a man—or a horse—by quality of character rather than breeding alone."

"It's easier with horses," Brendan said, thinking of the muddle he'd left behind in London.

Carlisle laughed. "Oh, is it not! I've known horses to do foolish things, but for sheer, incomprehensible stupidity or malice—or breathtaking wisdom or kindness—there is no match for *Homo sapiens*. And a man may be a blend of both. But to answer your original question, if you wish to return to London, I could ask Mr. Presgrave if he would be willing to take you up as a passenger. If you prefer to hire a post-chaise or catch a stage, I can have you driven up to Ashford or Medway. I would be happy to take you back myself, but I mean to stay here until Queenie has foaled, so you must make up your own mind on that account."

Brendan weighed the risk of displeasing his mother and sister against the chance to see what sort of foal that lovely mare would produce with the peerless stallion Nightshade as its sire. "Is she very near her time?"

"Matthews believes it will be very soon, perhaps even tonight, and I've seldom known him to be mistaken."

"I see." Brendan decided to pay close attention to his job. The road to Twin Oaks curved around at this point, with a copse of trees on one side and a shallow bank into an orchard on the other. A long visit was out of the question, but perhaps he could spare another day or two…

"You need not decide at this moment," Carlisle said.

If his brother had uttered those words, in that humorous tone of voice, Brendan would have felt himself being made fun of. But with Carlisle, he had the sense that the older man perfectly understood the tug between family obligation and the temptation to await the arrival of a lovely foal.

"It would be foolish to begin a journey today, in any case," Carlisle added, "so you may as well sleep on it."

"Thank you, sir, I shall— Hey!" A thickset, rough-looking man had just appeared from a clump of trees, stepping into the road with both hands raised to flag them down. Brendan brought the horses to a halt as quickly as he was able, and the man stepped aside in time to avoid being run down. Brendan would have said something about his lack of caution, but he realized the fellow was looking at Carlisle. He also noticed that the man had a pistol thrust into his belt, and he looked as though he would not take much convincing to use it.

"'Good day to you, Major," the stranger said. "If you have a few minutes, there's something I'd like to say to you."

Carlisle's expression was serious, but not alarmed. "Of course, Mr. Jenkins. How may I be of service?"

So this was the Wise Old Owler himself, innkeeper cum smuggler-king. Brendan gave what he hoped was a polite nod; it earned him nothing but a sizing-up.

"Introduce me to your friend?" Jenkins suggested.

"But of course, my apologies. Mr. Townsend, this is Mr. Jenkins, owner of the Wise Old Owl, who has just suffered the loss of his eldest son. Mr. Jenkins, Mr. Townsend is the brother of a man with whom I served in the Penninsular War. He is here as his brother's agent on a matter of horse-breeding."

"Can he keep his mouth shut?"

Brendan suppressed an indignant retort, knowing that Carlisle needed to talk to this man.

"He can, but I warn you—Sir Thomas Livingstone has commissioned me to investigate on his behalf, so you must bear in mind that I represent the Law in this matter."

"I thank you for the warning," Jenkins said stolidly, "but this one time I'm on the side o' the law." His heavy jaw was set, and he showed no emotion, but Brendan sensed that it took him some effort to remain impassive. "You know my son was murdered."

"Yes. You have my condolences."

"Thankee. But what I'm here to ask for is your help. And the reason I'm here, instead of meetin' you in my own place, is that I'm having to doubt my own men. I don't want no word gettin' out that I was here—I just want to tell you that the man you want is Joe Bowker."

"I've heard the name," Carlisle said. "What can you tell me about him?"

"He means to take over the business," Jenkins said. "And well you know what business I mean, so I'll not waste your time on that. What you need to know is, he killed my boy. I don't deny I'd rather see him dead at my hand, but I've always fought shy of bloodshed—"

"I rather think you mean you've avoided outright *murder*," Carlisle interjected. "I can think of a number of injuries to government servants that have coincided with my pack animals going missing."

"Accidents do happen." Jenkins' jaw jutted out like a caricature from a broadsheet. "But if you'd listen—he's threatened me and mine before this. I'm willin' to give the law a chance, because my boy Tom—" His voice caught. "My boy, he told me he'd give the business his best shot, but he wasn't going to be a murderin' sort of man. He'd agreed to take the reins if I'd keep my neck out of the noose. I've come to the time of life where I don't see too good at night, and—"

"I hate to interrupt you," Carlisle said, "but if you wish this meeting to remain private, we had better be quick about it or get off the road and out of sight. I appreciate your coming forward, but what I most need to know is where Joseph Bowker may be found."

"That I cannot tell you. If he's doin' what I told him to do, he's down at the Thames, shipping some merchandise."

"I don't suppose you'd tell me if that merchandise happens to be legal?" Carlisle inquired mildly.

"I don't suppose I would." Jenkins grinned suddenly. "Because it's nothing I've ever laid eyes on. Now, if he's *not* doin' what I told him to do, I think he may be lyin' in wait, hopin' to bag himself another Jenkins, which is another reason I'm talkin' to you."

"I see. Well, Mr. Jenkins, unless you have a witness to support your accusation, I may not be able to help you see justice for your son. Would you be able to communicate with me in any way, if you were to see Bowker back in the neighborhood?"

"I might. Trouble is, I might not, because I think this Bowker's got at some of my men. I don't know who it is that I can rely on out of my own crew. My son Roger, I trust him, save that he's but a lad of fourteen."

"That's old enough to run errands."

Jenkins bridled. "And young enough to have *his* head bashed in. No thank'ee, sir! My wife's keepin' him close around the house, now, and I don't blame her. What I'm thinkin' is, if you can send that man of yours down to the Owl, I can have a quiet word with him when necessary."

Carlisle nodded. "That should serve. Or if you need to contact me in a hurry, send word that you've a barrel of beer ready to send along to Twin Oaks—if you have one."

Jenkins' face lightened slightly. "Oh, aye, we've got that."

"I'll be at the Owl tomorrow, for the inquest. If there's anything you need to tell me, you can do it when I offer my condolences." Carlisle reached out his hand. "I *do* condole you, Mr. Jenkins. It's no small thing, to lose a child. You and your wife keep young Roger under your eye until we have this matter settled."

The suspicious expression on Jenkins' face softened, as if such sympathy was something he'd never expected. "I will, sir. And I thank you."

Carlisle nodded, and said, "Very good. Let's get along home, Mr. Townsend."

With a nod to the smuggler at the side of the road, Brendan raised the whip once more and signaled the horses to move along.

As Carlisle had expected, Brendan decided he would postpone his return to London for a day or two. James, he said, would understand his absence and make apologies to his mother and sister.

According to Carlisle's custom when he was at home, the cook had prepared a light repast of cold meats upon their return. The meal finished, there they were, the rest of the day stretching out before them.

"I could offer you a game of cards," Carlisle said, "but as we have both expressed disinterest in that pastime, I hesitate to suggest it. Billiards, perhaps?"

"If you wish." Brendan glanced out the window of the breakfast-room, which looked out upon a field behind the stables. "If I were not here, what would you do?"

"Review my accounts," Carlisle admitted. "This makes me very grateful you *are* here. Or if I could not bear to be indoors on such a beautiful day, I might go for a ride."

He congratulated himself on guessing rightly when the younger man's face brightened. "Could we? I ride in London, of course, but that's either watching for traffic every moment or idling along in the Park—not real riding."

"A man after my own heart," Carlisle approved. "I need to put a saddle on Nightshade and give him some exercise. Matthews generally sees to that, but I would not wish him to forget me."

It took little time to change into riding gear, and while the assistant groom Jem was saddling Nightshade, Brendan was given the choice of Carlisle's two hunters, Whiskey, a chestnut mare whose coloring matched her name, and Sailor, a pale grey gelding. He sensibly asked which had been ridden last and, upon learning that Whiskey had been exercised that morning, asked to ride Sailor.

They must have made a pretty picture, Carlisle thought as they started out on a circuit of the estate, mounted on black and white as though representing living chess pieces. But he had little time for poetic metaphors; Nightshade was feeling his oats and seemed determined to remind his master that he was no mere gelding.

Brendan noticed Nightshade's prancing, and laughed. "He does want to stretch himself! Would I stand a chance if we were to race?"

"Not of winning, perhaps," Carlisle said, "but Sailor has good bottom. Do you see that coppice of trees yonder?"

Brendan glanced in the direction he indicated, nodded, and his horse suddenly leapt away with a surprising burst of speed. Carlisle blinked, taken by surprise, then gave Nightshade his head, to follow at his own pace. As that was neck-or-nothing, they soon overtook the grey and his rider, though not as quickly as Carlisle had thought they would. He still reached the trees at least two full lengths ahead.

Brendan rode up, laughing once more as Sailor settled into a walk beside the black horse. "Much good my cleverness did me! What a prize you have there, sir! If that foal has his sire's power and his dam's beauty, only a fool would care about the papers."

"That is my hope—though I should have to be hard pressed indeed to part with any of them. I've had half-a-dozen offers for this fellow, from gentlemen who'd replace me with a jockey. The next time you visit, I would like to see what you think of him as a mount."

"You would allow me to ride him?" Brendan asked in surprise.

"I would indeed—and you may be sure that is not an invitation I extend very often."

The young man's face fairly glowed with pleasure. "Thank you, sir!"

Carlisle found it difficult to believe that Brendan was actually related to James Townsend. James had been a good soldier, no question of that, and an excellent officer—but Carlisle often suspected he had chosen the Cavalry because he thought it glamorous, not because he wanted to spend his days on horseback.

Brendan, on the other hand, rode like a centaur. He had that natural grace a horseman needed, the sense of balance that enabled him to lean into Sailor's movements and guide him almost as though he and the horse were a single living creature.

"I never saw you signal Sailor to gallop," Carlisle said. "You really do have a feeling for them, do you not?"

"That's in the blood," Brendan said in an offhand way. "I can take no credit for it."

"How so? Your brother—forgive me—is a competent horse-man, but no more than that."

"Oh, James is a typical English Townsend. The horse-sense is from my mother's side of the family; her grandmother was the daughter of an Irish horse-trader. The family tale is that when my great-grandfather was bound for the American colonies to help his younger brother establish a homestead, he found himself on a ship with Brendan McMurdo, his horses, and his daughter Fiona. No one in the family knows precisely what happened, but when he left the colonies to return to England, the horses stayed on the homestead but Fiona went with him, as his wife."

"That's very romantic," Carlisle replied.

"I hope it was, for her sake. The family must have been in a taking at finding the heir not only married to an Irish girl but about to become a father. They must have eventually accepted her; my mother remembers her grandparents being very happy together. And it does seem to hold true that those in the family who have her Black Irish coloring have a feeling for horses, and the blond Eng-lish types, like my father and brother James, do not."

Carlisle nodded. "And your sister?"

"Oh, she enjoys riding, but she maintains that the side-saddle is an instrument of torture, even though she accepts that a lady could hardly ride in any other manner. She challenged me to jump with a side-saddle once, when we were young, and I had to own that it's devilishly uncomfortable." He nodded at Carlisle's incredulous expression. "Yes, I felt a damned fool and got off the thing as soon as ever I could—but when a fellow's sister issues a challenge, what else can one do?"

"Pray that one's friends are nowhere in the neighborhood!"

Carlisle answered immediately. "I know that I have met your sister at your brother's home, but she gave no impression of having such an independent mind."

"Oh, Elspeth is a real lady," Brendan assured him. "Which means that she, like my mother, has more under her bonnet than a pretty head of hair, including the wit not to let a man know it. She's just beginning her first Season. That is why I must go back very soon, to squire her around to Almack's and such, but it appears she is already expecting an offer at any moment. I hope he comes up to scratch promptly—if he does, I will be off the hook, and he will take over escort duties."

"You sound fairly confident of your liberty."

"If I were offering odds, I would make book that there will be an announcement in the *Times* by May Day. I have met the gentleman, and he seems a good sort, apart from an inexplicable craving for my sister's company."

"I am sure that he will consider himself fortunate if he is accepted," Carlisle said, still bemused with the absurd mental image of Brendan on a side-saddle. "She sounds like a delightful young lady."

He had been thinking of Brendan as an adult, but that young man's response was all boy. "Oh, she's all right, for a girl. Would you care for another race?"

Major Carlisle kissed divinely. Brendan had known he would, and the reality was even better than the expectation. Those long legs, hard and strong from hours in the saddle, twined with his own as they moved urgently together between the sheets. Brendan ran his fingers through the bronze-gold hair, pulling that lean body against his own. He rolled onto his back, bringing Carlisle atop him, his body humming with pleasure—but someone was calling. Damn them!

"Mr. Townsend?"

Brendan blinked at the glimmer of a candle beside his bed.

"Yes, what— ?"

"The Major said you wished to be waked when La Reine began foaling, sir. It's time."

He was suddenly wide awake, dreams forgotten, and threw back the covers. "I'll be ready in a moment."

"There are some rough clothes here, sir… do you require assistance in dressing?"

Brendan laughed, shoving his feet into the homespun trousers. "A valet for these? Thank you, I can manage. How does it go? Is she well?"

"I know almost nothing of the stables, sir, but the Major seems concerned. He told me to say he will see you in the foaling box."

Brendan tucked his nightshirt into the trousers and pulled on a pair of battered boots that the footman provided, then followed him downstairs. He shivered in the chill spring air, but a bright, nearly-full moon gave light enough for him to reach the stables without difficulty. As he entered, he could see that several lanterns were hung around the sides of Queenie's foaling box.

He passed the other stalls, noting that the horses in them were all awake and alert, well aware that something important was going on. Brendan came up to the box quietly, hearing not only the murmur of voices, but the anxious note in some of them.

"Get her up, then," Carlisle was saying. "If we can help the foal slip back inside and then shift him a bit—"

"I tried that already, Major," Matthews said regretfully, "and it didn't work. He's a big 'un."

"We'll have to try again. We must do *something*."

In the circle of light inside the foaling box, Carlisle and Matthews knelt beside the laboring mare, with the two stable-boys hovering on either side. A hodgepodge of odors filled the stall, mainly crushed straw and sweat, and wisps of steam were rising from the horse's heaving body.

Queenie was clearly in distress, restlessly blowing great huffs of breath, down on her side with Carlisle at her head. He had hold of her halter, urging her to rise, but it appeared she had no intention of doing anything of the sort. Carlisle glanced over his shoulder and saw Brendan. "Good morning, Mr. Townsend. Would you be interested in giving us a hand, here?"

"Anything," Brendan said. "What shall I do? What's happened?"

"The foal's stuck—a leg bent back, and it's going to take both of us to shift him. Every time we try, she knocks the boys down—they're simply not big enough to hold the poor girl. Can you help me get her upright?"

"Of course." Brendan went round to the mare's far side, lifting her head as Carlisle wrapped both arms around her neck. Together, they coaxed and wrestled her into a sitting position. Brendan dropped to his knees beside the mare to prevent her lying back down as her master soothed her. He found it a trial to concentrate on the animal; Carlisle wore nothing but a pair of old buckskin riding breeches, and the subtle contour of the muscles in his chest and shoulders made it obvious that his tailor needed to do very little in the way of padding. The appeal was not only physical, either; the concern evident on his striking features made Brendan wish there was some way he could offer comfort.

There wasn't time for that, of course, nor would such foolishness be welcome; the only thing he could do was what was asked of him. Poor Queenie could use a bit of comforting, though; her eyes were wild, surrounded by white. "Hello, my lady," he said, one hand on the halter while he stroked her neck. "This must be very strange for you. It certainly is for me."

She cocked her ears toward him, as if unable to believe this foolish human was babbling at her while her caretakers were doing rude, unexpected things at her nether end.

"It'll take both of us, sir," Matthews said. "I can't get hold of either foot."

"Terence, over here, if you please!" Carlisle said sharply. The lad scrambled to hold Queenie's halter; Brendan scratched her forelock and gently twisted her ear. She rolled an eye at him, and he played with the other ear. He didn't want to put a twitch on her, but she needed distracting.

"I've got hold of a jaw," Matthews said. Glancing down, Brendan could barely see the groom; he was lying on the floor with only part of one shoulder visible over the mare's haunches.

Carlisle was smearing something on his own arm—some sort of grease, Brendan thought—and a moment later he lay down beside his stableman. Brendan knew that Carlisle must be reaching inside the mare to shift the foal, and was just as glad he could not see what was going on.

"All right," the Major ordered. "I feel the edge of the hoof, you push his head—*damn!*"

He shouted just as Queenie groaned and flung her head back; Brendan could see the ripple of a contraction run across her steaming flank. "What's happened?"

"Trying to squeeze my arm off, the ungrateful beast," Carlisle said. "Can't fault her, she doesn't understand we're trying to help. Ready for another try, Matthews?"

"Aye, sir."

"All right—got the little fellow's nose? On the count of three. One, two—"

Brendan tightened his hold on the halter, and put his own forehead down against the mare's. "That's the girl, let them help…

"Three!"

Queenie muttered and twitched again, and once more there were epithets uttered at the other end of the mare.

"Again," said Carlisle.

It took countless more tries, and all of them were sweating as hard as Queenie by the time Carlisle called out that he had the leg. Queenie was making quite a lot of noise; Brendan was sure she was swearing, and he did not blame her in the least.

He was never able to say, in the years after that night, how many hours he had spent hunkered down beside that roan mare, cosseting her while she pushed out her firstborn. But when they were finally able to free the foal's foreleg, everything became easier. The rippling contractions along Queenie's belly seemed to cause her less strain, and after a minute or so Matthews said, "There's the first leg."

Carlisle slapped him on the back, and patted Queenie's rump. "Come on, girl, the worst's over."

She grumbled, grunted, and Matthews said, "And the other."

Brendan couldn't see anything of the birth, but he could see that something was happening. He rubbed Queenie's nose, as much to reassure himself as her. "That's a good girl, you'll be fine."

"There's the nose," Carlisle said after a long time had passed.

And after another long wait, Matthews said, "Take that other leg, sir, let's just help her a bit."

As if sensing the end of her struggle, the mare surged up, scrambling to stand on her feet and pulling Brendan with her, and at that point he saw his first glimpse of the foal—two ridiculously long, thin legs, and a wet little head with its ears slicked back.

He laughed aloud, and Carlisle looked up, a grin on his face that was an exact match for the one Brendan knew must be on his own.

"Ever seen this before, Mr. Townsend?" Carlisle asked.

"No," Brendan said. "My father never breeds his own horses, he's always said a stallion is too unpredictable and dangerous to have around."

"He's probably right, for the most part. If Nightshade weren't such a good-natured fellow… Ah, that's it, sweetheart, push now…"

The foal inched out, and then suddenly there was a last squelching *whoosh* of movement, and a shape that seemed too big to come from inside this trim little mare was lying on the floor just behind her, still tethered to her mother by the umbilical cord. Matthews was on his knees beside the foal, using a damp rag to clear the birth fluids from her mouth and nostrils.

The ordeal was over. A dark-colored filly with white markings lay on the straw behind her dam, and Brendan's legs had fallen asleep. He didn't even realize that, until he tried to take a step and nearly fell over. Philip Carlisle caught him, lending a steady arm until he could stay on his feet.

"They need to rest, now," Carlisle said. "And I think we do, too." He went back to the mare's head, stroking and praising her, but her attention was now on the new arrival.

"How long will it be before she can get up?" Brendan asked.

"Not long. Ten or fifteen minutes, an hour, at most. Matthews knows more about that than I do."

"We need to keep 'em both quiet until the cord goes slack," the stableman said. "Cut that too soon, they could both bleed out. There'll be—"

The mare shuddered all over and another, smaller object plopped to the ground. "Afterbirth," Matthews said shortly. "That's good. When Queenie's got to know her little 'un, you can come back and visit. They need some time to get acquainted. Come back when it's daylight—this little princess will likely take an hour or two before she can spend much time on her own four feet."

"Princess?" Brendan asked.

"That will do for the moment," Carlisle said. "Come along, Mr. Townsend. I warned Peters that we'd need a quantity of hot water before the night was over. I don't grudge Queenie a bit of the effort, but I mean to have a wash right now. Matthews, you come along as soon as you're able."

The groom only nodded as he rubbed the foal dry with a bit of sacking, and Brendan envied him the task.

"I had a bath-room put in beside the kitchen," Carlisle explained as they walked back to the house. "One of my neighbors has a scientific turn of mind, and he had a notion that running a pipe from a cistern on the roof to a storage tank behind the stove could provide warm water for washing, without requiring the servants to carry it upstairs, cooling all the while. I thought the experiment worth a try."

The thought of warm water and soap made Brendan very happy. "Does it work?"

"Fairly well, I believe, but you can judge for yourself. There is a bath-room upstairs as well, of course, but if I've been getting filthy outdoors I find it more convenient to just wash up before going any further into the house, and of course the servants appreciate running ten steps instead of two flights. The water is much hotter, too. I often use it when I've been out in the stables, and I believe Peters soaks his lumbago in the hip-bath from time to time."

Brendan started to laugh, but it turned into a yawn. "I am sorry. I was just imagining what my father would say at that notion. Scrub up in the same room as the servants?"

"Well, from what you said earlier, your father would not be found lying beside his groom in a foaling box in the wee hours, up to his armpit in—"

"No!" Brendan began to laugh again, and found he couldn't stop. "God, no," he gasped, and took a deep breath, forcing himself to be calm. "I think I must never tell him about this adventure. Although he only told me to finish college before I wasted any more time in the stables, and, you know—I *did* finish college!"

Carlisle shook his head, smiling. "Please do keep it to yourself. My servants already think me somewhat slack-twisted in matters of my own consequence, and I should not wish to scandalize the Viscount. Though if I were to tell him about this evening's excitement, I should have to praise your conduct. You not only kept your head, you kept Queenie far calmer than the boys were able to, and that made the job easier for Matthews and me. Ah, here we are, and I see Peters has provided not only hot water, but clean towels, slippers, and even dressing-gowns. The end of a perfect evening!" He led the way through a back doorway, into a spartan bath-room with stone floors and two tubs of water.

And then Major Carlisle dropped his filthy breeches and stepped into one of the tubs, and Brendan found himself blushing like a schoolgirl. He turned hastily to the other tub to cover his embarrassment, and busied himself with soap and washcloth.

He wanted to look, but he did not dare.

✤ CHAPTER 8 ✤

The sun was blazing through his bedroom window when Brendan finally opened his eyes. Nearly noon, he guessed. He wondered whether Major Carlisle was up and about, and found himself embarrassed once more at the memory of the night before.

He'd made the mistake of glancing over when Carlisle had stepped out of the tub, his body wet and glistening in the candlelight. He was a handsome, well-built man, and despite the fact that he must be close to forty he was as sleek and lean as a thoroughbred, the most gorgeous thing Brendan had ever laid eyes on. He'd had to engage in some quick work with the towel and dressing-gown to disguise his own body's reaction.

It was time to get back to town, immediately, before he did anything stupid. Not that he was likely to have the chance. Even if he were foolish enough to consider trying to seduce the Major, he had no notion of how one went about such a thing. Probably just as well, too.

He had only had time to pull on his stockings and trousers when he heard a discreet tap at the door. "Yes, come in," he called.

"I am sorry, sir." It was Peters, condescending to a duty below his station, delivering a tray that held a silver pot and a china cup and saucer. "Major Carlisle has gone to attend the inquest, and has instructed me to offer you breakfast in the small dining room. Will you require any assistance?"

"No, thank you. If I may have hot water I can shave myself. I shall be down as quickly as possible."

"Very good, sir."

Brendan poured himself a cup of what proved to be hot chocolate, and carried it over to the windowsill, which was low and deep enough to serve as a seat. He gazed out through the mullioned panes at the garden below. Twin Oaks was not the largest estate he'd ever seen, but the groundskeeper did his job well. The lawn just below his window was bordered along the drive by a low formal hedge, and a couple of low flowering trees—cherries, he guessed—were just breaking into bloom.

He called "Come!" to another tap on the door, and this time it was a young chambermaid carrying in a can of hot water. He thanked her as well, musing as he shaved that Carlisle's little whim of requiring the servants to knock was actually a very good idea. It was no wonder, when one thought about it, that servants' carrying tales was always a concern. They had admirable opportunity to gather gossip-fodder, when their duties required them to burst in on their employers without any warning.

While shaving, Brendan realized that he had not asked Carlisle to inquire whether Presgrave, the coroner, would be willing to allow him to ride back to London in his carriage. Perhaps he would do that anyway. If not—well, he'd simply have to ask the Major when he returned. He could not stay at Twin Oaks any longer, much as he liked the place, and much as he would like to stay around and see how Queenie and her foal were doing.

If he hurried, perhaps he could spend a few minutes at the stable after he'd had something to eat.

After a meal that he swallowed too quickly to pay much attention to what was on his plate, Brendan was unsurprised to find his host already returned from the village and leaning on the fence beside the gate, watching Queenie and her new filly. "Good morning, sir!" he called. "Or is it afternoon?"

Carlisle glanced over his shoulder. "Nearly one. Did you sleep well?"

"Far too well, to lose the morning that way. I cannot believe that I was such a slugabed."

"It was only lacking an hour or so to dawn when we retired," Carlisle said, his attention back on the horses. "She'll be a quick one, I think. See how she stands—legs well under her, and only half a day on her feet!"

Brendan nodded. The mare and her baby made a beautiful picture, the coppery-gold dam with her cornsilk mane and tail contrasting with the inky-black filly—a true jet black, without a trace of the brownish baby fur that most black foals were born with—tagging close at her side. "It amazes me that horses can carry their young ones to such size. Compared to cats or dogs...even a large litter still comes out one pup at a time."

"Indeed. I must thank you for your assistance last night, Mr. Townsend. We could have distracted Queenie with a twitch, I suppose, but I wished to keep her as free from distress as possible."

"She seems well enough now." The foal had decided it was time for a drink, and Queenie was nudging her little one into place at her udder. "In fact, one would never guess this was her first."

"Her foster-mother taught her well." Carlisle straightened, turning himself away from the fence as though pulling away from a strong magnet. "And now I must repay your courtesy with consideration, and return you to your home." He cast a longing look back over his shoulder. "I would prefer to stay here, of course, but when I spoke to Ezra Jenkins at the inquest, he told me he had received a message from a friend of his in London. It seems that the elusive Mr. Bowker has gone to London Town, and appears to be stopping there for a few days."

"I should not have stayed here so long," Brendan admitted, "but I cannot be sorry. Do you mean to pursue Bowker in the city?"

Carlisle shook his head. "No. Taking the chase out of this district and into London would mean hiring a Bow Street Runner, and even if I were to do that, there are no grounds for an arrest. He'll have disposed of the cargo by now—brandy, Jenkins told me. No, he must be caught in the act. Jenkins has decided that he will bide his time and watch his back until his enemy returns. In the meantime, we may as well drive back to London ourselves and see what we may do to resolve your friend's problem with the offensively insistent innkeeper."

"That sounds almost like the title for one of the novels to which my mother is addicted," Brendan said. "Though if it were, the innkeeper would be a revenant spirit, and would be routed by a virtuous curate."

Carlisle winced. "Ye gods." He added tactfully, "I have met your mother, a most charming lady. I should never have guessed she had a taste for that sort of ... entertainment."

"I think ghost-stories are her only vice, besides hats," Brendan said. "And she hasn't much time to indulge in reading at the moment, with my sister's campaign underway. Speaking of which, do you mean to leave today?"

"Yes, as soon as we may. I had one of the grooms take Romulus and Remus out to the Knight's Inn yesterday evening, and stay with them; I thought you'd need to go home today, even if Queenie hadn't foaled. That was why we were shorthanded last night. We can change horses there, and be in town before dark. Might you be ready in half an hour?"

"I am ready at any time convenient to you, Major. You are too kind to offer your assistance; the more I consider what I have asked of you, the more I wonder at my own presumption!"

"Not at all," Carlisle said quickly. "I have enjoyed your company, and truth be told, I have seen too many good men ruined by blackmailers. If I am able to help foil one, it will be a genuine pleasure."

"Still…" Brendan knew he should stop babbling. "I do thank you."

Carlisle made a dismissive gesture, and changed the subject by directing Brendan's attention to a row of handsome oak saplings he had recently caused to be set along the drive, and their conversation turned to the more pleasant topic of landscape design.

In a very short time they were on the road once more, this time riding inside the carriage with Edward up in the driver's box. Carlisle, despite his preference for driving, had turned in late and risen early, so he made himself comfortable on one of the well-padded seats and was soon sound asleep.

Brendan did his best to distract himself with a borrowed book that concerned itself with the health and diseases of horses. It was interesting enough, but he could not keep his mind fixed on the pages. He had discovered in himself a considerable reluctance to return to London, and Tony, and Tony's tiresome problem. He did not want to introduce Carlisle to the indiscreet Mr. Hillyard, or take him to that disgusting club. He wanted to keep Philip Carlisle as far from any of that as he possibly could, keep him from being contaminated by it.

He had been so desperate to find help with the problem that he had not thought things through as he should have. What if Tony were to let something slip that revealed their relationship? What would Carlisle think of him then?

A fine time to worry about it—too late now. And he was probably deceiving himself if he thought Major Carlisle had not already guessed why he was so concerned for Tony. Carlisle was tolerating him for some reason—perhaps out of respect for James—but what did it matter? A man was known by the company he kept, and a man of Carlisle's position would hardly find any basis for friendship with a younger man of such poor judgment.

Just as well, too, because what Brendan wanted was far more than friendship. It was difficult to sit here and not stare at the strong, lithe figure curled on the seat opposite, the clean line of jaw, the eyebrows two strokes of darker brown beneath the honey-gold hair. Brendan's fingers itched to reach out and brush an errant lock away from Carlisle's sleeping face….

He caught himself, shocked at the very thought. He was a fine one to criticize Tony, and all the while sit here harboring thoughts that, if he were to act on them, could only give monstrous offense to a gentleman who had offered him nothing but kindness.

Brendan forced his eyes away from Carlisle and back to the book, but it was hopeless. A pity he had not asked to be awakened earlier; sleep was the last thing on his mind now, and the thought of riding like this for hours, with no conversation or any other sort of distraction—

A happy thought sent him rummaging through the pockets of his riding coat, tossed on the seat beside him. Although the weather had been too fair for him to need to wear it, he had put his sketch-book in one pocket and a small box of pencils in another. He might not be able to concentrate on a printed page, but his mind's eye was full of the happy tableau in the paddock, and he could draw at least some of it from memory.

He did a few preliminary sketches first: a study of La Reine's elegant head, her large, luminous eyes and the delicate white blaze between them. Princess' head was next, the proportions so different in a foal, the color ... well, of course he could not make her dark enough with only a bit of lead, but the blaze so similar to her mother's was easier to remember. He could see, in the shape of the baby head, how like her dam she would be when she began to grow up.

When he had completed the likenesses to his own satisfaction, he began to consider the design of a more complex picture. His mind was full of images from the night before: the great curve of the mare's side as she lay in the straw, the uncertainty in her eyes, the moment of birth... Philip Carlisle's face, tense and focused, as he watched the new foal arrive in the world, anxiety and anticipation blended equally.

No, he could not draw *that*. But when Brendan looked at the formerly blank page of his sketch-pad, he saw that not only could he draw Carlisle that way, he had.

He would have rubbed out the crude sketch, except that he had, in a very rudimentary way, captured a pretty good likeness. He was seldom able to do that with drawings of human beings. Horses were easy; humans were not, and he had never seen anything so beautiful as that blend of strength and gentleness as Carlisle had shown the night before. He would cherish that memory, and never show the picture to anyone else.

Perhaps, though, as a sort of thank-you, he might do Major

Carlisle a drawing of himself and his new arrival as he had seen them earlier: *Carlisle with one foot on the bottom rail of the gate, one arm on the top rail … yes. Head up, face keen…*

The page was too small for much detail, but the line of his body showed how the animals within the paddock had all his attention. And a bit beyond the rail, Queenie—not challenging or oblivious to observation, but aware of Carlisle's presence, even though the lion's share of her attention was on her foal. Princess was easiest to draw, though Brendan had to find his rubber eraser and re-draw her legs a few times. There was a fine line between an accurate representation of a newborn horse's legs and a caricature.

He sat back at last, pleased with the sketch, if not delighted. It would do as the basis for a more finished pen and ink drawing, when he had time to sit down and indulge himself in his hobby. Drawing horses was never as pleasing as riding, or even watching them graze and frolic together, but it was more fulfilling than drawing pictures of stone cherubs above an altar.

It was really too bad that the education of a young gentleman did not include the instruction in watercolors that was part of a young lady's training. Princess could be depicted well enough in black ink on white paper, but Queenie was a golden thing, and ink could never capture her full beauty. A pity James Seymour was no longer alive; there was a painter who might have done her justice.

Philip Carlisle shifted in his sleep, and Brendan considered him once again. Surely there could be no harm in doing a quick study of his face, if he did it with the intention of making a reference for the finished portrait of a man and his horses? It was the likeness that mattered, after all, not the pleasure the act of creation gave the artist. That was a private matter, and would never be anything else.

But he finally wearied even of drawing. Putting the sketch pad away, he leaned back against the well-padded cushions and closed his eyes; sleep came almost immediately.

Philip Carlisle awoke slowly, wondering what was wrong until he had enough wit to realize that nothing was wrong at all; it was simply that the carriage had slowed down, and the peaceful country road outside his window had been replaced by the bustle of a coaching inn's yard. He sat up and stretched, smiling at the sight of Brendan Townsend slumped awkwardly against the squabs in the opposite seat.

He cleared his throat. "Mr. Townsend? We have arrived."

There was no response. He tried again, but Townsend's utterly blank expression was that of a young man who had not gotten enough sleep and was determined to rectify the error. Finally Carlisle chuckled and reached across to shake his guest's shoulder.

Brendan righted himself, apologizing profusely, as the carriage came to a stop.

"No harm done," Carlisle said. "I only just awoke, myself. We're at the Knight's Inn and should have time for a quick dinner while the horses are changed. Shall we?"

The words were hardly out of his mouth when Edward opened the carriage door and let down the steps. Dutifully stifling a yawn, Brendan followed him out of the carriage and into the inn.

They had some cold beef and bread and ale. When they returned to the yard, Edward was just climbing back into the box. Carlisle made certain his coachman had been able to find nourishment, then climbed back inside. He knew his own strength well enough, and was not the sort of man who was too proud to admit that at twoscore years of age he was at less than his best from a late night and two mugs of ale.

"Well, Mr. Townsend," he said, as the carriage jolted into motion, "I must apologize for my lack of scintillating conversation on the first half of our journey. I trust you were able to amuse yourself?"

Brendan nodded, but he looked slightly embarrassed. "Sir, I am not certain whether I should ask your permission or your pardon," he said. "I had a notion.... "

He looked so abashed that Carlisle finally grew impatient.

"Speak up, please! Unless you mean to ask something completely outside of reason, I am hardly likely to object."

The boy actually blushed. "I merely wondered, sir… would you mind if I were to make a drawing of La Reine and her filly?"

Carlisle did not know what he had expected to hear, but it was certainly not that. "Of course not! Are you an artist?"

"I… I would never claim that, sir! I draw a bit, for my own amusement, only. And I have a book on drawing with ink… Most often, I only sketch with pencil. But Queenie is such a beautiful creature, I could not resist." He fumbled with his coat, and drew out a sketch-book, proffering it like a spaniel with a gnawed pheasant. "There, you see?"

Before him, on the flat white surface, Queenie's coquettish personality was as apparent as though she were there before him. A little to one side was Princess, big-eyed with wonder at the new world she had just entered. Carlisle turned a page, and saw himself, leaning with one foot on the gate, marveling at the astonishing gift he'd just been granted. The open emotion on his face, somehow conveyed with just a few deceptively simple strokes of the pencil, was almost embarrassing.

He was about to turn another page, but Brendan held out his hand, and Carlisle felt obliged to surrender the book.

"I thought I might do a pen-and-ink drawing of them," he said diffidently, "and then it occurred to me that, as they are your horses, I really ought to ask your permission."

"My *permission?*" Carlisle reached for the book again; reluctantly, Brendan opened it to the page with the two head-studies. Once again, the likeness drew a smile from him. "Did you draw all this from memory?"

"Yes, sir. They are but rough sketches— preliminary studies. The final work would be more finished."

"My permission." Carlisle repeated, gazing at the stray bit of forelock that never would lie straight on Queenie's face. "My dear boy—you are no businessman. You should by rights be asking me how much I would pay to have you draw them."

Brendan cast him a look of doubt. "I had thought to do it as a token of gratitude, sir."

"Gratitude? For what?"

"Your help, of course. This problem with my friend…"

"Well, I think you might wait until I have actually accomplished something, before thanking me. But I am quite serious about your talent."

Brendan shrugged self-consciously. "I have no training, Major. This is nothing more than a hobby."

"It could be more than that, if you chose. I have seen plenty of paintings of horses, Mr. Townsend. There's one in my study—I must show it to you one day—of a horse that my father owned, a big bay hunter. It's a splendid painting, quite a handsome animal. But it looks nothing at all like Pharamond. An artist who is able to draw a horse that resembles a proper horse is to be commended. An artist who can draw a horse that looks so much like one particular horse that a stranger could pick her out of a crowd…" Carlisle shook his head and gave back the sketches. "You said you were seeking a useful occupation. I think you have found it."

"You cannot be serious, sir."

"I can, and I am. If you were serious, of course, you would need to take lessons, perhaps serve an apprenticeship. But why not? It is not so respected a profession as architecture, but you would have the same chance to create something of lasting worth and beauty."

Brendan opened his book, studying the first sketch. "It is rather like them, isn't it?"

"Very much so. And to answer your question—yes, of course. I would be delighted to have you draw Queenie and her foal, or any of my horses that might take your fancy. They might not sit as still for you as a human subject would, but neither will they ask you to make them thinner or handsomer."

Smiling, Brendan put the book away and changed the subject, asking how Carlisle had come to meet his brother James. That led to a series of reminiscences about the Peninsular War, the long series of campaigns across Europe and the great naval battles.

"I thought to run away to sea when the war first started," Brendan confessed. "I was just old enough—ten or eleven. But my brother Andrew was already a midshipman, and he advised me to reconsider."

"For what reason?"

"A very good one, I assure you. I have never been able to set foot in anything bigger than a rowboat without becoming pitifully seasick."

Carlisle grimaced in sympathy. "Not a useful tendency in a mariner."

"No. Andrew wrote me back and assured me that I would never do. By the time I learned that Nelson himself had the same problem, my father had already decided that Eton was more important than my patriotic duty."

"With your two brothers at war, I imagine your father thought it wise to keep you close at home."

"Perhaps. But I am very glad my brothers both survived." Brendan glanced out the window, his face troubled. "Major, speaking of family, there is something I need to tell you... about this other matter. When I was at the Arbor, I recognized one of the others present, a man who seemed very interested in Tony's ... performance."

"A relative of yours?" Carlisle guessed.

Brendan nodded, one short, tight jerk of his head. "An uncle. My godfather, in fact." He glanced up, meeting Carlisle's eyes for just an instant. "I am fairly sure he did not see me, but if we were to return there at an hour when the club was open, and he was present, I do not see how that could be avoided."

"It's good you thought to tell me," Carlisle said. "We shall have to consider a diversionary action when we plan our campaign. When you are back with your family, you must see if you are able to ascertain whether he is in town. I will learn what I can about the club's owner. But even if we cannot keep your godfather away, did you not say everyone is masked?"

"Yes, half-masks, that covered the hair and face down to the upper lip. But I recognized him regardless—and it wasn't just from his watch-fob, though that was how I knew for certain. His figure, his voice… they were unmistakable."

"To your artist's eye, perhaps. When did he last see you?"

"Oh, a couple of years, at the very least." The look of worry lightened. "Do you think he might not recognize me?"

"In a mask, with nothing but your chin showing, and, I'll wager, more height and muscle than the last time he saw you? I think it a good chance. He may not be present, in any event, and I mean for us to be in and out as quickly as possible. You must be careful to keep silent if he should be present, but I cannot imagine any of that club's patrons are there every night."

The relief on the younger man's face was so strong that Carlisle felt a twinge of unease. Had he really been at that club merely because he was too green to detach himself from an unsuitable companion? There was no reason to doubt that, but young Townsend's concern for this Hillyard seemed … excessive, for want of a better word. Loyalty to a friend was one thing, but what else might lie between them?

Well, whatever it might be, or might have been, letting it lie was the prudent course of action. Carlisle reminded himself that Brendan Townsend's personal faults were no business of his. *After all, Brendan has a father, and older brothers…*

Whose help he had avoided…. Why did this charming, good-natured young man avoid revealing this secret to the people who knew him best? Why was he more willing to confide in a stranger?

Carlisle smiled with a confidence he did not quite feel, and began to tell Brendan about a Mameluk-trained Arabian he had bought from a captured Frenchman, then sold to a general whose mount had been shot from under him. Brendan's thoughts were apparently easy to redirect; unfortunately, Carlisle's were not.

◖ CHAPTER 9 ◗

"Brendan! Where have you been?"

His sister's accusing tones halted Brendan on the mid-point landing of the stairway. He knew his guilty face did not convey the half of his culpability. "Only out in Kent. But I am home, Ellie! And by the time you need me as an escort, I shall be ready, with bells on."

"I have been driven nearly to distraction these past two days," she said, following him up the stairs. "How *could* you just vanish that way?"

"I apologize most humbly," he said, continuing up to the gallery so they might talk on a level. "That is no excuse whatever, of course, but I do apologize, and I can only say that I would have been the shabbiest sort of friend if I had not behaved like the shabbiest sort of brother."

"Indeed, you have been!"

"Do you mean to tell me that Mr. Edrington was unwilling to walk with you in the park without me in attendance?" he asked.

Despite her effort to look stern, a smile broke through. "No, not at all… but it was still most unhandsome of you."

"Ellie, I had intended to return at least a day earlier, but the opportunity to do a good deed arose quite unexpectedly." He set his portmanteau down—he had not bothered to wait for a footman to carry it upstairs—and gave his sister a hug. "You are looking very well!"

"Thank you, but I am in a turmoil. Brendan, Harry has asked Papa's permission to speak to me!"

"A bit late, don't you think?" he teased. "I have seen him speak to you any number of times these past few weeks, and you seemed to enjoy his conversation."

She gave him an admonishing tap on the arm. "Beast! You know what I mean. He wishes to *speak to me.*"

His sister was so earnestly serious that he could not resist twitting her a bit more. "Ellie, I do remember your mentioning that he had asked you for permission to ask our father for permission to address you. After such an impressive quantity of permission, you surely cannot expect me to be surprised that he has screwed up his courage to make an offer."

The look she leveled at him was almost the equal to his mother's most basilisk gaze. "Brendan, when he asks—and I believe it will be very soon—I would like *very much* to be able to give him an immediate answer. Have you forgotten your promise?"

He searched his conscience for anything he might have promised, and neglected to do, that could have put her into such a taking. It burst upon him suddenly, and he slapped his forehead. "Yes! That is, no, I did not forget, but I only just remembered, because I have already performed my duty on your behalf. Yes, my dear. I asked Norwood to make discreet inquiries of the Honourable Harry's valet, and if you will only let me live to see another sunrise, I will discover whether he has gathered any useful intelligence. I should have done so before I left, but there was simply no time, and I truly am sorry."

She answered with a sigh of relief.

"But where's the girl who was in no hurry to receive an offer?" he asked. "When you first asked me about this, you said you were enjoying your light flirtations."

"I was. But—" She clasped her hands together almost as if in prayer, and brought them to her lips. "Brendan, the most amazing thing has happened. Harry has been so attentive and so thoughtful, and when he looks at me, it seems as though the very *sight* of me makes him happy… and I confess I have begun to feel the same way when I see him in a crowd. I believe I have fallen in love, Brendan, and now it seems silly to continue flirting with other gentlemen when I only want to be with Harry."

He hugged her to give himself a moment to get his face and his emotions under control. "My word," he said lightly. "You have made the leap from the schoolroom to a woman of serious purpose at an astonishing pace!"

"I know," she said soberly. "Mama says I should not be hasty, and I am trying not to be—and if you find out something dreadful, I *will* be sensible—but I hope you do not, so please ask Norwood as soon as you possibly can, my *very* dear brother!"

"I am wise to your wiles, young lady, but I will seek him out as soon as I've had a moment to change."

Her smile was answer enough, and after bestowing a kiss on his cheek she darted back downstairs.

Well, that was one minor crisis averted. If only his own problems could be resolved so easily—and if only he did not feel about Philip Carlisle the way his sister felt about Edrington! Not that the sentiment was returned, no chance of that, but— No, best not to even think along those lines. He had better not allow himself to look as moonstruck as Elspeth did, or his mother would begin to ask unanswerable questions.

As soon as he had the chance, Brendan took himself down to the butler's pantry, where he found Norwood busily making a list. He waited until the pencil was set aside to say, "Am I interrupting?"

Norwood leapt to his feet. "Mr. Brendan! No, sir, not at all. I was merely making notes on some matters relating to your mother's house-party."

"House-party? In honor of my sister?"

"Indeed, sir." Norwood's well-disciplined features softened into what was almost a conspiratorial grin. "Regarding that matter you confided in me, sir."

"Ah. A house-party, with perhaps an Important Announce-ment."

"Just so, sir."

"When is it to be?"

"In a week's time, sir. I believe your mother sent out the cards of invitation some time ago."

"Rather foresighted of her, wasn't it?"

"I believe the party has been in train for some time, sir, and the announcement is not, as yet, a matter of certainty."

"Well, out with it, then!" Brendan said. "You hold the key in your incomparably competent hands. You do not have the air of the skeleton at the feast. Is it good news, then?"

Norwood inclined his head, refusing to abandon his dignity. "Very much so, sir. It could hardly be better. The Honourable Mr. Edrington is a man of moderate habits. He is an inveterate whist player, but does not indulge in deep play. He is not by any means an abstainer, but his household has never seen him dis-grace himself, and he keeps his hands to himself when it comes to females in service in his father's home."

"What, *no* petticoat-adventures?"

"There *was* a brief affair with a member of the muslin com-pany last year, most discreet, and expected in a gentleman of his age and station. It did not last long, sir; his valet says the parting was amicable and the gentleman generous. This Season, it ap-pears Mr Edrington has determined that the time has come for him to settle into the matrimonial state, and his father's estab-lishment is also in high anticipation of an Announcement."

"Fair wind and plenty of it, as my brother would say." Bren-dan was more relieved than he had expected to be. "Excellent work, Norwood." He passed an appropriate reward to his hench-man. "Thank you."

"There is only one thing, sir," Norwood said. "I cannot believe your sister would quibble at this, but apparently Mr. Edrington has a pet to which he is much devoted."

"So long as he doesn't bring it on their honeymoon, I doubt

she would mind."

Norwood's brows drew together. "I do not *think* he would do that, sir, but apparently he is quite fond of the beast…"

Brendan decided he could not waste a moment in reporting the mainly good news to his sister, but when he looked into the sitting room in search of her, he found only his mother. "Good afternoon," he said, bestowing a kiss upon the parental cheek. "That's a very diverting headdress."

As her dark hair had begun to fade at the temples, The Viscountess had adopted the current fashion for turbans. This one, a violet wrap shot through with silver threads and topped by an ostrich plume of moderate height, went quite nicely with her dress, which was pale grey with a stripe of a similar color.

"Thank you, my dear. I find the turban so much more soothing to my feelings than caps, which always make me feel quite elderly. Though of course I could never have grandchildren if my own children were too young to give them to me. Immie and Jamie are such darlings, I cannot regret growing old."

"Old?" he said. "Nonsense. You are quite the youngest grandmama I know. I shall dance with you at Ellie's wedding. Which, I gather, is becoming more of a certainty with each passing day."

"Yes, young Harry," she said. "I confess I had hoped for a title, but really, this Season…" She shook her head. "He is a fine young man, he can take good care of her, she likes him very well, and what is *most* important, he enjoys her sprightliness. That Fridayfaced Fenwick boy…I could not be happy with the thought of him married to my most cheerful child. When he takes Holy Orders they should encourage him to conduct funerals. He is *such* a dismal creature. But very earnest in his vocation, I am sure," she added, as though trying to be fair.

"James and Anne mentioned him," Brendan said. "I believe Ellie has a friend that she thinks may suit him better."

"Yes, she had Millicent Peabody over to dinner last week, and we invited Mr. Fenwick, as well. I think they would do very well together. He has taken it into his head to do missionary work, and, Brendan, she was in positive *raptures* at the notion of him carrying the Gospel to the benighted. I think that Mr. Fenwick has quite won her heart."

He laughed. "I had no idea Ellie was such a dab hand at matchmaking. Did he seem susceptible?"

His mother's eyes twinkled. "My dear, if a presentable young lady looked at you as if you was Nelson and she was Emma Hamilton, what would you do?"

Brendan grimaced. "If you must know, I'd run as though pursued by seven devils. Lady Hamilton is not at all my style."

He was rewarded with peals of laughter. "I must be glad of that, I think!" she said when her mirth subsided. "But Brendan, have you met *any* young ladies who interest you?"

Brendan suppressed a sigh. He could hardly say, *No, Mama, but I am madly in love with James' commanding officer.* "Not as yet, Mama, and truly, I think that is just as well, don't you? If I were to marry, I could never support a wife in any sort of style. Indeed, I begin to think I am not the marrying kind." *That, I think, should become my motto. One hears it often enough.* And it struck him, suddenly: who could say? Perhaps some of the gentlemen on the town who made that claim did so for the very same reason he did himself.

"You are young, yet," she said. "And it is very sensible to avoid matrimony if you have not fixed on a career. Or have you?"

He could ask for no better chance to test the waters. "Mama, what would you say if I were to tell you that I was thinking of studying art?" When she frowned, he added, "A friend saw some of my sketches, and thinks I might have a real talent for painting portraits."

"You do draw beautifully," she said thoughtfully. "And of course, so long as you were respectable, not taking mistresses and other men's wives like Lord Byron..."

"I shouldn't think of it," he said honestly.

"Then certainly, why not try your hand at it? If you really wish to be a portraitist and can learn to draw a good likeness, perhaps

you might begin with our Family. I have never been really satisfied with the portrait your father commissioned… and now there
are the grandchildren. I should love to have a picture as they are
now, so sweet and happy!"

"I could sketch them, I think, but if you truly want a portrait
it would be best to commission it soon. They might be full-grown
before I have the skill." He smiled, wondering what his mother
might say if she knew he would most likely start with the family
horses. "Thank you. I was afraid you'd think it a mad scheme."

"It is not so steady as the Church would be," she admitted,
"but that is not really what you wanted, is it?"

"No, I'm afraid not. Mama, have you seen Ellie about? I
wished to ask her something, but perhaps you can tell me—am I
required for any socializing this evening?"

His mother nodded. "If you would care to escort us, we are to
meet the Rownhams for a theatre party this evening, to see
Keane in—oh, I forget the name of the play; I believe it is Shake-
speare, and he does that so beautifully."

"Certainly, Mama. Will it be just the three of us?"

"Yes. Oh, Brendan, I nearly forgot—I should have mentioned
this to you before, but are you aware of my house-party, the week
after next?"

"I believe I have heard something about it, yes."

"I just received a letter from Grandmama, and it is *most* pro-
voking. After taking rooms at Bath and not budging for nearly a
decade, she has decided she will honour our house with her presence; she plans to arrive tomorrow, and she expects to have her
old rooms. That is to say, *your* rooms!"

"Then have them she will, I suppose," he said. "You can
scarcely turn her away. She must be nearly ninety!"

"Yes—*far* too old to go jauntering around the country. I own
I had not expected her to accept, but, you know, I *had* to invite
her. And with her companion, and her abigail, and her dresser,
and who knows what else—I am afraid I don't have any notion of
where else to put you!"

"Don't worry, Mama. At worst, I can take a room at an hotel."

"Thank you, dear. I was thinking perhaps you might possibly stop for a few nights with that friend of yours, the one you were staying with when you first came to town."

The thought of Tony curdled all his comfort. Brendan knew he would have to talk to him again. He felt no pleasure in the idea. Far from asking to share lodgings—and intimacy—he might be perfectly happy if he never again saw that young man. "I don't think so," he temporized. "I believe he may be out of town. But never fear, I shall find a place to lay my head."

He excused himself, but was still unable to deliver his intelligence to his sister; she was dressing for dinner, and this was not news that should be shared in the presence of her maid.

At loose ends, Brendan sat down and dashed off a quick note to Major Carlisle, explaining that he might not be resident at the family home for a few days. He sent a footman off with the message and thought no more about it until the man returned with an unexpected answer.

"Come and stay with me while you are dispossessed," the Major's note suggested. *"This inconvenience may serve our purpose better, as you will have neither family nor servants wondering where you may be at odd hours."* He invited Brendan to call the following day, thus relieving the footsore footman of another journey.

So that was one dilemma resolved.

It was not until later that evening at the theatre, when his mother and her friends had gone off at intermission to visit some acquaintances in their box, that Brendan finally had the chance to speak to Elspeth without the danger of interruption.

"Well?" his sister demanded, as soon as the door to their box had closed behind the wanderers.

"Harry is a veritable paragon of masculine virtue," Brendan said. "I don't know how you managed to lure him in, Ellie." He paused, as though considering. "I know you are far too fair-minded to object to his few peccadillos: the glass eye, false teeth, and the ghost that wanders his home with its head tucked under its arm."

"I believe the law may allow me to plead extenuating circumstances for fratricide," she said in an equally agreeable tone. "In your case, I might even win a verdict of self-defense!"

"You really are deadlier than the male," he said in admiration. "If I handed James such a hum, he would do no worse than offer to thrash me."

She smiled. "Thrashing one's brother is unladylike, sir. We of the weaker sex must be courteous until we run mad from frustration, and then it's 'cry havoc.'" She seized him by the arms and gave him a shake. "Brendan, *will* you stop playing the fool? Though I can't help feeling reassured—I know you are not cruel enough to tease if you had learned something *dreadful.*"

"Of course not. As to whether it's dreadful, I can only say I was relieved to learn that the Honorable Harry has one human weakness, however minor. What do you think of poodles?"

She blinked. "I cannot say I ever do think of poodles—Oh, Brendan, he doesn't!"

"He does. And he has the creature shorn so that it resembles a sheep, which I gather is his idea of a joke. But to give the dog its due, it is apparently very amiable and well-behaved. His servants are generally fond of the animal."

"Well, I'm fond enough of animals myself, so if it can refrain from chewing my slippers, we should deal well enough. How in the world do you suppose he settled on a poodle?"

"The story," Brendan said, "is that Edrington happened to see Poodle Byng driving along in the Park with his namesake beside him in the carriage, and made a humorous remark. A friend of his, who happened to be a friend of Byng's as well, challenged him to live with a poodle for six months and see if he still thought Byng so foolish. So he did."

"And he took a fancy to the creature," Elspeth finished.

"Apparently so. And it's just the one dog, not a pack of the beasts, so you must make its acquaintance and make up your own mind."

His sister smiled, her eyes sparkling. "If keeping a poodle is his worst peccadillo—I think I already have."

"You were not considering buying any of these properties, I hope." Ellis Stanford, Philip Carlisle's man of business, handed back the list Carlisle had given him the day before, and offered his guest a chair.

Carlisle sat and glanced at the paper. "Not I, no. A young acquaintance of mine, an Army connection who's come into a bit of money, asked my opinion. I've never heard of any of these establishments, so I told him I would ask someone who had a better basis for making a judgment. Personally, I would not wish to invest in a tavern."

"Oh, it's not a bad notion, on principle. There are worse investments." Stanford opened a decanter on the sideboard in his office and poured deep amber liquid into a crystal glass. "Sherry?"

"Yes, thank you. If the principle is sound, what makes these shady propositions?"

"It's exactly that. Those four inns all have something a bit unsavory about them. I showed that to a friend of mine, a barrister, and two of the establishments are suspected of being meeting-places for buying and selling stolen goods. One is nothing more than the front for a brothel, and the last… I'm not certain what goes on there, but it has a peculiar reputation."

"Hm." Carlisle privately congratulated himself on his ability to spot a wrong 'un. Three of the taverns on his list were ones he had selected based on his own estimate of their quality; the fourth, of course, was the Cock and Bottle. "I suspect some Captain Sharp must have thought my acquaintance a Johnny Raw. I wonder if any of these places are really for sale at all."

"Oh, I suppose any of them might be—if a buyer had enough of the ready and didn't look too closely at the books! But I'm glad to know you're not the pigeon about to be plucked. I felt sure you had more sense."

"Indeed, I do. And I must thank you again for this quick work. If my acquaintance is still considering the investment after what you have told me, I shall suggest he ask his man of business to look up the owners before signing any papers."

"Tell him to have his man of business give the information to a solicitor, and look into the legal history of the place. Better yet, tell him to steer well clear of the lot of 'em!"

"I'll do that, Stanford. Thank you."

They spent a half-hour or so reviewing Carlisle's various investments and considering possible alterations, and then the Major took his leave. He had established one fact: Richard Dobson was sole owner of the Cock and Bottle, making the situation slightly simpler but at the same time more of a challenge. There'd be no reporting an extortionate employee to the owner; this villain was on his own turf and entrenched.

By the time he reached his home, Carlisle had decided on his plan of attack. He sat down to list what he knew of the situation and make a basic sketch of the club—Brendan could help him adjust that, when he arrived—and write down the details he needed to learn before they set a time to make their move.

Carlisle knew that he ought to meet with Brendan's friend Tony Hillyard. *Who sounds like a complete loose-screw.* He was not looking forward to the occasion, but Hillyard knew Dobson by sight and could describe the man's inner office, the lines of approach and retreat. Since Brendan had never even met Dobson, Hillyard was the only source of this vital information.

He was also, unfortunately, their weak link, and, from all Carlisle had heard about him, the only one of the party inclined to panic. For all that he seemed a quiet, gentle youth, Carlisle was sure Brendan Townsend could be counted on to stand fast in a crisis.

And his talent! Carlisle had no artistic ability whatsoever, but he did have a deep appreciation of good art, and he was amazed that Brendan had been able to remember so many details about a pair of horses he had known for little more than a day.

It would be interesting to see whether Brendan chose to pursue the idea of art as a serious career. At two-and-twenty, he was badly in need of some direction. Carlisle had seen enough young men that age, casting about for their life's purpose in the Army. For some, that was the proper career; others stayed for a year or two, then sold out as soon as they could without creating an embarrassment.

Brendan Townsend would have been one of those who left. A decade ago, Carlisle would have considered that a regrettable circumstance, but the mortar and pestle of war had ground away some of his prejudices. It took a certain kind of man to throw himself into battle and come out with his humanity intact—there were certainly men who did one and not the other, who either crumbled and went home branded as cowards, or lost their humanity and became pitiless and cruel. It was said that war made men, and that was true enough, but it also might break them.

Carlisle was old enough now to know that there was more than one kind of courage. He could count on the fingers of one hand the number of men he knew who would stay and help, rather than make themselves scarce, when a foaling mare was in distress.

He could count on that same hand the number of men with whom he felt truly comfortable. An only child, he had wondered what it would be like to have brothers; by the time he went to school, he had learned that a man measured himself by competition with other men. He had found a certain comfort in the Army, a sense of being part of something important, and occasionally a real friendship. He had found men he could admire, and a commanding officer that inspired him to something close to worship. He could...*almost*...understand how an emotional young man like Brendan might, in the all-male world of University life, form an attachment....

Carlisle caught himself, shocked at the direction in which his thoughts were tending. He had no evidence at all that young Townsend's romantic life was anything other than conventional. Just because Tony Hillyard had spent his time at a tarted-up molly house did not mean that he had seduced Brendan Townsend.

It did not *mean* that.

But the circumstances did suggest it, quite strongly. No man who valued his reputation—or, indeed, his life—would take another gentleman with him to a molly house unless he was reasonably certain that the other man was at the very least tolerant of such activity. And was it not much more likely that a molly would visit such a place with his lover—or at the very least, someone he was trying to seduce?

Well, what of it? What business is it of yours if Brendan Townsend was misbehaving with young Hillyard, or, indeed, half the members of that Godforsaken club?

Or, conversely, what was wrong with hoping that such an agreeable young man was not, in fact, engaging in activity that was roundly condemned by the Churches of both England and Rome, behavior that could destroy his reputation and life if he were to be caught at it? Was it not perfectly understandable that any man who considered himself his brother's keeper would hold an earnest hope that this was not the case?

Carlisle wished that James Townsend had sent Brendan to someone else for advice. And yet... at the same time he was glad that he had not sent him elsewhere. There were too many others who would have the same suspicions and act on them, bringing down the scandal and danger that Brendan was trying to avert. There was not likely to be anyone else who would see the rare combination of sweetness and talent in the boy's character, who would want to help and protect him.

With a deep sigh, almost a groan, Carlisle abandoned the list on the desk before him and buried his face in his hands. He could not let go of the tiger's tail, but it was foolish and dangerous to involve himself any further.

Well, he had been foolish before, and at least no one was shooting at him.

Not yet, anyway.

◖ CHAPTER 10 ◗

Brendan woke with a ridiculous thrill of anticipation. The knowledge that he would be spending the next few days at Major Carlisle's home should not have filled him with the same excitement as Christmas morning had inspired when he was a child, but try as he might, he could not entirely suppress the feeling. He had not looked forward to anything so much in ages.

Mindful of his duties, he made certain that his social calendar was clear for the day. At the breakfast table his mother informed him that the nonpariel Mr. Edrington—he really had to stop thinking of the poor chap as the Honorable Harry, if he was going to become a member of the family—was invited for luncheon and might reasonably be expected to take advantage of the opportunity to make an offer for Elspeth.

"Your sister means to go walking with him in the park afterwards," his mother said, "and if they are engaged at that point, your presence would be somewhat superfluous."

"What if he loses his nerve?"

"Then she will probably find she has the headache and does not care to go out in the bright sunshine," his mother said. "But I had a note from him this morning asking what color dress she meant to wear, so that he might bring her a posy to match."

Brendan was impressed. "Thorough, is he not? What did you tell him?"

His mother laughed. "Oh, bless the boy—I told him to choose

something white, with fragrance, and she would be happy. I don't know what my girl means to wear to receive his proposal, and at this moment, neither does she. She had a muffin and a cup of tea and ran back upstairs to consider her momentous decision. I believe she has scattered every dress she owns about her room. *I* think she should wear her pink promenade ensemble with the matching pelisse."

"But, Mama—what difference does it make what dress she wears?"

"To Harry, not a whit. To Elspeth…" His mother bestowed upon him that fond smile that meant she thought the had the perspicacity of a pilchard. "Son, when a young lady receives an offer that she means to accept, every detail of the event is important. It is her first truly *adult* decision, and it will change her life forever. To have everything just so…" She sighed. "Your father made a sad botch of the matter, you know. We had just returned from a lovely stroll, and he said, out of the blue, 'I wish you will marry me so I do not have to go home all alone.'"

"That does not sound objectionable at all!"

"Yes, but he said it as though he meant to wed me on the spot. Besides that, I had a pebble in my shoe and it was *such* a warm day. I was exceedingly uncomfortable! Oh, you laugh, but it would have been so lovely if I had been cool, and sitting gracefully in the shade."

"Oh, *poor* Mama," he said, stifling his laughter.

"Off with you, you unsympathetic rascal! I'll finish my tea and go see if I cannot help Elspeth come to a decision."

"Give my sister my love, and wish her luck." Brendan made his escape, happy for Ellie but feeling a sad, wistful twinge as his earlier anticipation dissolved into melancholy. He would never have that sort of good fortune. He could neither make an offer for the object of his affection, nor ever hope to receive one.

The situation was hopeless, really. He should not have had his portmanteau sent to Major Carlisle's home. He should be seeking a set of chambers in Albany or one of the other fashionable districts, establishing himself as a gentleman on the town, an independent young man.

And he would do that soon, but with his grandmother's arrival imminent, a speedy removal was the better part of valor. Grandmama—his father's mother—was always inclined to treat her family in much the same way Queen Elizabeth had treated those subjects who were honored by her royal visitations. Having lived through two such ancestral visitations, Brendan could only be deeply grateful to Major Carlisle for sparing him the opportunity to experience another.

The Major was out when Brendan arrived, but the butler, whose name he had never learned, showed him to a handsome chamber where his case had already been unpacked, and offered him refreshments, which he declined, and the freedom of the library, which he accepted with alacrity. Before he could take advantage of that offer, however, Carlisle returned home, entering through the front door just as Brendan was following the butler down the front stairway.

"Good morning, Mr. Townsend!" Carlisle said, handing his hat and stick to the butler. "Are the accommodations to your liking?"

"Very comfortable, thank you." Brendan felt anything but comfortable, suddenly conscious once more of how very attractive the older man was. "I must thank you again for your hospitality."

"Oh, think nothing of it. I enjoy your company. I do not often have house guests, and in any case, this arrangement should facilitate our endeavor."

"I hope it does. You spoke of a ...fishing expedition, on the way back to town. Has it met with any success?"

"Yes, a little. Come into my study, there are some matters we need to discuss." Carlisle led the way back to the room where they had first conferred only a few days earlier, and, once again inviting Brendan to have a chair, sat behind the desk. He offered refreshment, but Brendan declined, eager to learn what he had to say. "I have the name of the owner of that building," the Major said. "The man your friend has run afoul of is, in fact, the owner."

"This will be more difficult, then," Brendan said.

"Perhaps—but as I've said, that does mean he cannot easily retreat. I have drawn a sort of map of the place, and hope you'll correct any errors I have made."

He laid two sheets of foolscap on the desk between them. "This is the interior as you described it, and this is of the streets surrounding the building. I drove past there this morning. Are they accurate?"

"The street is, of course. This interior…" Brendan took pencil in hand and made a few trifling corrections—adding a vestibule, lengthening a hallway, noting where a doorman stood on duty at all times. "But I know nothing of what lies beyond the front rooms, sir. Tony Hillyard may know; he's been through that curtain and even in Dobson's office, I believe. Would you like me to ask him for that information?"

"If you wish. I had planned to ask him myself, but I would not object if you prefer to attend to that chore."

He seemed puzzled. Brendan toyed with the pencil, not certain whether he should express his concern, whether Carlisle might be offended. "Major, I have given this matter a good deal of thought, and as much as it pains me to say it, I fear we cannot rely on Mr. Hillyard's discretion. He is … what did you call him, feckless? You are exactly right. And worse than that, he is selfish and irresponsible."

"I had gathered that already," Carlisle admitted, "from his behavior toward you. If you wish, of course you may ask him for the information we need. But I shall have to meet him at some point, I think."

"Yes, I suppose you will. Still… I am reluctant to introduce him to you before the last possible moment. I know, from my own experience, that he has no compunction about drawing others into his problems. To reveal your identity to him…" How could he explain the profound uneasiness he felt at the notion? "Sir, I realize this may seem foolish, but for all I know he might show up here on your doorstep the next time he gets himself into trouble. I was wondering whether you might perhaps instruct me in a course of action, and let me deal with the matter myself? That was all I'd ever meant to ask for, after all—your advice."

Was that a look of approval in the Major's eyes? Brendan hoped so. "I appreciate your concern, Mr. Townsend, and indeed, it might be well if he does not meet me until the very last moment. I confess I would prefer that; it will save me ringing a peal over that young nincompoop. But the plan I have in mind requires that you go into the club with Hillyard and lull Dobson into a false sense of security—let him think that you have agreed to his demands and mean to sign his infernal book, while I wait in reserve. Oh, one moment—" He made a brief note on a list at his elbow. "That is another thing I need to know: will Hillyard be permitted to bring two guests with him into the club?"

"I don't know, sir. He told me that the rule allows him to bring any guest in three times, after which the guest must buy his own membership if he wishes to continue."

"Find out, if you can. This might be accomplished if I were to go with him in your place, but if this villain is expecting you, a stranger would put him on his guard. Did he actually see you, on your visit there?"

"I cannot be certain. Very likely not; I was not introduced, at any rate. Tony says Dobson does not share the habits of his clientele, so it seems unlikely he would mingle with them."

"Preferring instead to simply profit from their need for secrecy," he said with asperity. "The more I learn of this specimen, the less I like him. To err is human. To cynically profit from others' errors…" He shook his head. "I think that is even worse. Very well. You must also ask whether Hillyard can contact Dobson in advance of your visit, to let him know that you have agreed to his disgusting proposal and make an appointment for him to meet you."

"*What?*"

"Only a ruse," Carlisle assured him, "to put the villain off guard."

Still shaken, Brendan asked, "But, sir—put him off guard to what purpose?"

"So that he will be in a suitable frame of mind to respond favorably to my suggestion that he abandon his plan for either you or Mr. Hillyard disgracing yourselves in his establishment." Carlisle smiled, and it was not a cheerful smile. For the first time Brendan had a notion of what it might have meant to face the Major in battle.

Tony Hillyard was in his room when Brendan stopped by the hotel. Brendan's discomfort at the thought of this encounter was eased by his relief that Carlisle had been willing to stay in the background until his participation was absolutely necessary. Brendan might have had no confidence at all in Tony's discretion, but he had every confidence in Tony's ability to see what was perfectly plain. If Tony caught even a glimpse of how Brendan felt about Carlisle, even though the feelings were not reciprocated, he might throw a jealous tantrum, which would do none of them any good.

Tony attempted to embrace Brendan as he walked through the door, but Brendan pushed him away—not harshly, but with finality.

"That's a fine way to greet a friend!" Tony protested. Left at loose ends for several days, he seemed to be feeling anxious and quarrelsome.

"This isn't a friendly visit, it's strictly business—the business of saving your reputation. Or are you no longer concerned with that?"

"I suppose I must be, mustn't I?" Tony asked waspishly. "My dear Papa is beginning to turn the screws—says if I don't propose to Lady Constance soon, I must move back home."

"Well, I can hardly help you with that," Brendan said, nettled at Tony heaping yet another grievance on his shoulders. "Come, let us sit and discuss this in a reasonable way. There's some information that I believe only you can provide."

Tony sat, looked at the floor plan of The Arbor, and added

some necessary details. He listened, frowning, to Brendan's explanation of Major Carlisle's plan of attack. "That sounds very fine—if it works! But what is it he means to say to convince Dobson? What if this scheme fails? A fine spot to leave me in!"

Brendan found himself observing his one-time lover the way he might watch a dog worrying a bone. He felt peculiarly detached, no longer personally involved in Tony's plight. "You must admit it's a better notion than anything you've been able to suggest," he said, letting the annoyance he felt creep into his voice. "A man would think you *wanted* to be coerced into performing for those voyeurs!"

"You don't care about me at all anymore," Tony accused.

He was fishing for a declaration of devotion, and Brendan had none to offer. "That's neither here nor there, is it? You asked me for help, I found help—and you are doing your best to act as though I've made the situation worse! Honestly, Tony, if I hadn't given my word to help you—" He didn't even bother to finish the sentence. He *had* given his word, and there was nothing to be done for it at this point. He went to the window, looking down to the street below, wishing he were down in the street below, out in the country—anywhere but here.

Tony insinuated himself closer, trying the coaxing tone that had used to work so well to overcome Brendan's scruples. "Bren, why bother with this hugger-mugger business? All you have to do is spend a few minutes with me onstage—"

Brendan spun, shoving him away, and Tony sprawled across the bed. Fighting down his anger, Brendan said, "Mr. Hillyard, you must disabuse yourself of that delusion. You were fool enough to do it once—"

"Twice," Tony muttered.

"Dear God!" Brendan yanked the chair from the table, and sat straddling it, the high wooden back a literal barrier between them. "You're a bigger fool than I thought."

"What was I supposed to do? You'd vanished, and I couldn't put him off forever."

"And what did you accomplish? Did he give you back your paper?"

"Of course not. He said the patron who'd requested a repeat performance was not there that evening."

Brendan rubbed his forehead. "Well, there's no undoing it. I suppose that may serve. It will certainly make Dobson less suspicious when you return with me and an anonymous gentleman. Are you allowed to bring two guests at once?"

"Yes. Up to three. Anything more than that and one must reserve a private room and pay a fee for the privilege."

"That will not be necessary," Brendan said.

"Oh, why bother?" Tony sat up on the bed, his shoes leaving dirt on the coverlet. "Perhaps I should simply continue my career there until someone blows the gaff. I don't suppose they really hang anyone for sodomy these days."

"Do not deceive yourself," Brendan warned. "It does not happen often, but when it does…You do know that one of my brothers is in the Navy?"

Tony nodded. "Yes, and I hear they all have a jolly time together."

"I doubt you heard that from a sailor. Well, the Navy does not hang men *often*, either. But when a man is caught disgracing himself, an example is made to discourage others, and so it is on land. When you are caught—and if you persist with this mad behavior, you will certainly be caught—would you prefer being exposed in the stocks, or sentenced to prison? Never mind your father's feelings—I expect you think he deserves it, and perhaps he does. But what of your mother, Tony?" He knew it was a maudlin appeal, but if Tony cared about anyone, it would be her. "Her health is not strong. Such disgrace would kill her."

Tony waved his hand dismissively. "It would never come to that. Your uncle…"

Brendan simply stared, and at last Tony flushed. "You said your uncle is rich and powerful—"

"*Tony.* You didn't approach him—?"

With a scowl somewhere between guilt and defiance, Tony said, "No, I haven't—not yet. But what if I did? If you mean to abandon me, I shall need a friend."

"If you think him your friend or believe that he would protect you, you are a fool. He would denounce you, Tony. He would claim you had approached him, and his testimony would put the nail in your coffin."

Brendan could not sit still; he rose to pace around the room. "You threw my rank in my face the last time we spoke, and I'll throw it back at you now. Your being a merchant's son has never made the slightest difference to me—but it would weigh heavily against you in court."

"I'm sure my father—"

"Oh, really? From what I've seen of him, from what you've told me, your father would disown you. And even if he did not, all the ill-will felt against men such as your father, those who've made their fortune in trade and are trying to move into Society, would be unleashed upon you. You'd be the perfect sort to punish as an example—outside the *ton*, the son of an encroaching mushroom. Even if you were not condemned to hang—and make no mistake, that possibility is *very* real—you would spend time in prison, certain sure. And there is no way you could keep the matter secret from your father."

Tony pouted—an expression Brendan had once found charming. It held no appeal now. "What makes you so certain your uncle would denounce me?"

It occurred to Brendan that what was perfectly obvious to him might well not be so to Tony. "He would do it because he would have no choice—no, not even if he regretted it bitterly. He has a *wife*, Tony. A wife, a family, even grandchildren. He has a title, a position of respect and consequence in Society— everything to lose, and nothing to gain. Even if he loved you, which is most unlikely, he would not stand up in court and claim you as his lover. He could not. It would mean his death as well as yours."

Tony's face fell as he realized that Brendan spoke the truth. "And what of you, Bren?"

Brendan had to tell the truth, no matter how painful. "I have a family, too."

He went back the window, watching the street below with all its players moving in their neatly ordered circles. "And my duty to them …"

"Comes before me."

Well, what the devil do you expect? He made himself stay calm and simply said, "Yes, Tony, it does. I would not hurt them for the world."

"Oh, of *course* not. I quite understand. You don't love me, either, do you?"

Brendan ignored the sneering tone and kept to the truth. "I thought I did, once." He laughed. "But at the time, I thought that you loved me. And now I know better."

"That's a hard thing to say."

"Yes, is it not? But a hard truth is better than a pretty lie. Tony, if you had truly cared for me, if I'd been anything more to you than a plaything—or perhaps a playmate—you'd never have taken me to The Arbor. You'd not be pressing me, even now, to do something utterly repugnant to me."

He sighed, weary beyond words of this stupid game. "I promised I would help you, and I will, but you cannot sit by like a whining child and wait to be rescued. We have a plan. I think it stands a good chance of success, but you must play your part—and you *must* decide whether you will take this help or throw the chance away. I need to know that *right now*. If you don't give me a straight answer I'll be out that door in an instant and give you the cut direct if ever I see you again. Yes or no, Tony—which will it be?"

CHAPTER 11

Brendan left his former lover enjoying a fit of the sullens. He was pleased to be able to think of Tony as a *former* lover, and had reached a point where he wondered what on earth he had ever seen in him. He returned to Major Carlisle's house with all the information he'd set out to obtain, and a determination to reward himself afterward by spending some time in Hyde Park with Galahad. The fashionable hour of the Promenade had already passed, so he would have less chance of being hailed into conversation with his contemporaries. At this moment, polite social discourse was not one of those things Brendan would wish for.

But he did not disdain all company. As he had hoped, the Major decided to join him with the horse he kept stabled in town, a neat bay hack named Carmen that had neither Nightshade's flash nor Queenie's charm, but was calm and steady even when a cart full of caged, squawking chickens went past them in the opposite direction.

For all the conversation that had passed between them out at Twin Oaks, he and Carlisle were both oddly quiet as they rode through town. Once they had determined that they had nothing to do but wait until Tony Hillyard notified them of the date of his appointment with Dicky Dee, they ambled along together in agreeable silence. It was as though having made and confirmed their plan, there was nothing left but the waiting. There was much that Brendan wanted to say, but propriety forbade it.

Brendan should have felt elated, but for reasons he did not fully understand, his spirits were as low as they had been at any point in this predicament. The plan as it now stood did not require Tony to see Carlisle until the very night of their venture. Even then, they would pick him up after dark, in Carlisle's carriage. Once inside the club they would all be masked, so it was extremely unlikely that Tony could ever identify him.

The Major would be "Mr. Jones" to Tony; Brendan had suggested this subterfuge when Carlisle said he should be introduced at The Arbor as "Mr. Smith." Carlisle had accepted the idea without demur, and Brendan was much relieved. He had entered into this effort without really considering the consequences should something go wrong, but realized now that he should never have accepted Carlisle's help. What meant most to him now, besides keeping his own family out of it, was protecting this man who was becoming so important to him. He had no wish to be considered a mere boy being looked after by an older, more capable man, but a man himself, capable of considering the welfare of another. Still, it was good that an experienced strategist was planning this campaign.

Brendan considered that he was doing pretty well, for a man of no experience. He had accomplished everything that Philip had asked—

No, he admonished himself. Everything that *Major Carlisle* had asked him to do—and a little more, besides. And while he was still uneasy, even frightened, at the idea of going back into The Arbor, he felt fairly confident that they would succeed, and that he would then be free of Tony Hillyard once and for all.

He would be free…

Free to do what?

He could take classes in art, in painting. That would be interesting, he knew. He was beginning to imagine traveling to Italy, to get a glimpse of that most extraordinary place of worship, the Sistine Chapel. He might be able to discover whether he had any real ability or was only the merest dilettante. He might spend time in the halcyon meadows at Twin Oaks, hiding from the world among Carlisle's beautiful horses, recording their images on canvas so that their beauty might live for centuries.

The thought of all this was opening up doors in his mind, as though he had been living in a grand home with all but a small suite of rooms locked and barred to his entry. With nothing more than a few words, Carlisle had thrown open the doors and shown him a glimpse of wonder. Philip Carlisle had seen a part of him whose existence no one else had ever guessed.

And yet… and yet, Philip Carlisle, whose opinion had become so vitally important, imagined him to be a poor unfortunate boy, deceived and misled by a sodomite libertine, a lad of good address who had to be rescued from his own excessive friendliness. Here they were, entering the gates of Hyde Park, playground of the *ton*, and the man beside him had no idea who Brendan Townsend really was.

It was insupportable. Brendan could give himself credit for good intentions. He could, he knew, have simply told Tony to go hang. There was no proof that their friendship had ever been anything but platonic, and he could always say that he had no idea of Tony's immoral inclinations until his eyes were opened by that visit to The Arbor. He could lie himself sick and walk away scot-free of blame.

But he would have to live with himself if he did. And he did not know if he could manage that.

He stole a glance at Carlisle, and found himself meeting the other man's eyes. He was transfixed; the words simply spilled out. "I lied to you," he heard himself say.

Carlisle merely glanced about, as though checking to see if anyone was in earshot. "I doubt it," he said.

Brendan tore his eyes away. He felt stupid, gauche. His pulse was loud in his ears, and his face was burning. "By omission."

"Most people do lie that way," Carlisle said mildly. "Sometimes it is easier to let others think what they will than to cause turmoil and unhappiness by saying what one knows they would rather not hear."

Brendan glanced at him, sharply. "What do you mean?"

"There was a time in my life when I wanted nothing more than to put paid to my existence. If I had done it—if I had even said I wanted to do it—my action would have caused pain to many people. So I did not speak—a lie of omission—and eventually the desire passed, and no one ever knew."

Somehow, his words seemed to have two layers of meaning, and Brendan had never been good at that sort of conversation. But he did remember James had said Carlisle was a widower, so perhaps that was what he meant. "Was it when you lost your wife?"

"Yes. And another time. Another loss. It is interesting, don't you think, that with all the trivialities of our lives, men speak most seldom of the things that touch us most deeply?"

Brendan bit his lip. Carlisle was not looking at him anymore. His elegant profile was facing forward, his gaze turned to the other riders and the ladies in their carriages as the parade of Society took its well-regulated turns around the Park.

"I am not ..." He stopped, wondered if Carlisle's words had been a warning to keep his mouth shut. Would he ruin everything by speaking? Or would it be worse to hide his dangerous truth, and let this good and beautiful man risk disgrace and ruin through trying to help someone entirely undeserving?

Brendan took a deep breath, and let go of all the rosy hopes for the future. He could still study art, his mother had not objected to that; one way or another she would see to it that his father eventually understood that having a son who painted horses was not such a bad notion. But the rest of it... No. He could not reach out to take something that he had no right to ask for. There were other horses in the world, other places to paint. The family's manor would do well enough. He could not accept help offered in ignorance, with so much depending on his lie.

He tried once more. "If you choose not to follow the plans we have discussed," he said carefully, "I will understand perfectly—in fact, I would think you well out of it and hold no resentment. I can remove to an inn, and have my case sent there from your home. But I cannot lie to you, sir. My friendship with Mr. Hillyard… was not platonic."

He closed his eyes, and waited to hear the sound of Carmen's hoofbeats moving rapidly away. He heard only the steady clop of her steps, in counterpoint to Galahad's.

"I know," said Philip Carlisle.

Brendan could not speak. He hardly dared to breathe. They walked on steadily for a minute or more.

"I'm not so green that I failed to realize the circumstances," Carlisle said finally. "But it seems to me that this inconsiderate clodpole—whatever you may call him, he is hardly your *friend*—has given you a hard enough lesson. And in any case, it's not my place to judge."

Brendan had been prepared for anger, revulsion, or even cold dislike, but not for this neutral acceptance. He shivered suddenly, and Galahad shook his head in sympathy, bridle jingling. "Nonetheless," Brendan said, his voice unsteady, "I do feel as though I ought not take advantage of your generosity. I should not stay under your roof."

A note of humor crept into Carlisle's voice. "Do you also plan to procure a bell for yourself, and walk about shouting, 'Unclean! Unclean?'"

He knew the Major meant that as a joke, but it struck too close to the gold. "I—I feel as though I should."

"Please refrain, Mr. Townsend. Only the gossips would enjoy the performance, and you must know that such behavior would terrify my horse."

The request was delivered in such a dry, ironical tone that Brendan had to meet Carlisle's eyes once more. And when he did, he could not stop himself from laughing, and then apologizing yet again.

"I am not suggesting you continue this activity," Carlisle said, as matter-of-factly as though he were talking about a binge of deep Basset, "and, God knows, certainly not with Mr. Hillyard."

"Absolutely not," Brendan said. "When I consider his character,

I cannot believe that I was so stupid as to…" He shook his head, disgusted with himself.

"I assure you, every man alive has some mistake of that sort in his past. More likely with a barque of frailty, but everyone errs. Women, gambling, drink, adventuring—did you never get into trouble as a boy?"

"Not really. I could always see where things would lead, and it never seemed worth the consequences."

"You might have been better off if you had been a hellion, and got it out of your system."

His jangled feelings finally back under control, Brendan nodded. "I believe you are right, Major. How did you become such an oracle?"

"When one spends twenty years the Army," Carlisle said, "one sees a seemingly endless procession of young men making mistakes, over and over again, always the same sort of mistakes. And whether it's cards or bad judgment in battle or a petticoat entanglement or something similar, each of you thinks he is the only young man who has ever been so abominably stupid. You are not unique in that respect. I do not believe there is anything you could possibly do that some other young man has not already attempted, and botched even more thoroughly."

A sudden memory made Brendan smile. "James did say that if you could not help a soldier with his problem, the problem could not be solved."

"Did he, now?" Carlisle's tone was grim, but his expression was not. "I shall have to thank Captain Townsend for that encomium, when next I see him."

"He'll appreciate your gratitude, I am sure. And your magistrate in Kent clearly feels the same way. Still… I believe it would be proper for me to remove to other accommodations."

"Oh, for the love of God! " Carlisle cried, his patience apparently at an end. "D'you think you're *contagious?* We have a job to do, young man, and as I said in my note, we shall find the task much easier if you do not have to extract yourself from the bosom of your family when the flag goes up. Leave if you must, but don't do it on my account."

"Are you certain?"

"Yes! We have enough in the way of complications from that loose-screw classmate of yours." He shook his head and said nothing for a little while, then went on, more calmly, "I do not intend to remonstrate with you or harangue you with Scripture. I have observed that you are what my grandmother would have called 'a well-behaved young man.' And even if you were not, I'm quite capable of defending my virtue against any unwanted advances. Stay until the job is done."

Slightly dizzy with relief, Brendan could only say, "Yes, sir."

With the tension behind the unspoken lie dissipated, their conversation became more normal, which meant that it reverted to horses. Carlisle noticed a small scar across the back of Galahad's left foreleg, which led to an explanation of the odd circumstance of a piece of snapped carriage-wheel being flung halfway across the road, the extent of the injury, the time it took to heal, and the herbs used in the poultice. Brendan was so relieved to have such commonplace matters under discussion that he became quite animated when describing Galahad's efforts to remove the medicinal pack.

When they began exchanging anecdotes of idiotic horse antics, Brendan felt he had come home. He knew better; he knew that Carlisle's tolerance was not to be taken as a sign of anything but the man's determination to complete a task he had undertaken, but he was nonetheless grateful for not being treated like the pariah he felt himself to be.

After another half-hour or so of exercise, with night beginning to fall, they returned their horses to the mews behind Carlisle's town house and walked around to the front door.

"May I offer you some refreshment?" Carlisle asked.

"Yes, thank you—if it would not be too much trouble."

"None at all." The Major led his guest into a spacious, comfortable front parlor, a room Brendan had not seen on his earlier visit, where the curtains were drawn against the night. A branch of candles burned upon the mantle on either side of a portrait of a beautiful, liquid-eyed woman with stunning auburn curls arranged in a style of some years past. Brendan thought the room pleasant, if a bit old-fashioned; one of the chairs had been upholstered in a fabric very much like one his mother had used in her own sitting room many years earlier.

"I hope you will not be too uncomfortable staying here until we resolve your difficulty," Carlisle said. "My home is large enough, if not in the pinnacle of style." He glanced around the drawing room, obviously ignorant of whether the furnishings were a la mode or sadly outdated. "I never had much interest in such things—my wife always looked after that."

"It's lovely," Brendan said. "And quite comfortable."

"Thank you. Port?"

Brendan nodded, and thanked his host when he handed him a glass.

Carlisle waved his hand as though displaying the décor. "Since her death, I've kept it this way—I've had no interest in refurbishing." He glanced at the portrait hanging behind him, and added, "Nor in much else. I really must thank you for taking me out of myself with this little puzzle."

"She was beautiful," Brendan said. "You must miss her very much."

Carlisle's smile was sad, reminiscent. "As I would miss my breath. It would have been our fifteenth anniversary, this Midsummer's Day. I can hardly believe she's been gone for ten years."

"I'm sorry."

"No, it's I who should apologize. After ten years, one would think…" He sighed. "I always feel a bit of guilt at this time of year. Lillian made me promise I would marry again. She said that our son would need a mother, and that I—"

"You have a son?" It seemed strange that Carlisle had not mentioned him before now. The boy must be away at school.

Brendan wondered what he would look like—a sturdy child, tall and fair like his father, or a lively redhead?

"No." Carlisle's mouth tightened. "He survived his mother by only a few hours. Something wrong with his blood, the doctor said."

Brendan was silent. He could scarcely imagine the grief of two such losses coming so close together. No wonder Major Carlisle had been so sympathetic to Jenkins, the smuggler.

"Losing him as well… Well, that gave me the excuse I needed to break my promise. Since I had no child, I saw no need for a new mother. I decided I would never marry again," Philip said, and added in a low tone, "I could not bear to face that loss another time."

"I should think not," Brendan said.

"That was the time I spoke of—when I wished that I might end my life. I hope you do not think me too great a coward!"

"Not at all. I understand—" Brendan shook his head suddenly. "No, I cannot understand. Forgive me, please, I do not mean to pry, but—how do you bear the loneliness?"

Carlisle shrugged. "I have my horses, my books…friends at the club, my charity work—and, of course, the occasional venture into criminal investigation."

And yet he'd said he had no interest in anything. But it was possible to keep busy without necessarily having much interest in the activity—anything would be better than brooding over such a loss. "Of course," Brendan said with automatic courtesy.

Carlisle raised an eyebrow; Brendan could see him school his features to polite tranquility. "Oh, you must not think me a recluse, Mr. Townsend. I count myself rich for having had five years of happiness. There are many who've never had as much."

"I wish you'd had more," Brendan said, then sought a different tack. "I do appreciate your hospitality, more than I can say. My mother suggested I seek lodgings with Mr. Hillyard, and of course that would never have done."

"Certainly not. Would you care for a game of billiards before we dine?"

"Only if you will not be bored beyond measure by playing against a hopeless amateur. Riding is the only activity at which I excel."

"We shall be evenly matched, then," Carlisle said. "So long as we do each other no injury with the billiard cues, we may count the attempt a success."

The sky was lit by flashes that spoke of cannon fire on the ridge behind their camp, but Captain Lockwood never flinched at the occasional blast that struck too close to their tents. "Good work, Ensign Carlisle," he said. "I shall write your father and let him know what a bright, observant young man he sent me."

"Thank you, sir." Philip was near to bursting with pride. He'd known that the oddly-scattered stones had meant something, that the arrangement had been intentional, no accident, and he was enormously relieved that the Captain had confirmed his tentative guess. What a man Captain Lockwood was, and how lucky he was to have drawn this assignment! The Captain even looked like a hero – tall, slender, his dark eyes and hair making him look so strong and serious. His expectations were high and his praise rare, but infinitely precious for its scarcity.

"Thank you, Carlisle," the Captain said. "We shall go into battle tomorrow forewarned and forearmed, thanks to your keen eye."

"Thank you, sir." Philip said again. He hoped he sounded matter-of-fact, but he could not keep the grin from his face.

"You're a good lad. Let's hope tomorrow sees you safe, and us to victory." And the Captain leaned down and kissed him, quickly and gently. "Off with you, now."

Philip didn't want to go. He wanted another kiss, wanted to beg the Captain to allow him to stay the night. But he knew that was impossible, and he meant to be a good soldier, so he obeyed his orders. He ran back to his own tent, his body tingling from head to toe and his blood thundering in his ears. The Captain had kissed him!

And then the cannons began to roar—

Carlisle sat up in bed, the clap of thunder dying off in the distance. *What in God's name— ?*

Rain from a spring storm slapped on the windows, and a flash of lightning lit the room, followed by another, quieter burst of thunder. And his body still tingled with the memory.

Captain Lockwood... Good God. He had not even thought of Lockwood in years. He had practically worshipped the man; his first commanding officer had been everything that Carlisle had hoped to be, a sterling example, and the best teacher he could ever have wished.

Captain Lockwood had died in that battle. Forewarned, forearmed, it had not mattered. The enemy had simply outnumbered and outfought them. Even the hidden cache of ammunition was not enough.

Half the regiment had perished. A mere Cornet, Carlisle had been the only officer to survive that day. It was burned on his memory. That kiss, so gentle, so full of promise...

That never happened.

Or had it? Shaken awake at this late hour, full of longing, Carlisle could not remember for certain. Knowing Captain Lockwood and his rock-solid integrity, he could be sure it had not. Even if the man had wanted to, Carlisle knew he would not do such a thing to a youngster under his command, a boy whose wakening manhood had become confused with hero-worship.

But dreams could be peculiar things. Sometimes they told you truth that was not fact. It almost did not matter whether the Captain had kissed him or not. Philip had wanted him to, had wanted it desperately—not only in his dream, but in that distant past. If Lockwood had survived that battle... what might have happened then?

Nothing. Nothing would ever have happened, because Ensign Carlisle would never, not even on pain of death, have revealed his feelings. And Captain Lockwood, even if he had been inclined that way, would never have taken advantage of a boy who had not yet reached his majority.

As things turned out, that question mattered not at all. While home on leave, Philip Carlisle had been introduced to Lillian Winter, the sister of another junior officer, and fallen head-over-heels in love with her. His attachment to Captain Lockwood was, if he thought about it at all, remembered as a keen enthusiasm for the Army and adulation of his commanding officer. All that was very normal, very acceptable. Philip had not even needed to deliberately set the other feelings aside; the joy of finding someone who loved him, whose intimate presence made him feel alive, brought him to manhood in a way that nothing else ever could. His love for Lillian had left no room for anything else.

But Lillian had been gone for ten years, now. Ten terribly lonely years.

Society's matchmaking ladies had left him alone for two years after his bereavement; for another three, they tried to find him a new wife. They did not succeed. Eventually, they gave up. They said, *Major Carlisle, poor man. He has buried his heart with his wife.*

When he first heard that expression, it suited his feelings exactly. He had genuinely believed it to be true.

Now, for reasons he could not comprehend, Brendan Townsend was making him feel alive again, under circumstances that were completely reversed. Now he was the older man, and Brendan was ...*not* a child. Younger, perhaps, and less mature, but physically and intellectually a man grown.

And in this particular matter, more experienced than Carlisle himself.

"I'm quite capable," he had told Brendan, *"of defending my virtue against any unwanted advances."* Well, that was true enough.

But what in God's name was he supposed to do if he *did* want those advances?

⟋ CHAPTER 12 ⟍

The streets were quiet; the time was a little past midnight. Brendan wished he could see the faces of the two men sitting with him in the hired carriage driven by Major Carlisle's coachman, Edward. Carlisle himself occupied the seat opposite, quiet, composed, ready for anything. Beside him, Tony fidgeted, his attitude toward Carlisle that of a dog meeting a new arrival in the pack—one who was unwelcome, but too formidable to fight.

"Tell me, sir," Tony asked suddenly. "What is your plan if he should laugh in our faces?"

Carlisle's voice was steady, his manner commanding and slightly aloof. If Brendan continued his analogy of a hunting pack, Carlisle would be the unquestioned leader. "I do not think he will be likely to laugh. You have only to do your part—get us through the door and into his office, and return to the carriage when I tell you to go. You need not concern yourself with any untoward events; I will deal with those."

His certainty calmed Brendan like a swallow of good brandy; Tony only sat back without replying. The carriage rolled inexorably along the cobblestones, past the Cock and Bottle. It pulled up to a stop just long enough for its three passengers to get out.

"Fifteen minutes," Carlisle reminded Edward, who nodded, clucked to the horses, and drove slowly around the corner. He would meet them at the end of the alley on the other side of the row of buildings, down the passage from the hidden exit.

The Major's voice was crisp in the cool evening air. "Are you ready, gentlemen?"

"Yes," said Brendan, surprised that his voice was steady. "Let us get on with it."

Tony led the way into the mollyhouse. The night was dark, their hats shaded their faces, and the entrance was a blind doorway. Tony gave a coded knock upon the inner door, and when a window in that door slid open, he proffered his token of membership, a coin with a notch cut out of the edge. "Mr. Scarlet and two guests, for The Arbor," he said.

"Good evening, gentlemen," said the man on the other side of the door. "Please wear these at all times. When you have put them on, proceed through the door to your left, and up the stairs. Mr. Scarlet may have informed you, gentlemen: if you should recognize another guest, please do not address him except by his house name."

"Thanks for the warning," Carlisle said in a gruff voice.

Three wide strips of black velvet were passed through; Brendan donned his in silence, as did the others. When their faces were covered from brow to nose, they left the normal world and went up a flight of steps to The Arbor, passing through another door into a spacious, well-lighted vestibule with a hallway leading away toward the back of the building and a set of paneled doors to the left. These, Brendan knew, led into the room where Tony had given his alarming performance. From somewhere else down the hall came the faint notes of a piano.

The light thrown by candles on every available surface was dazzling after the dimness of street and vestibule, and Brendan was surprised at the heat of the place, something he had not remembered. He felt strangely disoriented, but Tony seemed quite at home, greeting the masked attendant and asking if Mr. Dee was in this evening.

"Yes, Mr. Scarlet," the man replied. "He told me to watch for you and your friend. Who's the other gentleman?"

"Oh, another friend. I'll introduce him. I told Mr. Dee I

might be bringing someone along, you know. Do you need to show us in?"

"I'm afraid I cannot leave my post, sir. Please, gentlemen, help yourselves to refreshments. Mr. Scarlet, do your friends have names?"

"Smith and Jones, they have no imagination." Tony collected a glass of champagne from a low table beside the entrance. "Come along, gentlemen. If you're considering membership I must say it's well worth the extravagant price."

Brendan followed without availing himself of the champagne. He felt stimulated enough without it, and half-sick with nerves. Major Carlisle showed no sign of anxiety; he merely followed Tony down the short hallway to a paneled door. There was another door just across from it, and from within could be heard a low moan, and then "Oh, yes... harder!"

Tony turned, apparently distracted; Brendan gave him a jab with his elbow and nodded toward the door. As Tony knocked, Brendan darted a glance at Major Carlisle, but his face might have been carved from stone.

Someone called "Come in!" and Tony entered, with Brendan at his heels. Carlisle stayed on the far side of the door, where he could not be seen from within.

"Mister Scarlet," said the man behind the desk. "So very good to see you again."

"I brought him," Tony said, just as he was supposed to.

Brendan was no longer afraid; he was disgusted. So this was Tony's dragon—a plump little man with a weasel's smile, his thinning pale hair combed and pomaded into an oily attempt at a Brutus. His office was beautifully furnished with a mahogany desk and a Turkey carpet; heavy draperies hung at the grand window, and stone lions snarled on either side of the fireplace, where a coal fire crackled busily. Handsome surroundings, but their elegance made their inhabitant look even commoner than he was. A bit of Brendan's pity for Tony's plight turned to scorn. What made him think he had anything to fear from this scheming scrub?

"And Mr.—?" the scrub went on, looking at Brendan.

"Smith," Brendan said, not trying to conceal his contempt.

"Yes, that will do well enough for your house name, although there are half a dozen of your kinsmen already among us. But our policy requires you to sign the membership book with your *real* name." He made a great show of taking a key from his watch-pocket, unlocking the drawer of his desk, and producing a leather-bound registration book, of the sort used at the better hotels.

"Smith," Brendan repeated. "Strange as it may seem to you, there are any number of us around. And why should I need to sign your book? I was under the impression that I was not required to become a member until the third visit."

"Only members may perform," Dobson said. "Under the circumstances, however—" He glanced up in irritation as a couple stumbled down the hall, grabbing at one another's clothing. "Shut that door, would you?" he snapped to Tony.

Before Tony could do anything, Brendan stepped around him to the door and pushed it to, but left it open a crack so that Carlisle could still hear what happened inside. "Thank you, I prefer privacy myself."

"I should think you would. As I was saying, under the circumstances, since Mr. S*carlet* says you have no interest in membership, the fee will be waived."

"How very kind of you."

"But you must sign the book."

Brendan shrugged, feigning concession. "Oh, very well. You realize, do you not, that if you were to point to me in court and say, *"Ecce homo,"* I would call you a damned liar?"

"Court? You wrong me, sir!"

"Of course I do." Brendan said, mocking the tone of false sincerity.

With a smile so smug Brendan longed to knock it off his face, Dobson put the book on the desk before him and opened it to a page that held only one other name. "If you would just sign here … You will see this page is reserved for you and Mr. Hillyard.

Since membership is offered only by invitation from a trusted member, we keep separate pages in the register for gentlemen who are known to one another, so that you can see there is no double-dealing."

"Such as blackmail?"

Dobson recoiled. "What an ugly word!"

Brendan felt as though he had stumbled onto a stage and into some bizarre melodrama. "Is it not," he said. He picked up the pen Dobson provided, dipped it in the standish beside the desk, and scratched "Ninian Smith" on the line below Tony's name. "There you are."

"Excellent." Dobson set the book to one side and said, "Very well, Mr. Smith, off with the mask, if you please."

The sense of unreality increased. Thank God Carlisle had guessed how this strange charade would play out. "I do not please."

He found himself speaking as he thought Philip Carlisle might speak, from a position of personal authority, and it gave him a strength he did not really feel he possessed. "Mister—do let us call him Scarlet—persuaded me that his life would be ruined if I did not cater to your extortionate demand. As far as I am concerned, he ought to call you out and have done with it."

"You refuse?"

"I commend your perspicacity. We are at a point of 'this far, and no farther,' sir. I will give you one performance, and you will give my friend that page from your infamous ledger, and our association will be at an end."

Dobson cast an ugly look at Brendan, and turned to Tony. "So this is what you call cooperation?"

"I had no idea he would take this tack!" Tony protested. "I never—"

The door slammed open, and Major Carlisle stormed in. "Tony! Leave this place immediately, or you will be disowned before you are an hour older!"

Tony looked so thunder-struck Brendan wondered if he was about to faint, but he rallied enough to gasp, "Yes, sir!"

He scurried out as though his coat-tails were on fire, and in the few seconds it would have taken him to reach the exit stair, Carlisle lit into the molly-house keeper with all the fury of an outraged father. "You *cur!* You vile whoremonger!"

Dobson leapt to his feet. "I beg your pardon!"

"As well you should! What right have you to drag my son into this festering cesspit?"

Brendan heard footsteps in the hall. Any place such as this must have a few bravos to keep order… but no, it was just a man in evening-dress, standing in an awkward crouch as he hastily did up his trouser buttons. Another man peered in behind him.

"I do not drag anyone in, sir. This is an exclusive establishment. Your son—if he is your son—came here of his own free will."

"Perhaps he did, the first time." Carlisle leaned against the desk, towering over Dobson. "He has done many foolish things. But I know he did not come here tonight because he wished to. He was here because you forced him to, with your bloody blackmail!"

A gaggle of masked faces crowded the doorway now, but no one attempted to enter. And Brendan noticed that the first man who'd been there was now gone.

He moved around the edge of the desk a step or two, as though putting distance between himself and this angry intruder. As Carlisle reached across the desk to seize Dobson by the lapels and berate him further, Brendan quietly slid the ledger-book off the edge of the desk and tucked it under his arm inside his coat, holding it tight against his body.

Dobson didn't notice. He was trying to wrest himself free, sputtering, "But you're not even his father!"

"No," Carlisle said softly. He tilted his head slightly, toward the door. "But they don't know that, do they?" With a fierce grin, he shoved Dobson back into his chair. "Goodbye, and good riddance. Come along, Mr. Smith!"

He did not need to ask twice. As Brendan hurried after the Major, he realized that the entire exchange had taken only a little over a minute. They pushed their way through the growing muddle of men in the hallway, most of whom were also heading for the exit, the air filled with their anxious muttering.

Brendan's heart leapt into his throat as their way was blocked by two large men whose function in the establishment was obviously that of keeping the peace.

Carlisle did not miss a step. With a backwards jerk of his head, he told the first bravo, "There's a madman in the office! Better be quick!" Then he reached back and hauled Brendan around in front of him. "You lead the way, you've been here before."

"Yes, sir." The excitement was racing in his veins. "I have it."

"I saw. Good work. Now, *move!*"

They were not alone on the stairway, nor in the alley, and, like most of the other men clattering down the stairs, they did not bother to take off their masks. As soon as they were outdoors, Carlisle motioned him aside, into a doorway of a shop that was closed and shuttered for the night. They stood there for a moment while a dozen men scattered into the darkness. Brendan checked once more to be sure the book was under his arm, and buttoned his coat up tight to keep it there.

When the rush had died away, Carlisle peered out, looked up and down the alley, and ducked back into the shadows long enough to take off the mask and stuff it into his coat pocket.

Brendan did the same. "My God, sir, that was splendid!"

"We're not clear yet," Carlisle said. "And we won't be until that damned book is burnt. I hope your friend had wit enough to find the carriage." He strode off down the alley, swiftly but not hurrying, and Brendan did the best he could to match his pace.

Edward had the carriage waiting as arranged, the door open and the steps down. Tony's anxious face appeared around the side of the door.

Edward grinned. "Was the raid successful, sir?"

"Yes, Sergeant. We have the enemy's flag, and a retreat is in order." Carlisle vaulted up into the carriage. And as soon as Brendan threw himself into the seat beside him Edward closed the door, and they were soon on their way.

"Did you get it?" Tony asked anxiously.

"Yes." Brendan patted his coat. "And not just the page with your signature, but the entire book! Safe and sound, until we're able to destroy the damned thing."

"All the names? Let me see!"

He reached toward Brendan; Major Carlisle brushed his hand aside. "You can't see anything in this light, Mr. Hillyard," he said. "And it would be better if you do not."

"But—"

"No. We shall drive you to your lodgings and bid you good-night. You may trust Mr. Townsend to witness the object's destruction."

Tony snorted. "Oh, so *you* will know the names of Society's sodomites, but *I* am not to be so privileged?"

Brendan could hardly believe his effrontery. "Tony! This expedition was to save your good name, not to endanger other—"

"Just why do you wish to see the names, Mr. Hillyard?" Carlisle interrupted, his voice cool. "What is it to you?"

After a moment's silence, Tony said, with unconvincing indifference, "Oh, mere curiosity, I suppose."

Carlisle laughed. "That is not a good enough reason. Forgive my want of nicety, but this foray was made necessary by your inability to exercise discretion. I think it would be a great mistake to allow you to acquaint yourself with the names inscribed in that ledger." He spoke in a mild, almost humorous tone, an odd contrast to what he actually said.

Tony shifted in his seat. "I should leave you now and find my own way home! What gives you the right to order me about?"

This was no time for Tony to throw a temperament. Brendan bit his tongue, knowing the Major would handle the situation better than he could.

Carlisle let the silence draw out long enough to take the momentum out of Tony's demand. When he finally spoke, the humor was gone. "You were willing enough to take my orders when it was your reputation at stake. You were willing to demand that your friend—who offers you a loyalty you do not deserve—debase himself to protect a good reputation which you also clearly do not deserve. I have the right to order you about, Mr. Hillyard, because I just saved your sorry neck—and because if someone did not tell you what to do, you would resurrect a scandal we have just contrived to bury. Damn you for a reckless, stupid fool—do you *wish* to hang?"

Somehow, the reprimand got through to Tony where all Brendan's exhortations did not. Tony hung his head. "No. No. I apologize. And…" he pursed his lips as though the words tasted sour, "I thank you for helping me."

Brendan closed his eyes and allowed himself to breathe once more.

"Every name in this register," Major Carlisle said, "belongs to a man whose very life depends upon his identity being kept secret. I do not intend to let you read them, nor will Mr. Townsend, nor I myself. I will not so much as open this book. It will go directly into the fire, and stay there until I can pound the ashes into an unreadable powder. And I shall ask Mr. Townsend to witness that I do exactly that."

"It must be that way, Tony," Brendan agreed. "That book could harm too many people—destroy dozens of families."

"In any case," Carlisle said, "he will have no further need of the membership list. Not after tonight. This will finish him."

"What do you mean?" Tony asked. "You may have the book, but he still has the club—and the mollyhouse downstairs."

"Does he, indeed? You did not see the number of gentlemen who gathered round to hear what I had to tell your Mr. Dobson. In a day or two, the word will have spread, and every man Jack of them will realize that he's been patronizing a 'safe haven' run by a rogue who has been blackmailing one of their number. Very soon, they will begin to wonder what would prevent him from doing the same to any of them. No, Mr. Hillyard. He may still keep the tavern, though he'd be wise to change the nature of its clientele, as the place has already acquired a smoky reputation in legal circles. But I should be amazed if The Arbor is still in operation by the month's end."

"Rolled him up, horse, foot, and guns!" Brendan exulted.

"I certainly hope so." The carriage drew to a halt, and joggled as Edward climbed down to open the door. Carlisle moved the curtain aside to peer out. "It seems you are home safe and sound, Mr. Hillyard. Of course you will speak of this evening's events to no one."

"Of course not! Do you think I'm an idiot?"

Carlisle did not answer that loaded question. "Goodnight, then," he said, "and pleasant dreams."

Tony stormed out, as much as one could storm on a wobbly set of carriage steps, and stalked into the York without looking back.

"Gratitude is not his strong suit, is it?" Carlisle remarked.

Brendan laughed. "No, sir, but at least he's gone. And I thank you with all my heart, even if he did not."

◖ᴖ᷉ CHAPTER 13 ᷉ᴖ◗

Philip Carlisle was pleased to see the back of Tony Hillyard. The only thing that did not please him was that Hillyard's departure meant he was left alone in the carriage with Brendan. The younger man was fairly bursting with enthusiasm and what Carlisle clearly recognized as hero-worship, but there was a warmth in his voice that made Carlisle worry that the sentiment might be something even stronger.

He would not have been so uneasy if not for his own excess of feeling. He had been wound up to a pre-battle pitch when they entered the club, and his vigil outside Dobson's door, waiting for the conversation to reach a cue for his entrance, had only turned the screw a little tighter. That was nothing; he had expected it, had used that tension to fuel his tirade at the club-owner.

But he had not expected the two men, slightly foxed, who had wandered down the hallway toward what Carlisle knew were bedrooms. He had not expected himself to be stirred by the sounds of their amorous fumbling, or brought to the point of painful arousal when they had given up attempting to open the door and simply began embracing and clutching at one another against the door itself.

And he had not expected to find himself now in a state where he had so often seen men after a battle—still at a high pitch of excitement, relieved to be alive and uncaptured, and desperate to find a willing partner and sexual release.

He suspected—No, he *knew*—that Brendan would be willing.

And he could not permit him to offer. But it was very difficult to have the young man sitting there beside him, close enough to notice the scent of his cologne, and not wish to touch him.

It was Brendan himself who broke the tension. "Thank God that's over!" he said, in such an annoyed tone that Carlisle was able to laugh. Then Brendan added, "You were brilliant, sir!"

"I must say the same of your performance, though I never expected anything less from you. I was quite relieved, even surprised, that Mr. Hillyard found himself able to follow the program."

"Perhaps he had no time to do anything but follow orders. When you explained what you wanted us to do, I did not understand why you meant to send him away so quickly, but now I understand. If he had stayed, he could never have resisted the impulse to open his mouth."

Carlisle nodded, glad for the distraction. "That was my expectation, from your description of him. What a spoiled brat! I can hardly wait to get home, send Edward and Goodbody off to their well-earned rest, and burn that damned book."

"Here, sir—please take it." Brendan said. He pulled the register out from beneath his coat and handed it to Carlisle. "I hope there is a roaring fire in the grate!"

"If not, there soon will be." Carlisle examined the heavy leather-bound cover and gave a short laugh. "I am afraid I misled Mr. Hillyard in one small respect."

"What's that, sir?"

"I do not intend to read this roster of infamy, but I will need to open it for the sake of efficiency. I indulged in a bit of exaggeration to impress Mr. Hillyard with my sense of purpose. This damned thing won't ever burn unless we tear off the covers."

Brendan's shout of laughter was enough to dispel the last of Carlisle's inappropriate desires. He would, however, have to be cautious around the boy, keep his own guard up. The one saving grace in the situation was that even though he knew of Brendan's proclivities, Brendan was not aware that Carlisle had that same potential, and the element of adulation could serve to keep him at arm's length.

"I must thank you again, sir," Brendan said. "I truly do not know what I'd have done without you."

"I suspect you would have come up with something similar. Your idea of making me the Man of Mystery was a capital notion. That added to my authority; you were the familiar old school companion. That handicap of not having Mr. Hillyard's respect meant you could not command his obedience. But command is also something one learns, and you have not had the opportunity."

"It's easy enough with horses." Brendan sighed. "It seems I have a great deal more to learn when it comes to human beings."

"If your father did not keep a stallion," Carlisle said, steering the subject carefully into safer waters, "you may have been spared certain lessons in horses being as stubborn and reckless as any human. Of course, when one encounters both a problem horse and a problem man, the difficulty is exponential."

"Every problem horse I've met did have a problem man somewhere in the picture," Brendan said. "Have you not found that to be true? And somehow, the horse ceases to be a problem when the man is elsewhere."

"I have noticed that myself. When I was a captain, one of my commanding officers was a man of more bluster than real ability, and he bolstered his uncertain authority by insisting on riding a stallion."

Brendan smiled. "I think James may have told me about that gentleman. Not by name, of course."

"That does not surprise me. Your brother had a very nice little mare who was spared from battle and sent home in disgrace when she was found to be increasing after an assignation with 'Britain Victorious'."

"So that's why James named that colt 'Rendezvous'!" Brendan snickered, then lost his composure altogether.

Carlisle did not attempt to discourage his mirth. If sex was one way to dissipate post-battle tension, laughter was surely another.

It was not much farther to his house; Edward let them out at the door and took the carriage off to the mews, to be returned the next day. Hiring a vehicle might have been an excess of caution, but Carlisle knew that there were few varieties of scandal that would make a fouler stink that what they'd been meddling in, and he'd meant to confuse the trail as much as possible. Edward had arranged the loan through a friend, with the hint that his master meant to pay a visit to a lady whose excessively observant neighbours would have recognized the Carlisle carriage.

Covering one sort of misbehavior with another was perhaps not the most original strategy, but it should prove effective to even the most thorough investigator. To Edward himself, and to his butler Goodbody, Carlisle had given the half-truth that he was helping one of young Mr. Townsend's friends retrieve an indiscreet letter from a blackmailer.

Goodbody had stayed up to open the door, even though he'd had orders to take himself to bed. As he and Brendan were relieved of their outer garments Carlisle repeated the order, and requested that brandy and two glasses be brought to his study. "Oh, and I meant to mention this earlier; is there a fire in the grate?

"Indeed there is, sir. And the refreshments are there as well." To Carlisle's raised eyebrow, he said, "I had anticipated your success, sir."

"You are an optimist, Goodbody."

"Not at all, sir. A realist."

"Well, we have one last task to perform, which we have given our word will be done in strictest privacy. And I will not have a fatigued major-domo running my establishment, so off to bed with you!"

"Very good, sir." He bowed slightly and headed off to the back stairs, while Carlisle led Brendan through the parlor toward his study.

Goodbody had done his job with his usual quiet efficiency. Decanters of brandy and port sat on the serving tray, with appropriate glasses. Flame flickered in the coals, adding that light to a lamp on the desk and a branch of candles on the table beside the tray.

He poured brandy into two glasses and offered one to Brendan. "To our success!"

"Hear, hear." They sat, Carlisle behind his desk. A timid move, he chided himself, but where else was he to sit? Brendan took the same chair he'd occupied on his first visit. He looked about him, and noticed the painting above the fireplace. "Is that the picture you mentioned—the horse that does not look like himself?"

Carlisle glanced up. "No. This is Speedwell, a hunter I had for years. That other painting I mentioned hangs in my library in Kent. Speedwell went to war with me. I lost him eight years ago, in Portugal."

"I'm sorry."

Carlisle shrugged. "That is war. I stayed on until Bonaparte was finished, then sold out. I remind myself that even if he had lived, he would most likely have died by now. He would have been over twenty."

"They're contradictions, are they not?" Brendan said pensively. "So very strong, but so vulnerable."

"Yes. Still, though their lives are short, they live every moment to the full. There's an honesty to horses—and dogs, too."

"They have what we have lost."

Carlisle turned to look at him; Brendan smiled. "I've not gone maudlin drunk, sir, only reflecting on this evening. So much deceit, so much distress, and all of it caused not by the thing itself, but by the law's condemnation."

Carlisle took a sip of brandy, let it warm him through. He felt as though he should argue the point, but he was forced to agree, in principle. "Such behavior does break the marriage vow," he offered.

"If the man is married to begin with, it does," Brendan agreed. "But the wedding vows don't seem to count for much if a gentleman chooses to keep a mistress." He glanced at Carlisle and said quickly, "I apologize, sir; I did not mean to imply you would do such a thing."

"No offense taken. I was never so much as tempted to stray. But I do agree, the law is unreasonably selective, and some theologians hold differing views. I once heard a parson preach a sermon that claimed the sin of Sodom and Gomorrah was inhospitality and greed, rather than the more usual fault."

"And how did the congregation take it? Tar and feathers, I should think."

"No, he prefaced it with the justification that it was for children's ears, to give them an explanation until they were old enough to understand the whole story. Still, what he said made sense, and since my mother sent me off to war with a Bible and there were times it was the only thing I had to read, I did."

"All of it?" Brendan asked, wide-eyed.

"Yes." He did not think it necessary to explain that he had been searching for a loophole, hoping that his own soul was not damned forever by his warm regard for Captain Lockwood. "And of all the abominations in Leviticus, it does seem peculiar that one act should be so reviled in this modern day. Men shave every morning; we cut our hair, we eat pork and lobster... every bit as bad as sodomy, according to the Bible. And as you say, Leviticus prescribes that a man who commits adultery should be put to death, along with his mistress. We'd see a great many empty seats in Parliament if that part of the law were to be interpreted as literally."

His glass was empty, but it had not been a very large drink. He thought another would not hurt. "What you must consider, though, is not what the Bible says, but how Society interprets what it says. When the great majority eat pork and consort with mistresses, those transgressions will not be punished. When you consort with someone like Mr. Hillyard—"

"Never again!"

"Or anyone not a woman," Carlisle said. "You risk not only reputation, but your very life. If you were my son—"

"I am *not*," Brendan met his eyes, and Carlisle looked away from the intensity of feeling he saw there. "Please, sir—I admire you more than I can say, but I cannot see you as my father."

"Just as well, since your own should be with you for some time yet," Carlisle said wryly. "Still—I admire you as well, and even if I did not find your companionship agreeable, I should fear for your safety if you continue to seek ... affection ... in such hazardous company."

Brendan emptied his own glass, and nodded when Carlisle proffered the decanter. He gazed down at the amber liquid, as though
seeking an answer in its depths. "You say that as though I have a
choice, sir. I do love my sister—she was a jolly playmate in my childhood, and I still enjoy her company. But apart from dancing and
conversation, women hold no attraction for me. They are pretty to
look upon, as horses are—and in matrimonial terms, they have as
much appeal. I wish it were otherwise."

He took a deep drink, and smiled sadly. "I have had enough
brandy to say this, and I beg your pardon in advance. If I could find
a woman half as beautiful as—as yourself, sir, I would marry her.
But that will never happen."

Carlisle cursed himself for bringing up the subject, and tried
not to think about how lovely the boy's speaking eyes were, under
those jet-black brows. He felt he should say something, but what
words were there to close the door he'd opened by bringing up
this subject?

"I do not think I shall ever marry," Brendan said without waiting for an answer. "Thank God I'm not my father's heir. As for seeking affection…I believe the military term is 'forlorn hope.'"

He shook his head, as though the subject was more than he
could stand, and glanced around. "This is a pleasant room. It suits
you. And there's a symmetry to ending our business in the room
where it began, don't you think?" He set his glass down carefully,
and Carlisle judged his condition as slightly in his altitudes but well
in control. "Shall we burn this dangerous book, sir, and call our business done?"

Philip nodded, and put his own glass aside. It was a pleasant
room, but he'd not thought of that in choosing it for this task. Why
had he done so? It was a little more private, but there'd be as little
danger of interruption in the front parlor, and that room had a better fireplace for this sort of thing.

Of course, that room also had Lillian's portrait hanging above
the hearth, and for some reason he shied away from involving her
in this, even so obliquely. What would she have thought of this

night's adventure—theft and destruction of evidence that would have allowed the authorities to root out a nest of sodomites?

He had to believe that she would approve. Of all the women he had ever met, Lillian had had no trace of the peevish meanness that so many ladies of her class were pleased to call virtue. She had always received the news of scandals with sorrow at the pain it caused the innocents, not the gossips' thinly veiled satisfaction at someone being caught out, the chance to feel superior to their fellow mortals.

If Lillian were alive, he would burn this book, bid Brendan goodnight, and go to his bed in the expectation that she would be waiting there to learn whether he had saved someone from disaster. He knew that. And he knew, too, that if she were alive he would not be feeling so uneasy.

But she was not. As he knelt to move aside the firescreen and stir up the coals, Philip Carlisle knew that he had reached the moment of accepting that Lillian was gone, and would never be returning.

"May I?" Brendan said behind him. "It occurs to me that if I were to tear the covers off, you might keep to the letter of your promise."

Carlisle laughed. "By all means." He took the bellows and puffed air into the newly-agitated coals, hearing the sound of tearing paper behind him.

Brendan knelt beside him with the pages in one hand, torn through across their width. "I thought they would burn better this way," he said.

"So they will." Carlisle took one of the sections and fanned out the pages, placing them face-down in the fire. The outer leaves flared immediately, curling into ash; the inner pages took a little longer. When that was down to a thin strip of scorched paper at the spine, he repeated the process with the second half.

"There must have been at least a dozen men there that first night," Brendan said. "Perhaps twice as many. And all of them much like my uncle … respectable, upstanding gentlemen who would roundly condemn sodomy if anyone asked their opinion. How many men are leading that double life, do you think?"

"I would not venture a guess. I wonder if I should place an advertisement in the *Times*, anonymously, of course, assuring the members of the club that Mr. Dee's register had been burned."

"That would set many minds at ease. But how?"

"I shouldn't think it would be too difficult— phrase the notice in a way that suggests the fire was accidental, and if they wished to renew their membership they should apply to him. The poor devils who heard my tirade must be wondering who will be the next to feel the pinch." Carlisle picked up the poker, lifting the partly-burned pages to be sure the fire reached every one. "I suppose most men have secrets of one sort or another. How many gentlemen are so virtuous that they have no sins they might wish to hide?"

He could almost feel Brendan's eyes upon him, even as he felt the heat of the fire upon his face. "And please, my dear sir, do not cite me as a pattern-card of virtue. I've made my bargains with the devil. Think of those pack mules I loan to the free-traders."

"I can only think of the night Queenie gave birth," Brendan said warmly. "She'd have died if you hadn't set aside your dignity and helped Matthews. She—or Princess."

Carlisle blinked, genuinely puzzled. "What else could I have done?"

"My father—most gentlemen, I think—would have cursed their ill luck, told Matthews to try to save the mare, and walked away. Some damned fools would have cursed Matthews. But you helped him." Brendan sat back on his heels. "*You* could have done nothing else. I think that is when I realized that I love you."

And to Carlisle's horror and secret delight, Brendan leaned over and pulled him into an embrace, their lips meeting in a moment of intimacy that sent a flare of desire through Carlisle, jolting him to his core.

The kiss was too brief, then Brendan broke it off, leaning back. "I—I'm sorry. No, I'm *not* sorry. It was wonderful, but I was wrong, please forgive me."

Carlisle shook his head. "No. You needn't apologize." He had no idea what he was going to do next, but the thought flitted through his mind that from the time his old desires resurfaced in that fateful dream, this moment had been inevitable. But he had no idea what to do next, nor indeed what Brendan wanted him to do. The passive state was alien to him, but so was the notion of acting without a clear goal in mind.

"I thought…" Brendan rocked back on his heels, a bewildered look in his dark eyes. "I thought you would—would be angry, call me out."

"No fear of that. I despise dueling, and I seldom indulge in melodrama."

Brendan sat there for a moment, then pushed himself to his feet and dropped back into his chair. "No," he said, as if answering some inner debate. "I cannot. I must not."

Carlisle did not try to convince him, one way or the other. He merely picked up the poker again and did what he had said he'd do, making sure the incriminating membership register was nothing more than a pile of crumbled ash.

When he rose, he saw that Brendan was finishing off what appeared to be a little more brandy than he ought to be drinking. Carlisle pulled a second chair close, retrieved his own glass, and took possession of the decanter as subtly as he could. "Young man, that was a remarkably foolish thing to do."

"I couldn't agree more, sir. You are kind to call it merely foolish."

Yes, Carlisle thought, a little drunk, but only to the point of *in vino veritas.* "Why?"

"Because I am a—a lover of men, and I have never felt about anyone the way I feel about you." Brendan bit his lip. "I might plead that I did it because I had had too much to drink…" he shrugged, recognizing the weakness of his own argument. "But I drank deliberately, to get my courage up. And as my mother would say, a second mistake does not repair the first."

Carlisle took that as an opportunity to stopper the bottle and set it aside. He thought he might regain control of the situation with a fatherly lecture, but he could feel the ground slipping away beneath his feet. "Some things can only be learned as the result of making

mistakes. And very few of us are disciplined enough to avoid suc-
cumbing from time to time. What matters most is the company one
keeps when drinking."

"Yes, I know that now." Brendan looked down at Carlisle's hand
where it lay in his lap. "I feel quite safe now, in your hands."

"As well you may," the older man said, "because if you begin to
look too fuddled, as you do now, I would lock up the bottle and send
you off to bed."

Brendan reached over and slipped his hand into Carlisle's.
"Alone?" he asked.

Carlisle's breath caught in his throat. Two violent impulses
seized him: one, to draw his hand away immediately; the other, to
pull Brendan close and kiss those half-parted lips once more. The
conflict left him motionless, but he did not release the hand that
held his.

"I—I am sorry," Brendan said, flushing. "Please forgive me, that
was an infamous request."

"No…" Carlisle still felt frozen in the grip of his emotions.

"You—" Brendan swallowed. "I thought I was being so discreet,
and I'm sure you guessed from the start. Everything you have said
to warn me against Tony, you should say to yourself, about me. I
am surely no better."

"I think you are." Carlisle smiled. "Even if you and Tony were
both mad for women, you have character that he lacks. As for the
other matter…do not distress yourself. I am no better, either." Gazing into the soft dark eyes, he could only think how different Brendan was from Lillian—and how strangely similar. "I simply never
had your opportunities… or your courage." He leaned forward a
little, and Brendan reciprocated, and their lips met.

Brendan pulled back abruptly. "No. No, sir, I must not, you have
been too kind—"

It might have been the brandy, the high emotional fervor of
the evening, or the loneliness that had been Carlisle's constant
companion for the past decade. Perhaps it was all three. "If you
don't wish this, then go. But I'm eighteen years your senior, and

you need not fear for me."

Brendan pulled him close as a drowning man might, and his kiss was Paradise. They clung to one another, embracing so fervently that the chairs they sat upon began to creak.

"Not here." Carlisle managed to resist the intense attraction. "We must go upstairs. If you wish—"

Brendan stared at him as though mesmerized, his pupils huge and dark. "Yes. Please. But the servants— ?"

"They never come up unless I ring. Are you sure?"

"Since the moment I first saw you."

Somehow they managed to remove to Brendan's bedroom, which was the nearest, without waking any servants. A small part of Carlisle's mind was warning that this was a terrible mistake and he must stop immediately, but he could not heed it. For the first time in ten years he felt alive again, consumed with affection and desire for this beautiful young man.

He locked the door after they entered; locked, and slid the bolt home for safety's sake. "I'll not ask again if you are certain, but if you should change your mind—"

Brendan spun and threw himself against Carlisle, wrapping both arms around him. "Please," he said hoarsely, "please stop asking me to run away. Send me off if you will, but I should rather be dead than endure your indecision."

He took Carlisle's face between his hands, and kissed him. The faint tang of spirits from the brandy, the taste of passion, the smoothness of that hungry mouth devouring his own… Carlisle surrendered his wish to stay in control; he let the slim young body mold against his, accepting this unfamiliar role as object of desire. Need surged through him as Brendan's hands slid down and squeezed his arse, and his hips thrust forward involuntarily. His own hunger was fanned by the desperation in the younger man's touch.

"How— ?" he mumbled against Brendan's lips. "I don't know… I haven't…"

Brendan laughed, a brief puff of breath. "It must be the only thing you don't know … Come, I'll show you."

They undressed each other by the light of a single candle. Carlisle wondered if his body would be a disappointment, then forgot his concern as he gazed upon the perfect form of this boy who would be his lover. *Not a boy, though;* the strong shoulders were equal to his own, the chest dusted with a sprinkling of dark hair, the slender hips, strong thighs… he looked away from the dark patch of hair above the thighs, but his eyes were drawn back to the strong young cock standing upright.

Why now, after all these years, should he think back to that night before a battle, and the surge of mingled pride and desire he'd felt then? Was it just that Brendan Townsend bore some chance resemblance to a man he'd loved, without ever realizing it until he'd lost him?

Then he looked up, and saw that Brendan was looking just as avidly at him. "You're perfect," Brendan breathed. "My god, I can't believe this,"

Carlisle felt himself flushing. "Too much brandy," he said.

"Too much time spent wanting you." Brendan held out a hand, a dark Adonis in the candlelight. "Please?"

He stepped forward, pulled down the brocade bedspread, and climbed between the sheets. "Come, then."

Brendan pursed his lips and blew out the candle, then slid in beside him. Carlisle gasped as their naked bodies met. "My god— !"

"No, only a fool."

They kissed again, and Carlisle was surprised once more as Brendan shifted around to lie full-length atop him. His body felt aflame, every tiny movement setting off flares along every nerve. Their cocks ground together and he groaned with pleasure.

"You've never been with a man?" Brendan whispered, undulating against him

"No, never." And Carlisle realized he was glad of it. For this to be the first time… it was right.

"Will you think me a whore if I show you things?"

"Never," he repeated, touched that Brendan would care. He

could sense the face hovering just above his own, feel Brendan's tension. "What is it? What's wrong?"

"I feel like one," he whispered, with a catch in his voice. "I wish you were my first."

Carlisle reached up and caught his face, pulled him down for a kiss. "My dear boy," he mumbled against Brendan's lips, "it's better that one of us knows what he's doing. Perhaps… perhaps I'll be your last." He knew it had been the right thing to say as Brendan collapsed upon him with another of those endearing, whole-body embraces. It had been a stupid thing to say, Carlisle knew; he was eighteen years older, and likely to die first. That was only natural, and of course he would not want this sweet passionate creature to be alone for the rest of his life.

What was he thinking? There was no way they could be together like—*God in heaven!*

Brendan had slid down just a bit and caught one nipple in his mouth, grinding his belly against Carlisle's cock while his own slid between the older man's legs. The sudden assault on Carlisle's senses stopped all thought, and when that hot, teasing mouth slid down to his over-excited organ, Carlisle could not bear it. *Too soon, too soon…* his fingers tangled in Brendan's hair, meaning to pull him away, but his lover's fingers kneading his arse shredded his last remnant of self-control. He pulled him closer instead, thrusting up until he could stand it no more, and climaxed like the Royal fireworks bursting in the dark.

He came back to himself slowly, his chest heaving as though he'd run a mile. "Oh… why did … Dear boy, how could you… what shall I—"

"Shh." Brendan rolled to one side, nestling in Carlisle's shoulder. "You needn't do anything." Carlisle felt a bit of fabric wipe against his thigh. "There, mustn't give the servants gossip-fodder." He relaxed again, burrowing his face against the side of Carlisle's neck. "Thank you, so wonderful…" Brendan mumbled, and in a moment he began to snore.

໑ CHAPTER 14 ໒

Carlisle's eyes snapped open in the darkness. It was late, he knew—the dead-still hours between midnight and dawn. There was a warm body lying beside him, the gentle pulse of breath against his collarbone. He could hear Brendan breathing softly, and he felt cold all over as he realized what he had done. *Dear God!*

How—? Why did I—the brandy?

But he had not been that drunk. No, he might blame the brandy, but he could not believe that lie. He'd known what he was doing, and he'd done it anyway.

But he could not remain here in another man's bed. The servants would be stirring soon. They should not come in, but if one chanced to see him leaving, in the clothing he'd worn the night before—no. He must not be found here, under any circumstances.

He carefully disentangled himself, slipped out from under the covers. Beside him, Brendan murmured but did not waken. The chill of early spring seeped into Carlisle's bones as he fumbled about in the dark, collecting his clothing.

Just as well he kept only a skeleton staff here in town.

Feeling like a burglar in his own home, he slipped silently from his guest's bedchamber and back to his own. When the door was shut, and the key turned, he finally felt safe enough to light a candle.

The mirror showed him a haunted face, the face of a hypocrite. A scant handful of hours earlier, he had been excoriating the keeper of a den of sodomites.

Now he was one of them.

He turned away from the mirror, wondering what on earth he was going to do. If he had any sense of honor at all, he would get his service pistol and put a period to his existence. If he wanted to make a thorough job of it, he would shoot Brendan, and then himself.

The very thought was nearly a physical pain. No. He could not do that. It was not Brendan's fault at all; he might have awakened the hunger, but he could never have done so if it had not lain sleeping within Major Philip Carlisle's heroic and widely-respected breast. No, there would be no blaming the young man for his own nature. He was merely young, and affectionate, and wholly beautiful.

And so was what they had done together. If this was sodomy— it was no wonder that it was fought with such violent prejudice, for there was nothing in Carlisle's experience that surpassed the wonder of it.

But he had loved Lillian, too—loved her deeply and honestly. And they had made love with that same sort of wondrous joy, and he had looked forward to that joy manifesting itself in their child.

Who had died, after his birth had taken his mother's life.

How could Carlisle dare to displace Lillian's sacred memory with this? What he felt now… how could it be the same?

But it was the same; the trust, the tenderness—there was no difference.

Lillian had told him to love again. Not only for the child's sake, but for his own. And if he had been the one to die, would he not have told her to do the same? Would he have been so selfish as to demand that she never find joy again?

Was it possible that the sex of one's lover could make so little difference? Could it truly be a matter not of bodies, but of souls?

Even if that was the case, though, Society would not understand, or appreciate… or forgive. It had not been so many years ago that a man of the India Regiment, and his lover as well, had been hanged on the merest circumstantial evidence, and the testimony of a man they had insisted was a liar. How could he, in any honor, expose someone he loved to that horrible risk?

If Carlisle himself could put aside his long-ago infatuation with Michael Lockwood, if he had been able to find and love and marry a good and beautiful woman, then surely Brendan would be able to do the same. It would be better for him. It would be so much safer. And Brendan did not carry a curse in his blood; he might sire children and have a normal, happy life.

But only if this ended. Here and now.

In four long strides, Carlisle was at his desk, seeking pen, ink, and paper. He would leave Brendan a courteous note, worded in a way that would make the meaning perfectly clear only to the two of them. He would leave before Brendan woke, and he would stay away until he knew the boy had returned to a sane, conventional way of life.

Brendan was only two-and-twenty, and he had spent nearly all his time with other young men. What did he know about his potential? It would only take one young woman, the right woman. There had to be at least one reasonably eligible girl who could set the boy on the right path… or at least provide him with reasonable companionship and a proper, conventional household.

James Townsend was a good man, a steadying influence. He would be far better suited to guide his younger brother and steer him into a way of living that would allow him to keep living.

Carlisle sat for a time and thought, and then dipped his pen into the inkwell.

Brendan stirred as the morning light and warmth made an impression on the south-facing bedroom. He drifted up to drowsy wakefulness, knowing he felt happy but not remembering why.

As consciousness returned, and with it the memory of the night before, he stretched luxuriously. Philip! Philip, golden and warm and slightly tipsy, intrepid in the face of danger but tentative as a maiden in bed, admitting his inexperience and letting

Brendan take the lead, giving him the honor of being the first.

Brendan's cup overflowed. He had not in his wildest flights of imagination ever expected last night's events to happen. What an astonishing difference compared to his last encounter with Tony. How amazing to make love to someone that he could not only love but admire, someone he could look up to instead of worrying what sort of idiotic problem he would next be called upon to solve.

Philip.

Eyes still closed, he reached out, but touched only an empty pillow. Reality brought him back to earth. Of course Philip would have gone back to his own room; it would never do for them to be discovered in bed together. They dared not indulge in such luxury; every tryst would have to be as carefully planned as the raid on The Arbor. It would not be easy—but his life had never been easy, not since he realized he was a lover of men. Not easy, perhaps—but now, from time to time, joyful.

He closed his eyes, reliving each moment. He had imagined how it would feel to lie in Philip's arms, how his lips would taste, how that thick mane of hair would feel sliding through his searching fingers.

The reality had surpassed all imagining.

It had been exciting to be the one taking charge, leading his lover through their mutual exploration. He had never done that before. His only experience had been Tony's practiced—and, he now realized, rather mechanical—seduction.

What would happen when Philip felt confident enough to take the lead? Brendan had no doubt that he would. He could not imagine Philip staying passive for very long, for any reason.

His eyes opened suddenly, with a sudden burst of delight. There *was* something he could give to Philip, to him, and him alone, something Tony had never desired. Brendan felt a slight twinge of trepidation, for Philip was magnificently endowed. Still, Tony had always seemed to enjoy taking Brendan's cock inside him, and though Brendan had never felt any interest in allowing his erstwhile friend to reciprocate—nor, in truth, had Tony ever shown any interest—he felt sure that Philip would be most careful. He expected to enjoy it.

Indeed, if Tony's reaction were taken as an indicator, he expected to enjoy it very much.

Brendan dozed for a little while longer, reluctant to leave the sheets on which the scent of Philip's body still lingered. He threw an arm across the other pillow, rubbing his face against it like a cat.

Best not to stay abed too long, he reminded himself. He was a guest here, and it was the duty of a courteous guest not to delay the servants' work schedule. Giving the pillow one last affectionate squeeze, he tossed the covers aside and sprang out of bed.

He saw the folded notepaper propped against his shaving-case, and recognized Philip's handwriting. Perhaps he had needed to leave early on some errand? The note was not sealed, so it would not be—he suppressed a grin—a *billet-doux.*

He read the words quickly, and could not breathe. He read them once more, unable to believe what they said, or even comprehend the meaning.

Mr. Townsend—

It distresses me to tell you that I have been called away unexpectedly, and do not know when I shall be likely to return. You are welcome to stay at this house for as long as you wish, at least until your family's visitors have departed. I thank you for the pleasure of your company; do give my regards to your family and particularly your brother.

Please accept my apologies for this unintended breach of hospitality, and the informality of this note...

Carlisle

And that was all.

He stood there for a long time, the paper in his hand and a block in his throat that felt like a shard of glass. He could hear his heartbeat in his ears, but apart from that, nothing.

...the pleasure of your company... breach of hospitality...

When he was a child, his parents had hired a puppet show for the nursery. His birthday, Elspeth's—he could not remember the occasion and it hardly mattered. One of the puppets had gotten its strings tangled somehow, and while the other moved and gesticulated, the stricken marionette simply stood in place, paralyzed.

That was how he felt. He could not move, could barely breathe, and the only emotion that registered was utter bewilderment. Somewhere, far away, was a great mass of pain, anger, and confusion, but he could not quite reach it and was genuinely afraid to try.

He stumbled back to the bed, still feeling like a broken toy, and crept under the covers. He lay there for awhile, numb, the note crumpled in his clenched fist while the scent of Philip's body slowly faded from the pillow.

Eventually he noticed that the sun had moved, and the light on the bed was now playing across the floor. It was time to get up.

Time to go.

He looked at himself in the mirror over the dressing-table, and thought that he looked much as his maternal grandfather had when he was laid out in his coffin. That seemed right; everything within him felt dead, he had simply not had the sense to stop breathing and moving about.

Was this how true shock felt? Home on leave during the Peace of Amiens, his brother Andrew had once described a strange phenomenon called Shock of Ball—a thing that was said to happen when a cannonball passed so close to a sailor's body that it sucked the very life from him. But such a shock was supposed to cause instant death. This... this *numbness* was unnatural.

His mind shied away from that word, but the numbness receded, a little, and he realized he had to get out of this house. Conversing with Philip's butler would require more strength than he had to call upon. He had shaved just before the excursion to The Arbor, so his face would pass muster for a little while.

The room was well-appointed, with a small writing desk beside the window. It contained paper and pen, all he needed to write a short note to Goodbody. He expressed his unwillingness to put the household to any unnecessary trouble in its owner's absence, and requested that his luggage be packed and sent on to the Pulteney Hotel. He signed the note with a meticulous "B. Townsend," blotted it carefully with sand, and left it on the writing desk where the maid would find and deliver it.

He marveled at how well-trained he was. A true gentleman. He could write a courteous note even though he was barely aware of the floor beneath his feet.

Still feeling disoriented, he dressed himself and assessed his finances. After extracting enough for vails to the butler and the cost of sending his luggage, he still had a few pounds left, so there would be no need for an immediate trip to the bank. He would have funds enough to pay for his room at the Pulteney for a day or two, and to purchase a bottle of some sort of spirits for himself along the way. Getting blind drunk after a serious disappointment was a perfectly acceptable way for a young gentleman to conduct himself, so long as he was discreet. The staff at the Pulteney would not give him a second thought. No one would know him, no one would care. No one would ask the questions that might shatter the fragile shell that was keeping the pain encased within.

Brendan smoothed Philip's note and folded it away in the inner pocket of his waistcoat. He should tear it to shreds or burn it, but could not bear to think of doing such a thing. Perhaps later. Perhaps never.

He opened the bedroom door with care, found the hall empty. Moving quickly, he was down the stair and out the front door before anyone in the household made an appearance. The sun was excessively bright; no doubt that was what made his eyes water so fiercely.

"Two rooms, Cranton? That's *all?*"

"Afraid so, sir. Happen there might be another gent coming in later…"

Dicky Dee glared at his doorkeeper, then shook his head. He couldn't expect the man to go out and drag people in, not in an establishment that catered to such a particular clientele.

So… two couples had reserved rooms for the night. Only two! *Damn that sniveling Hillyard brat and his upper-crust catamite!* And the man claiming to be his father—who was *he*? A patron? A relative of Hillyard's? Or a close acquaintance of "Mr. Smith?"

Whoever he was, he had finished The Arbor, and all Dobson's plans. Oh, the molly-house was still there, the working-class clientele were still in attendance—for the moment. But business had begun to diminish there, too. That was inevitable. Some of the wealthier sodomites had a taste for the rough, which resulted in many of the downstairs mollies making personal arrangements with members of the upstairs club. That poisonous word *blackmail* was beginning to spread through both establishments. In another month, The Arbor would be little more than a memory.

It would—Dobson laughed mirthlessly—it would wither on the vine.

He was, somehow, not at all surprised to hear a knock on his door, and see a familiar form. It only needed that.

"Yes, my lord?"

His visitor closed the door carefully behind him, placed his hat on the desk and dropped his gloves into it, then made himself comfortable in the chair opposite Dobson's desk, not waiting for an invitation.

"May I offer you a drink?" Dobson essayed.

"No, thank you. I am concerned, sir. I understand you had a rather unpleasant incident on the premises recently."

"Yes, a…" Dobson chose his words carefully. "A member who was not content with our customs. He—"

"Don't humbug me," His Lordship said. "It was that lad I wished to see onstage, was it not? It seems to me you have handled the matter very badly."

"I—Yes, that's who it was. Why ask me, if you already know?"

"I was curious to see what sort of lies you might concoct."

Dobson was not in a mood to be sneered at. "My lord, the truth of the matter is that I was trying to be tactful. Since you have dispensed with that nicety, I feel free to remind you that I was exerting pressure upon that young man entirely on your behalf, and at your insistence."

"You dare—"

"I was doing so in order to find a way to give you what you demanded, without compromising the confidentiality of our membership list."

His Lordship leaned across the desk, looming. "You sank to *blackmail?*"

"I did not threaten him with the police; I threatened to tell his father. What would you have had me do?"

"As I told you!"

"He had no need for your money, my lord; he was plump enough in the purse to pay his own membership in the club. I did persuade him to repeat his performance—is it my fault you were not in attendance that night? If you had taken my suggestion, been patient, waited until he returned so that you might approach him in an ordinary manner—"

"Damn you!"

Dobson flinched as his lordship's fists came down upon the desk, and moved his chair back a few inches.

"I am finished doing business with you, Dobson," his visitor said. "I loaned you a thousand pounds to set up this establishment. You have repaid four hundred. I want the rest, and the interest, by the end of the week."

He had expected anger, even fury. He had not expected this. "But, my lord—even if I were to sell the place tomorrow, it would not be possible—"

"You heard me."

Dobson's ire was beginning to get the better of his patience. "And what will you do, my lord, if I cannot? Have me up before the debtor's court?"

He could not see the man's face, but what he could read—
eyes and mouth—were dumbfounded.

"Of course you will," Dobson said fallaciously. "The trial will
be a sensation—there's been nothing like it since the Vere Street
Club affair. How many men were hanged, then? How many man-
gled in the pillory? 'Your honor,'" he mocked, "'this man came to
me with a scheme to turn a set of apartments into an exclusive
mollyhouse, so that I and my sodomitical friends might cavort in
the luxury to which we are accustomed.'"

He laughed. "Certainly you may take me to court, my lord!
Why should you not? I am sure, if you can only find a judge who
is one of your disgusting fraternity, you might even win a writ requiring me to sell the property! Of course, your reputation is no
doubt so *very* high that it could withstand the scandal…" He was
certain that the face beneath the velvet mask was now apoplec-
tic. "No, you won't do that, will you?"

"What I will do, sir," His Lordship finally growled, "is file an
anonymous complaint against you, and see to it that the men you
batten on are warned in advance. The men who frequent this establishment can scatter. Yours is the only name on the deed of title."

Ah, threat and counter-threat. This was nothing but fencing.
"And your investment?"

"Well lost. I never gamble more than I can afford to lose, you
half-wit. Why do you suppose I gave you cash, without asking for
signed surety?"

Dobson snorted.

"You think I bluff, sir? You are mistaken. Were I to tell certain
men that you used your membership roster for blackmail, you
would be found out in that alley with your throat cut, and I'll be
damned if I don't think that a capital idea. There is but one thing
that can save you. *Where is that register?*"

Dobson felt his bones turn to water; the room suddenly
seemed oppressively hot. "Why, it should be here in my desk." He
tugged at the handle of the locked drawer. "I must find the key;
perhaps I left it at home…"

"Liar. Do not trifle with me. I have the tale from the lips of a man who saw it all. Someone took that book—that boy's *father*, if the story is true."

"It is not. That is to say, the man was not his father, I know that much. Some other molly, I'll wager."

"So a stranger, a man whose identity you do not even know, now has the signatures of the entire Arbor membership."

"Except yours, my lord," Dobson pointed out. "*You* are in no danger."

"I am here in this building right now, you fool! What if that man was an agent of the police?"

"Then I should have expected them to be here before now."

His lordship signed heavily. "You are worse than a fool. Do you think a warrant can be obtained out of thin air, and for such a charge, against so many men of consequence? The police would take their time, to be sure of tightening the noose."

Dobson began to feel solid ground beneath his feet once again. "I do not think a warrant will be obtained by anyone, my lord, not for any purpose. I believe Mister—" He caught himself, smiling. "I believe the boy who took your fancy asked another gentleman friend to help him obtain the book for his own protection. If they had any sense—and I'll give them their due, Wellington himself could not have done better—the book went into the fire before the sun rose."

"If I could be certain of that..." His lordship nodded once, and got to his feet. "Very well, then. You find out what became of that book. Find it—or find that boy, and arrange for me to meet with him. If he will give me his assurance that your clientele are in no danger of exposure, I'll see about helping you move this club to a safer place, to see if you cannot repay me, after all. You're an extortionate weasel, but you do run a good club."

"But—why should he assist me? Why should he be willing to meet with you?

A thin smile touched the lips barely visible at the lower edge of the mask. "Because when I spoke to him, the lad did not seem reluctant to make my acquaintance. I believe you merely botched the job, and I am convinced a little friendly persuasion would get the truth out of him."

Dobson thought rapidly. He knew where Tony Hillyard lived, and could no doubt find him. Whether or not he could convince him to meet with His Lordship—well, that mattered very little. The fate of the membership book—he could get that out of the brat by threatening to tell his father. It had worked before, it should work again. "What if I can get the truth from him, but he refuses to meet with you?"

"I must speak to him. You don't imagine I would accept your word, do you? Bring me the boy. Otherwise," said Lord Cedric, "I'll see that every sodomite in London learns that you black-mailed a man who revealed his identity and trusted your word to keep it secret. Your business will perish, if it is not already dead. And you will be fortunate indeed if that is the worst that befalls you."

⋐ CHAPTER 15 ⋑

Brendan pried his eyes open and thanked St. Gambrinus for finding him a room on the north side of the building, safe from the piercing shafts of the morning sun. His head hurt. Truth be told, his whole body hurt, and the dull ache in his heart defied all description, but for the moment he was grateful that the headache overpowered the rest of the misery.

What had awakened him? There had been a noise… There—a tapping!

Someone was at the door. He sighed and called "One moment!"

Wincing at the racket of his own voice, he grappled with the bedpost and hauled himself to his feet, a maneuver that required more physical coordination than he had at his command.

He found himself blinking stupidly at a maid holding a tray, but when she said, "Nine o'clock, sir. Your breakfast," he remembered that he had left an order for coffee and rolls to be brought up in the morning. He let her place the tray on the table and gave her a penny, then lowered himself carefully back onto the bed.

Why did I tell them to bring food? The very idea made his stomach—no, best not to think about it.

He had downed half a cup of coffee before realizing that the white object on the tray was a letter. A snake would have been more welcome, but he did not recognize the handwriting. It was not franked and he hadn't been asked to pay postage, so it must have been delivered by someone here in London.

Inside the letter was a second letter, and this handwriting he did recognize. He wondered blearily why his mother was writing to him, then realized that the first layer of paper bore a brief note, signed by Goodbody, Carlisle's butler, explaining that the enclosed note had been delivered to the house by a Townsend footman very early that morning.

He read the missive and groaned. How had he managed to forget that Elspeth's party was this very afternoon? *Have I really been here for two days?*

The brandy was at half-mast in the bottle he'd brought with him, so he concluded that yes, it could very well have been two days. There was no reason on earth, short of his own demise, that would excuse him from attendance at that party, and he had no intention of doing Ellie such a bad turn. He might feel like death on toast and he probably looked it, but he must make an appearance. Sodomite or not—and apparently not, at least not a very successful one—he was still a gentleman.

Tony Hillyard was a fool. Dicky Dee knew that the young man had left his previous lodgings—and he could guess why—but finding out where he had gone took no more effort than writing a note to Hillyard and attempting to deliver it at his former lodgings.

The landlady refused to reveal where he'd gone, but she was not averse to pocketing a sixpence to forward the gentleman's letter. She was already calling to the boy-of-all-work to come and run an errand as the housemaid showed Dobson to the door. After that, it was a simple matter to follow the boy, who obviously preferred to dawdle along on a beautiful, sunny day rather than hurry on his errand and run back to his place of employment.

The look of panic on Hillyard's face was almost worth the trouble of running him to ground. His first reaction was to attempt to slam the door shut in his visitor's face, but Dobson had expected that, and shoved both his foot and his shoulder through the doorway. "Now, now, *Mr. Scarlet*, you mustn't be hasty," he said. "I'm here with a business proposition."

"I should have you thrown out."

"No doubt you should, but if you do not hear me out first, you would regret it."

"Not as much as you would!"

"Your ability to bluff is improving. You must have been taking lessons from that gentleman who claimed to be your father."

Hillyard scowled and threw himself on his bed. "Very well. State your proposition and take yourself to perdition!"

"How very poetic," Dobson said. "I expect you can imagine what I want: that registry. You can tear out the page with your name on it, if you have not already done so. I suspect that won't matter very much, but one of the other members is demanding to see the book, and he has become excessively insistent."

"He's going to be excessively disappointed," Hillyard replied smugly. "He can't have it."

"I am willing to buy it back from you," offered Dobson.

"Oh, really? How much?"

"That would be difficult to say. You might have to conduct your negotiations in person. I am merely a go-between, as it were."

"Well, you'll just have to go on back and tell your member that he's fresh out of luck. The damned thing's been burned."

"*What?*"

"Of course, Dicky. What did you expect? You were blackmailing me, so who's to know what other lovely tricks you had set in motion? We decided that there was no good place to hide it, so my associates took the damned thing and burned it."

That would be good news, Dobson was sure—but he also knew that Hillyard was about as reliable as a rumor from a drunk. "Are you certain? Did you see it destroyed?"

"Not exactly…" Hillyard temporized. "But Mr. Smith and his friend were dead-set on throwing it in the fire, and I know Smith well enough to know that his word is as solid as the Rock of Gibraltar."

"So, in fact, you do not know. They might have kept it... for their own purposes."

"I *do* know. They were wild to destroy that book. As for using it for blackmail—impossible. They would not even let me look in it," he complained. "Said my discretion could not be trusted."

"So they are intelligent men," Dobson concluded. "Very well. I shall see if my client will take your word on this matter."

"He might as well," Hillyard said, shrugging. "I can't imagine they would be willing to talk to him. Washed their hands of the matter."

"They can afford to, can they not?"

"What do you mean by that?"

"I think my meaning should be clear even to you, Mr. Hillyard. I cannot prove that either of them was ever in my club before that night, and apart from charging them with theft—which you did not witness, so the matter is entirely my word against theirs—I have no hold over them."

"You've no hold over me, either," Hillyard shot back. "Not now, and you can be sure I'll give you no handle on me in the future, you bloodsucking leech!"

"Now, now... you'll do yourself no service with name-calling."

"Nor harm. You have no proof of anything now."

Dobson pasted a smile over his uncertainty. "Mr. Hillyard, I still know what you did as a member of The Arbor, and I can still have a little chat with your father—your real father."

"'The matter is entirely your word against mine,'" Hillyard said mockingly. "I daresay my father knows I stretch the truth from time to time, but when it comes to taking the word of a molly-house keeper against that of his only son and heir... I don't think you have much of a chance, Dicky."

Dicky Dobson had acquired a certain City polish when he went into the business of innkeeping. But his youth and childhood were in no way similar to that of this rich man's son, and he was not inclined to be sneered at. Seizing the arrogant young man

by his oversized lapels, he pulled him off the bed and onto the
floor and planted a knee in his chest.

"You listen to me, you soft-headed little sodomite," he spat. "I
must speak to the man who burned that book. Do you understand? My client is not going to take your word for it, and I would
not expect him to, because of all the two-faced lying bastards I've
met, *you* are at the very top of the list."

He bounced Hillyard's head on the floor for good measure,
then got up. "I want his name and direction, and I want it by the
end of the week, or we shall see who your father believes. If it
comes to that, I expect I could produce a very good likeness of
your signature. Would you like to see me try?"

Hillyard lay on the floor, gasping. He shook his head.

"I thought not. Get me that information, and you'll never see
me again. Fail, and you may not live long enough to regret your
failure."

Dobson left in high dudgeon, cheered by his ability to frighten
Hillyard as thoroughly as His Lordship had frightened him. He
hoped the little sod would have the information to him soon. If the
book was burnt, well and good…that rang true. If not, he would
have to consider another line of work in another city, and soon. He
might even have to think about leaving England altogether.

By the time Brendan reached his family home, it was nearly noon.
He had sent a note to his mother as soon as he was able to put pen
to paper, located a barber and had himself made presentable, then
found a coffee-shop and fortified himself with something non-al-
coholic. After consuming several cups of coffee and two sausage
rolls, he realized that he could not delay going home much longer,
and he set off in that direction, walking until he was able to hail a
hackney cab.

He had no idea what he was going to do.

What he must do was find Philip and talk to him. He had to
know whether there was anything he could possibly do to put

things right between them. If so, he would do it, no matter what that entailed. If not… He really could not see beyond that any more; he could not imagine a future without Philip in it, nor did he want to.

He should never have been reckless enough to attempt that first kiss. But Philip had not rejected him. He had seemed willing, even eager, after that awkward beginning. Their lovemaking had not been especially elaborate or sophisticated, but it had been the most overwhelmingly beautiful experience of Brendan's life. What a difference it made, to be with a lover who was intelligent and responsible, who could summon a threatening countenance at need, but in private show such painstaking concern for his horses and his household.

There was no comparison to what he'd experienced with Tony. That had been pleasant and exciting, the awakening of carnal knowledge with the thrill of the forbidden. What he and Philip had done together… that was love. Even if circumstances meant that they might never sleep together—two young men might share a bed and call it economy, but a man of Philip's stature could not spend the night with the younger brother of a friend—merely to spend an hour together from time to time would be more than Brendan had ever hoped for.

But why had Philip Carlisle fled so abruptly? Had he experienced a change of heart? He had enjoyed their congress, Brendan would swear to it… that final kiss pressed to his forehead, as he was falling asleep, drowsy and content… why would Philip have done that, if he regretted the experience?

Perhaps his reaction was simply a return to sober reality. It was one thing to have a drunken *pas de deux* with a love-struck sodomite. That could be blamed on the excitement of the moment and the potency of the brandy. Anyone might be curious, and they had both been drinking, but for a respectable gentleman who had been blissfully married to suddenly change his sensible celibacy and hare off after a male lover?

Put that way, it seemed quite mad.

But… still. Why could Philip not have simply gone off to his own bedroom, and, in the morning, taken his houseguest aside and told him in a calm and reasonable way that their misstep of the previous night was one that would not be repeated and could not be allowed to continue? *He must surely have known I would understand*, Brendan thought.

Had he simply been so mortified at what he had done that he could not stay and own up to it? Possible, but unlikely. They had each had a little to drink, but neither had been so drunk as to be irrational. If his Oxford education had done nothing else, it had given Brendan a pretty fair idea of his capacity for alcohol.

One thing Brendan did not believe—could not believe—was that Philip had merely taken him to bed out of curiosity. A man who could remain faithful to one woman for five years and then avoid women entirely for ten more was not a sexually driven man, nor one who acted on impulse. *There must have been something …*

Or perhaps there had been something. Brendan had been pitifully needy, and it could be that the kindly Major Carlisle had indeed taken pity on him, given him what he so desperately wanted—and then realized in the aftermath that he had acquired a limpet who would not be removed with anything short of blasting powder. *But I would not cling*, Brendan protested miserably. *I only want—*

Well, yes, he only wanted… and it was obvious that what he wanted was something that Philip was not prepared to give. How much of a hint was required to make it clear that his companionship was not welcome?

It was a hard lesson, but he had to learn it, and learn it well. If he wanted to have a true lifemate, a lover and partner to confide in, he was going to have to find a wife. And doing so was, thankfully, beyond his means, or he might have been tempted to make some unsuspecting lady miserable just so he would not have to be alone. The one he wanted did not want him; it was just that simple, and he must learn to accept that dismal reality.

By the time the hackney pulled up before the gates of the

Townsend's town home, Brendan had chased his dilemma around the track at least three times. He was almost relieved that there would be no time for further contemplation.

He paid off the driver and stepped from the miserable contemplation of his own thoughts into the bustle of a Society household in full-tilt preparation for a major ball. He went first to his mother's sitting-room, only to find the furniture rearranged to facilitate the festivities. A maid putting flowers into a crystal vase said that his mother was in the formal dining room, and it was there that he found her, in a blue morning-dress and matching turban, directing the setting of the table as though she were Wellington preparing for Waterloo.

Her face lit up at the sight of her youngest son. "Brendan! *Where* have you been? I was afraid you had been in an accident!"

He bowed, wincing as his lowered head suddenly began to throb. "My apologies, Mama. I was called upon to assist a friend in need, and could not avoid it. I did not return sooner for two reasons: I remember too many occasions when I was chased out of this very house for getting underfoot, and I am not feeling entirely well."

"You do not look well," she said critically.

"I'm sure I will be all right, though I have a bit of a headache. Is there anything I can do to assist you?"

"Not unless you can create an additional three hours between now and dinner time!" his mother said distractedly. "We shall be sixteen at dinner, before the ball. Our own family—Lucy and Richard will be here, which brings us to eight, and Harry's family—his mother, the Dowager Countess, his brother the Earl, the Countess, Harry himself, of course, and his younger brother Augustus, then your Grandmama and Cousin Violet, and my friend Edwina Postlethwaite and her husband—Ellie's godmother, you know. Thank heavens Harry's got a brother rather than a sister; I think young Augustus must escort Cousin Violet in to dinner."

"Is she still able to get about? The last time I saw her she seemed quite feeble."

"Oh, yes, Violet is still fairly spry. She is no older than I am, you know, at least thirty years younger than Grandmama. She only behaves as though she's an invalid because the old lady is so demanding. But don't you dare repeat that!"

"Soul of discretion," Brendan promised.

"And I am sorry, but I've put you beside Cousin Violet because you and Augustus will be at the foot of the table, beside me, and Violet has such a marked dislike of red-headed men that I am afraid she would put poor Augustus completely out of countenance. It will be bad enough for him to escort her, poor lamb. But I was able to put Ellie beside Harry, and made her promise to remind him to pay enough attention to Lucy. "

He should have been able to keep that array of friends and relations clear in his mind, but they all swam together. "Fear not, Mama, I can always ask our cousin about the Bath *on-dits*, and that ought to keep her occupied for as long as her voice holds out." He nearly asked her whom he was supposed to escort, but knew that she would tell him at dinnertime anyway, and that way he would not have to tax himself to remember.

The guest list was highly suggestive. Brendan asked, "Shall I assume from the contingent of Edringtons that Harry lived up to your expectations?"

"Oh, yes! He made his offer beautifully, Ellie says, and of course she accepted, so the ball will also be her engagement party."

He forced himself to smile; it was difficult to remember how to do that. "I'm so happy for her. I think she will enjoy the Season more, knowing she has made her decision."

"Yes, I believe you're right. Some girls prefer to wait as long as they can, but that dear child was never one to tease. I think she is happier having the matter settled."

A sudden fear struck him. "Will there be any other family at the ball?"

"A few, the ones who usually come. Was there anyone in particular?"

"Not really. I only asked because I thought I caught a glimpse of Uncle Cedric in town and wondered if he would be joining us."

"Oh, no. Do you know, I have not set eyes on your uncle in over a year. I think he dislikes big affairs as much as your father does—if it were not his own daughter's engagement party, *he* would probably send his regrets as well."

"Poor Papa," Brendan said, covering his relief with sympathy. "At least Ellie is the last daughter he has to launch."

"He is happy for her, in his way. He likes Harry very much." Brendan's mother frowned at him, a look he remembered well from childhood. "Son, I think you should go upstairs and lie down; you do not look well."

He started to argue, but realized that solitude was exactly what he needed. Then he remembered the dragon ensconced in his room and asked, "Yes, Mama, but *where?*"

She sent him up to his brother's suite. Both James and their father had escaped to White's and would not be home until the last possible moment before the party began. Viscount Martindale never begrudged his wife a moment of the social whirl she enjoyed so much, but neither did he feel any need to subject himself to it beyond what was absolutely necessary. Brendan did not have much in common with his father, but their emphatic preference for country life over the bustle of Town was one thing they shared.

He escaped to the relative quiet of James' bedroom and pulled the bed-curtains to shut out the light. He only wanted to get away from the bustle of preparation; he had not expected to be able to sleep. But once he was horizontal, his body took advantage of the opportunity. The next thing he knew, his brother was shaking his shoulder and ordering him to get up and do his duty.

Norwood was hovering at his elbow, ready to see Brendan properly groomed and shod. He had the requisite clothing in hand, and wasted no time making sure that Brendan would show himself a credit to the family. He submitted meekly; there was only one real arbiter of sartorial propriety in the household, and that man was Percival Norwood.

When Brendan finally escaped and found his sister down-stairs, he was glad to be looking his best; she deserved it. Elspeth was radiantly beautiful; her dress was mostly blue, light in shade but very rich, with an overskirt of some kind of lacework shot through with silver. She actually glittered, and when Brendan told her she looked like a fairy princess she only smiled instead of making the sort of joke he would normally have expected from her.

He remembered what their mother had said about a girl wanting everything perfect; it seemed as though Elspeth was getting her wish. The warm looks and smiles she exchanged with her betrothed throughout the meal certainly suggested she was happy.

For Brendan, though, the meal was hell. He could only sit and ask Cousin Violet inane questions, congratulate his mother on the quantity and quality of the food—what he tasted of it—and try to avoid watching his sister and Harry look at one another as though nothing and no one else existed in the world. *Smelling of April and May...* he had heard the expression for ages, but had never seen it expressed so perfectly. They were completely besotted with one another.

And what was wrong with that? They were *supposed* to be besotted. That was what young men were expected to do—fall madly in love with a suitable young woman, or at least work up a reasonable affection, and settle down, two by two, like Noah's Ark.

He didn't know how he made it through the ball. Before he'd fallen in love with Philip, he had been looking forward to this event, had expected to enjoy it on Ellie's behalf. As it was, he let himself slip back into that half-numb state and go through the motions, minding his steps in the dances, inviting the young ladies whose cards were not filled to take a turn on the dance floor—all the things a dutiful brother did to help make his sister's party a success.

I do not belong here. Family or not, this entire celebration was about a state of being from which he was barred. He would never stand bursting with pride and affection while his father announced to all their friends and relatives that his son and his new daughter were about to start a life together. He would never be allowed to claim his love before God and Society and begin a new life with well-wishing from friends and family. If his true nature were ever discovered, he would be cast out and condemned.

No wonder Philip had fled. What sort of fool would have stayed?

By the time the toasts were drunk, the final dance ended, and the guests beginning to call for their carriages, Brendan was in a state of despair blacker than Queenie's new foal. He wanted it all to be over, wanted to go and apologize to Philip, then walk off a cliff.

He could not do that. He could not even bring an end to his pain because suicide would devastate his parents and ruin his sister's happiness. It would be easier if he did not care about them, but there was nothing he might do to change that. He would rather cut off his own arm than hurt any of them. And he did not really want to die. He only wanted the pain to stop.

But he could not stay here. When everything was settled, he might simply pack himself up and go to Italy to study art. Or perhaps he might not study anything. He might simply go to Italy and never come back. If time truly did heal all wounds, he might one day find a purpose, or at least forget Philip.

Reality intruded itself briefly when the ever-reliable Norwood asked him whether he needed the family carriage to return to his temporary abode. He agreed, thinking he could redirect the driver to the Pulteney and say he was meeting friends. The family need never know he'd left Carlisle's home.

He buried his feelings and made a quick goodbye to his mother, standing with Ellie's godmother in a knot of chattering ladies. His father would be off with a few of his cronies, drinking brandy and playing billiards, so no effort was required in that direction. Brendan found Harry Edrington and offered another round of best wishes and congratulations, and at last managed to locate his little sister.

"Well, Miss Townsend," he said, taking her hands. "Are you prepared to retire from the chase and assemble your trousseau?"

"I am!" Still glowing with joy, she hugged him. "Oh, Brendan, I am *so* happy! I still cannot believe that this is happening to me…have you ever felt that way?"

"Frequently," he said. "I have the continuing delusion that I am actually Rodney MacEvil, the Pirate King. But I seldom tell anyone." He wiggled his eyebrows and cast his eyes to either side for dramatic effect.

"You have not been the Pirate King since you went off to Eton," she said. "Brendan, you look so sad. Is something wrong?"

He took a deep breath and shook his head. "Nothing serious. A friend of mine has been having some troubles, and I have been trying to help him settle them. I'm not sad, only a bit concerned."

"Well, if he's going to worry the life out of you, I hope you tell him to settle them for himself. I hate to see you so troubled. Especially now…"

Harry appeared at her shoulder. "My parents are leaving now, sweetheart. They would like to say goodbye to you… for now."

Elspeth glanced at Brendan, who shook Edrington's hand, congratulated him once more, and gave the obligatory warning that he had better take good care of his baby sister. Edrington responded with the usual assurances, and Brendan was at last free to make his escape.

CHAPTER 16

Another day at Twin Oaks, and Carlisle had still heard no word from Jenkins. So much for his excellent excuse for fleeing London like the coward he was beginning to realize he was.

Carlisle put down the book he was pretending to read and blew out the candle beside his bed. He wished mightily that Jenkins' mutinous colleague Bowker would return to Kent and resume his illegal activities so that there would be some excuse for action, something to do besides admire Queenie's foal and torment himself with indecision.

There was nothing else he could have done. He could not have stayed in London, with Brendan in the bedroom just down the hall, and kept his resolve. The temptation was too strong, the reward too sweet.

Brendan was a young man; in terms of loving, he was younger than his years. He must not be allowed to believe that just because he had been seduced by that parasitic Hillyard brat, he was incapable of forming a normal attachment to a woman. He might have to search for a long time before he found a woman who could share his love of horses, but if he were to find someone like Lillian, but with more enthusiasm for riding... Someone like his sister—well, no, Brendan needed to find someone who was not too much like his own sister, the poor boy had troubles enough.

Carlisle ground his teeth and got out of bed. As he had done the night before, he went to his dressing-table and found his pocket flask. *It's a bad habit, Major, drinking to put yourself to sleep.* He ought to get more exercise, or at least find a better book to read.

He had not had a decent night's rest since he had left Brendan sleeping and run away. Run away! Such a cowardly rout would have seen him cashiered, if it had been done in the line of duty. The more he considered his action, the more he regretted it. That infamous letter—what a slap in the face it must have been to a sensitive young man!

"I should rather be dead than endure your indecision…"

Carlisle was beginning to feel that way himself. But that was foolishness; neither of them would die. Brendan would live, and finish growing up. He would eventually realize that some kinds of love were not meant to last for very long, and other sorts were too dangerous to countenance. He would come to understand that a clean break was for the best. He would learn to redirect that energy, pour it into creating art the way that Carlisle himself had poured his heart into Twin Oaks. If all Brendan's passion and enthusiasm could be transformed into art…

If.

Brendan might just as easily be crushed by this second disappointment, so soon after the misbegotten entanglement with Hillyard. He had the fervor of youth, but he was also the sort who took disappointment hard. His drawings of Queenie and her foal had been the inspiration for a possible career, but what if he came to see his drawings as just another aspect of this mistake and Carlisle's rejection?

Philip Carlisle looked back on what he had done, and realized he had made the worst possible choices at every opportunity. He should have kept that desk between them, should have torn up the book himself, should have… should have…

He should not have fallen in love with Brendan Townsend, taken him to bed, and then fled like the worst coward on the face of the earth. But having done it, he saw no way to repair the mistakes, because any move he made toward Brendan would be a move that would endanger the boy. This was not a matter of choosing between a right choice and a wrong one. There was no right choice and there never would be.

Brendan awoke the next morning with his head free of pain and his mind clear, his decision made. He had to go find Philip. There was no other way he would ever know peace again.

He could guess where Philip had gone. Back to Kent, home to his horses, the only place he could have gone. And in addition to that, he still had the murder investigation to resolve. Brendan was certain Major Carlisle would never shirk his duty.

He had to see Philip one last time, speak to him, make certain that he had not done anything stupid or unthinking to offend the man he loved. He wanted to hope for a reconciliation, but that was beyond reason. All he could reasonably wish was to have things settled between them, so that if they happened to meet socially—which was likely, as Philip was one of James' oldest friends—there would be no cause for heart-burning.

Why had he fled so furtively? Had he feared Brendan would make a scene—did Philip think him as indiscreet as Tony? Was an explanation too much to expect? If Philip decided that the pleasure they'd shared was simply not worth the risk… well, it would be unfair of Brendan to try to argue him out of that fundamental decision. If he had resolved to end it, Brendan would understand. It would hurt, but he would understand.

Thirty-five miles was not an impossible distance for a lone rider. Brendan had considered the possibilities for travel, and decided that he wanted to be as independent and free of encumbrances as possible. He could ride Galahad, take the trip in easy stages, and stop overnight at coaching inns, making the trip in two or three days, depending on how well Galahad bore up on the journey.

He could send his luggage back home, tell James that he was off to Kent once again, and pack all that he really needed in a pair of saddlebags. He could not take much more than a few clean shirts, but he would not need much.

He would not be staying very long.

A light spring rain had washed the morning clear, and Philip Carlisle decided to take Nightshade out for a ramble before break-fast. The stable was too full of memories; even watching Queenie and her rapidly-growing Princess made him think of that astonish-ing sketched likeness, and the eager joy on Brendan's face at his honest praise. The light in his eyes, the disbelieving smile on his half-parted lips, which had been so unaccountably sweet…

Damn!

Was he going to be followed everywhere by those memories? After a week, the recollection was still painfully sharp and clear. He had never had this difficulty before; in wartime, he had learned to banish the horrors and clear his mind, to focus on the next task at hand.

But this was not the same, was it? These memories were more like his fond recollections of Lillian, although after ten years she no longer sprang to mind unless summoned.

Was he fated to wait ten years before these memories would fade? And how would he deal with living day to day? What would he do if he happened to run across Brendan in London, as was quite likely? He could not terminate his friendship with James Townsend without some rational explanation, nor did he wish to.

The situation would be intolerable He had acted on a craven impulse, and he would have to pay the penalty: seek Brendan out, offer his apology, and endure whatever recriminations the young man might seek to heap upon him. Lord knew he deserved them.

A bird burst suddenly from a low-growing shrub, and Night-shade sprang sideways, demanding Carlisle's entire attention to keep him from bolting. He should not have brought this rowdy lad out when his own mind was in such turmoil; Whiskey would have been a much better mount for a troubled man.

"You want to run, do you?" he said aloud. "I know the feeling. It's not always a wise thing to do." Not for humans, at any rate.

But a gallop would do them both good. He turned Nightshade toward the little rise that stood between them and the stables and gave him his head, letting the immediacy of sun, wind, and the powerful creature under his control block out all mental rambling. His breath sang through him, his blood sparkled like champagne. For the first time since he'd come home, he felt real happiness. *This* was life, the best part of it. All else was just the means to this moment of truth and clarity.

They crested the rise and he gazed down upon his home, the paddock just visible at the far side of the stable, the chimneys of the house rising above treetops. It was more than most men could ever hope for; he would be its steward for as long as his strength endured, and he would learn to be content…

Carlisle squinted as an unfamiliar horse appeared around the near side of the stable, the sun glinting off flanks bright as a new copper penny. His heart leapt, then sank, as he recognized the horse and its rider.

He restrained his first impulse, which was to turn tail and run, back over the hill, across the orchard, into the woods. Bad enough that he had waited for Brendan to appear, instead of seeking him out. It was his home ground, after all. He waited until he knew that Brendan had seen him, then raised a hand in greeting and nudged Nightshade into a slow walk down the slope. He wanted to gallop; his mount sensed that, but he could not allow it.

There was time enough to think while they slowly approached one another, but he found his mind strangely slow. All he could do was drink in the joyful, fearful sight and wonder what in the world he was going to do.

As Brendan drew close enough to make out detail, Carlisle saw that his coat was dusty and his face worn. Galahad, too, looked a bit jaded, as though he'd spent less of his time in the stable than he was accustomed to. To a cavalry officer, that combination of details suggested only one thing. "Good God, don't tell me you *rode* all the way!"

Brendan shrugged. "Not in one day. I am sorry. Should have written to ask, I know. Or stopped to get a bell..."

Unclean, unclean... The shaft struck home; Carlisle closed his eyes. When he thought he had control of his voice, he said, "Just as well you did not. You'd have frightened the horses."

A corner of that sensitive mouth quirked up, but Brendan did not speak. Carlisle wondered if he, too, was at a loss for the right thing to say. Finally he essayed a question on the most innocuous topic he could dredge up. "Shall we ride together?"

Brendan nodded, and Galahad fell into place beside Nightshade. Eventually Carlisle found it easier to say what was on his mind than to keep it in. "Please accept my apologies for the disgraceful manner of my departure. I was so far beyond point nonplus that I could think of nothing else."

"It is I who must apologize," Brendan said, "for putting you in an impossible position. I cannot apologize for what we did together—"

"No need," Carlisle interjected.

"Yes, there is; it was unfair to seduce you, after all you had done to help me."

"Seduce *me?*"

Brendan's glance flickered to him for an instant. "What else would you call it, sir? You'd never have made the first move. You were inexperienced, I was ... not. And I blush to admit I would do the same if we had it to do over, even knowing that there was no future in it."

Carlisle was nonplussed once more. "Why?"

"Trust," Brendan said simply. "For the first time in my life, I was with someone with whom I could be myself—*all* of myself."

"But your family, friends..."

"Know nothing of me, not in that regard. Major, I have been guarding my tongue since I was ten years old!"

Carlisle raised an eyebrow.

"Yes," Brendan said to his unasked question. "I have always

known, always had to be so careful… I cannot regret having known that freedom, that safety, just that once. I realize it would be presumptuous to ask to keep your friendship, sir, but I do hope there need be no lies between us, and no regrets."

"I should like that." He was glad that Brendan had appeared here, out in the open where they were able to speak freely, though he felt as though he still had to watch his every word. "I could not say anything in that letter that might raise the slightest suspicion in anyone's mind. I hoped you would understand that."

"I did understand. Of course I did. But what I still cannot understand…" He began to talk rapidly, his self-control dissolving before Carlisle's eyes, "I cannot understand how the man who would face down a blackmailer in his own den could not find the courage to—to do me the simple courtesy of rejecting me to my face!" He turned away for a moment, and took a deep breath. "I apologize," he said formally, under control once more. "I did not come here to throw accusations at you—"

"You have every right," Carlisle admitted. "What I did was disgraceful, and I have no excuse. I am not the hero you think me, sir!"

"I believe you are. At least, I thought so."

"My dear boy—"

"*Don't call me that!*" Brendan cried. He reined Galahad in, and turned to look Carlisle full in the face, and said, "Not unless you mean to act as though there's truth in it."

"It is the truth." He straightened, feeling as though a tremendous weight had gone from his shoulders. "It is, though at first I was not even aware of that. Not until…" No, that path was too dangerous to follow. "In any case, I hope you did not believe I became involved in the Arbor affair with the intention of winning the favors of the fair Mr. Hillyard!"

Brendan smiled, and shook his head. "No, by the time it came to that even I was no longer so gullible. But why did you take up the problem? It seemed to me even then, though I welcomed your help, that to involve yourself in such a matter was to take a considerable risk with no apparent reward."

"I asked myself the same thing," Carlisle replied. "And my first answer was that there is always some intrinsic satisfaction to be gained in foiling a blackmailer. I can think of few things so vile as battening off the failings of another. And Dobson was a particularly disgusting opponent."

"True, but you had never met him when you agreed to help me."

"I had met you, and I have a great regard for your brother. I did not want to send you off without at least giving you what advice I could. At first I thought you simply a good, loyal friend… perhaps too loyal. And then I began to fear that you had been ensnared by bad companions."

"Quite correctly."

"And, I confess… I was angry on your behalf, that you should put yourself at such risk for a man who treated you without any regard. What he did was infamous, tantamount to taking one's mistress to a brothel!"

Brendan nodded. "I felt that way myself. I had not realized, when we roomed together at college, that he saw me as little more than a great convenience. But in a way I must always be grateful."

Carlisle snorted. "To that brat!"

"Yes, indeed I am. However selfish his motives, he did show me my true nature. I had always thought myself a cold, sexless creature because I was never drawn to women, even the most beautiful. And if he had not taken me to The Arbor and shown me exactly who *he* was, and what little regard he truly had for me… I might yet be laboring under the misconception that he was my friend."

Carlisle nodded, but had no reply.

"So, then," Brendan said, "I suppose I must ask: is it your wish that we forget what passed between us, and establish a friendly but disinterested acquaintance?"

Carlisle meant to say, "Yes," but the memory of that night assailed him—arms around him, a warm, eager body pressed against his own, physical delight he had thought was denied him forever. His throat closed. He swallowed, not daring to meet the younger man's eyes. "I think that would be for the best, don't you?"

"That depends on how one chooses to define 'best,' I think," Brendan said wryly. "I have no doubt it would be the safest course of action..." He shook his head, much as a horse would when bothered by flies. "No, I cannot carry on this way. Major—Philip, I love you. I am well aware that we cannot have anything in the way of a *regular* connection, but I would be content with what- ever time together we could contrive. I do not wish to let you go ...unless that is truly what you desire."

Carlisle stared at Nightshade's mane, absently noting the way the hairs fell to one side or the other along the line of the spine. "We cannot always have what we desire," he began .

"I wish you would answer my questions." Brendan caught his eye, and held it. "That's the second you've evaded."

"It is? What was the first?"

"Why did you leave as you did? Were you afraid I would make a scene if you told me that you had made a mistake? I do not think it was because you suddenly took me in dislike for having been too bold."

"Not at all." If he was going to turn this young man's love away, he at least owed him honesty. "I was afraid, my— I was afraid for you. Did that sordid business in town not show you how danger- ous such a liaison could be?"

"It showed me how dangerous it can be to seek affection among strangers, certainly. I think that two men of discretion, who took no unnecessary chances and were faithful to one an- other, might do very well together."

"You say that now... Brendan, I must tell you something. When I was young, I felt as you do about my own regimental Cap- tain. He did not return my feelings—I doubt he ever guessed how I felt! But later, when I fell in love with my wife, he was forgotten."

"What became of your Captain?" Brendan asked.

"Killed in action."

Brendan pulled Galahad up short. "Philip, are your parents also dead?"

"Yes, for some years now."

"Brothers? Sisters?"

"None that lived."

Brendan blinked, and Carlisle could have sworn there were tears standing in his eyes. "My poor Philip, has everyone you ever loved died and left you alone?"

Carlisle cuffed him on the arm. "I was a soldier, you young sapskull! Of course I lost friends I loved."

"Still…"

"I chose not to marry again because the disease of the blood that took my son and wife also took both my brothers. Would you breed a horse that showed so poorly? Wife, mistress… legitimate or base-born child, I swore I'd never take that chance again."

He had not meant to say so much, but this conversation was in its own way more intimate than any he'd ever had with his wife. There were things one did not speak of with a lady. There were other things one never said to anyone—such as the fact that the night he'd spent with Brendan was the first time in ten years he was able to lie with anyone. He had never even dared try since Lillian's death, for fear that he might sire a doomed child.

Brendan looked suitably abashed. "I did not mean to imply your unease was irrational… It is only that, having spent my days among a flock of relatives, I find it hard to imagine life without any family. You have had far more than your share of ill luck."

"Well, that's true enough. But if that is my luck, I should hate to see it rub off on you. And I cannot help wondering whether you simply have not met the right lady. You are—"

"No younger than my brother was when he married his wife, and he had yearned after every pretty miss in the neighborhood since first his voice began to change. If I were going to fall in love with a girl, I am certain I'd have done it by now. I almost wish I could. My life would be much easier if I had not fallen in love with a stubborn country squire, but you are who and what I want."

"You would still be risking everything, and for what?" Carlisle wondered why he was arguing. The only proper thing to do was to ask the younger man to leave and never speak of it again, but he could not quite make himself do that.

"For something that makes me glad to be alive—yes, even if I risk my life and lose it! Sir, I have had half my life to consider the matter. In a hundred years' time we shall both be dust, and that condition will endure for a very long time. I would rather not live as though I were already in that state."

And that, Carlisle suspected, was what he himself had been doing since Lillian's death. "I wish I had your bravery," he confessed. "In matters of the heart, I believe you have more courage than I ever will."

"You have a great deal more to lose than I do, and people who depend upon you, whereas I have nothing much to offer, except myself—but I *could* promise you I shan't die in childbirth."

"You reassure me," Carlisle said wryly, but he smiled to take any sting out of the words.

With a fleeting smile, Brendan said, "That leaves only the matter of your immortal soul. I believe it is human malice, not God, that would condemn us, and I suspect you feel the same."

"You state my view precisely." Carlisle agreed, "but I would not underrate the danger of human malice."

"Nor do I. Still, you have shown Society that you are a normal man. I have no fortune to makes me a marriage prize—I should have to make myself a fortune somehow, or hang out for a rich wife, and it is no lie to say I'm too proud for that. I've used that excuse for some time now, and my relatives are beginning to accept that I'm not the marrying kind. I can ride with the best of them and am a fair shot with gun or pistol, so my manhood isn't likely to be called into question."

He checked Galahad, and turned to look Carlisle full in the face. "I only ask you, my dearest sir—shall we see whether we cannot contrive to have at least a little of what we desire, or would you prefer that I keep my hands and other appendages to myself?"

Carlisle hesitated. He knew how difficult it must be for Brendan to phrase the question so nonchalantly, and how carefully he must have considered the matter, to present it so precisely. "I believe that a young man as attractive and talented as yourself could do better than to throw in his lot with an old horse-nurse of a soldier," he said. "But…yes. If we can find a way, I should like to try."

He saw the light in Brendan's eyes, and wanted to pull him out of the saddle and into his arms. He laughed instead, but not with joy. "You see how it is? If we were ordinary lovers we might now embrace, but it is simply not possible." He held out his hand, and Brendan took it; if anyone were watching, it would look like a handshake, even though it was much more. "I wish that I could kiss you."

"Nightshade would take exception, I think," Brendan said. "As well he should, but we will find time for that." He took his hand away, slyly letting his fingertips stroke Carlisle's palm as he released it.

That simple gesture sent a thrill through Carlisle's entire body. Desire flared.

And there was nothing he could do about it. "You shameless flirt!"

Brendan grinned. "It's true. But very well-mannered, sir! May I stop here for the night, then? I paid my shot at the coaching inn and just rode in this morning—about five miles, I think."

Carlisle turned Nightshade toward the house, and Brendan followed. "You rode all the way from London?" Carlisle asked.

"I stopped twice. I might have come in last night, but my courage failed me, and I thought Galahad deserved the rest."

"Have you eaten?" When Brendan shook his head, he said, "Neither have I. Come back to the house with me. You must stay here, of course. I hope that we may find a little time and privacy, but other matters have prior claim. "

"The murder?" Brendan asked. "How goes it with Jenkins and his rival?"

"Bowker is back in Kent," Carlisle said. "I'm told a shipment of brandy came in last night, without Jenkins' approval. And it's hidden somewhere on my land."

⟪ CHAPTER 17 ⟫

Brendan turned Galahad over to Matthews, tossed the saddlebags over his own shoulder, and followed Philip back to the house. He did not know what was going to happen next, but he had his heart's desire and was content to let destiny take its course from here.

Destiny proved to be a fine substantial breakfast, and after two days of riding and subsisting on roadhouse provender, he was very grateful to have fresh eggs and home-cured bacon. Philip's foot touched his under the table, the only contact they dared attempt with the household staff buzzing about. It struck him that a man of substance like Philip Carlisle had less freedom, and certainly less privacy, than a couple of young men fresh out of college and dependent on parents—or, in Brendan's case, a modest competency.

"Do you have any idea where the cache is located?" Brendan asked as soon as the room was empty of anyone but themselves.

"There are only a few places that come to mind," Philip said. "The apple-barn, between the orchards and near the road, the gate-keeper's cottage, but Hubert swears there's nothing in his place, or the oast-house down near the edge of the woods."

"Also near a road, I imagine?"

"Of course—so the wagons can be brought in to take out the hops, after they're dried and sacked. That would be my choice—it's not visible from the road itself, and there are paths through that woods from almost anywhere you'd care to name."

"Including the shore?"

"I see you have perceived the pattern. Yes. The woods stretch around the boundary of my land on three sides. The climb from the shore is steep at the closest point, so their tubmen could not go far beyond the woods; they cache their goods, then return a day or two later."

Brendan nodded. "I hate to keep quizzing you, but do you know when that is likely to happen?"

"Jenkins tells me it may be tonight—it does help to have an informer with a grudge. We had a council of war yesterday, when he brought over a barrel of ale. He intends to confront Bowker over the brandy; I mean to steal a march on him and have the Preventives ready to move in and take the Bowker contingent before there's any more bloodshed. What would you say to a tour of my estate? We shall go armed; my plan was to take my stable hand Jem and try for a few of the rabbits that have been ravaging the spring peas. If we miss the rabbits and find contraband, so much the better."

A secondary plan began to form in Brendan's mind. "Tell me, sir, would either of those outbuildings be considered private places?"

Carlisle's eyes narrowed. "If I could be certain that the smugglers had not placed a lookout on the building, yes, they could be. Did you have something in mind?"

Brendan met his look, and smiled; the Major looked slightly uncomfortable. And was that just the suggestion of a blush? If it had been, it disappeared when a footman entered, bearing a silver tray. "The post, sir. Including a letter for Mr. Townsend."

Carlisle thanked the man and dismissed him, glancing over the two missives addressed to him. "Something from my man of business, and a letter from an old acquaintance," he said. "Who could be writing to you at this address?"

Brendan shook his head, equally puzzled, and opened the letter. "It's from Tony Hillyard," he said in surprise. "He— Oh, damn me for six kinds of an idiot, it never occurred to me to ask my brother *not* to tell Tony where I was—I never expected he'd come looking, and of course James didn't know he'd been involved in that other matter."

"What does he have to say?" Carlisle asked. "More of the old problem?"

"No." Brendan scanned the letter. "I believe he's attempting to let me down gently—can you believe it? He's decided to bow to his father's command and get himself leg-shackled; he has made an offer to the lady and she has accepted—there was never much doubt of that, from what he'd told me. Well, well. I suppose the Arbor affair put the wind up him, and he has decided to at least go through the motions of respectability."

"Who is the young lady?" Carlisle asked.

"Lady Constance, Olmstead's daughter. She's a few years older than he, and I think she must have been resigned to being an ape-leader. Poor girl."

"The word is that Olmstead's damned near on the rocks; there would have to be some sort of money trouble to make him willing to tie his daughter to a tradesman."

"A very well-heeled tradesman, I think, if Tony's spending habits are any indication. I do feel sorry for her, though, if she's expecting him to be much of a husband."

"Unless Olmstead has another daughter," Carlisle said thoughtfully, "Master Tony may find himself under the cat's paw. I've met the girl, and to say she's a managing sort would be understating the situation."

"Master Tony needs a minder." Brendan replied heartlessly. "And I have resigned that position. In his case, I think an ape-leader would be exceedingly appropriate."

"There are marriages made in heaven," Carlisle said, "and then there are those others…"

"Look on the bright side, sir," Brendan said. "This marriage may save two other young people from a terrible fate. And I know, that is a horrible thing to say, and I could never say such a thing to anyone but you."

Carlisle emptied his coffee cup. "I shall excuse your bad manners this once, young man, but in future you must watch that impertinence."

Brendan grinned. "Yes, sir. But only if you'll watch yours."

Carlisle glanced at the door, as though to be sure they were alone. He put his hand over Brendan's, and gave it a gentle squeeze. "Disrespectful brat," he said fondly.

"But *discreetly* disrespectful," Brendan replied, and was rewarded with a smile that warmed him through.

With a borrowed pair of brogans and an old shooting jacket left by some long-departed guest, Brendan joined Carlisle on a long tramp around the borders of Twin Oaks. The sun was at its height by now, so they went through the orchard to the woods beyond, then made for the oast-house, keeping to the edge of the path to avoid the soggy middle.

The woods reminded Brendan of how his mother had described Ellie preparing for the ball: patches of color were strewn everywhere, some flowering trees bright with lacy blossoms. The willows, as always, were first to don their leaves, while the larger trees had not yet made up their minds whether to go full-out in spring green or try for some more modish apparel.

"Why did you build it the oast all the way out here?" Brendan asked. "It seems very remote from the rest of your estate."

"It is, from the original property. My father and I speculated that the market for hops would increase, and not long before he died we bought some acreage on the other side of the road, part of an orchard that was not properly maintained. When the owner put it up for sale we bought it, cleared out the dead trees, and planted hops. Putting up an oast to dry the hops for shipping seemed the best course, so naturally, the closer to the fields, the better."

"I begin to appreciate what my father does with his days," Brendan said, "and why he never wants to leave the estate. I never realized how much work was involved."

"Proper management does take a good deal of attention. One

of the things I esteem in your brother James is that he under-
stands the responsibility of his position." He smiled. "I do not
mean to lecture. You'll work hard enough if you take up painting,
and it may be years before you reap tangible rewards."

"I suppose so. Still, it could only help to understand what others do. A portrait would be more meaningful if it were painted in
the proper setting." He knew it would sound like mere flattery if
he were to say that he now saw Philip as part of this place, but the
fleeting idea for a picture crossed his mind: Philip mounted on
Queenie with the orchard in glorious bloom in the background
and the woods rising behind him. That was who he was—a man
striving to protect the living things in his care, despite all the
death and misfortune that had surrounded him.

Of course that was too maudlin to say aloud. Brendan tucked
it away in his heart and said only, "I have never seen smuggled
goods. What is it we're seeking?"

"Oh, you've seen them," Carlisle assured him. "If you live in
England, believe me, you've seen them. But if the cargo is brandy
or gin, it will be in small barrels, about this size—" He held his
hands a foot apart. "The spirits are concentrated for shipment
and diluted at their final destination, so if you ever come across
a smuggler's tub, go easy."

"You said you thought there might be a watch on the cache?"

"Yes, it seems likely. I've an idea how to set their fears to
rest—you'll see when we reach the place. The oast-house is de-
serted now, of course; the hops are only beginning to grow. It will
be months before they are harvested and brought there to dry.
You can see the oast now, if you look—between those two chestnuts."

The stubby tower of the oast grew clearer as they approached.
When they came around a bend in the path Brendan could see
the long, low storage shed connected to it, which, Philip said,
contained the tools that would be used at harvest time. The long
fallow season made the place ideal as a storage depot for smuggling during any time but harvest.

Philip's voice rose in volume as they approached, his gestures wide. As they reached the door, he opened it and pointed up. "See? The floors are nothing but beams and lath, so the hot air rises through the hops and dries them." He then added, quietly, "Stand here, so you are visible from the trees, and act as though I am beside you, just within the door."

Brendan did so. Philip stepped within and leaned his gun against the door, then darted to the far side of the oast. He opened a door at that end, vanished for ten or fifteen seconds, then reappeared, ran back, and stepped outdoors as though he gone only a little way into the building.

"What was all that about?" Brendan asked quietly. "What was in that far room?"

"Barrels," Philip said with a satisfied nod. "Rows of barrels, at least a hundred, hidden beneath the cloth mats that we spread across the lath to keep the hops from falling through as they dry. As shipments go, it's a small one. I suspect our Mr. Bowker is a cautious man, or has not been able to recruit many of Jenkins' men for this double-dealing."

"What shall we do now?"

"I will take you on a tour of the other outbuildings of the estate. Don't frown, the only one of any significance is the apple barn, where we keep the cider-press. Like the oast-house, the place is a beehive in harvest time, and dead-quiet the rest of the year. *"Ah!"* He raised his gun and fired off a shot. "Missed."

"I saw nothing."

"Nor did I, but as we're walking about with guns we may as well at least give the impression we're after those rabbits."

Brendan laughed aloud. "We should have brought a dog to sniff them out."

"Not at all. Sniffing out rabbits would be fine, but what would we have done if we'd flushed a sentry back in the woods? There are times we're better off with our puny human ears and noses."

Another half-hour's walk brought them to the barn. The door screeched as it swung open on a cloud of fragrance, the sweet perfume of apples. "We still have some of last summer's harvest stored," Philip said. "But the place always smells this way, even when it's empty."

As Brendan's eyes adjusted to the dimness he caught a flicker of movement out of the corner of one eye, and turned to see a sleek tiger cat watching him from a stairway on one side of the barn.

"The resident rat-catchers," Philip said. "They come up to the house for a handout when the mice are scarce, and they earn every bit of their keep."

Unlike an ordinary barn, this one had only a couple of stalls in one corner, and what Brendan guessed was a tack-room. The ceiling was lower than usual, though the barn itself had looked average height from outside. "What do you keep upstairs?" he asked.

"Apples, of course."

"Would you show me?"

Philip shrugged, and then his eyes narrowed. "There is nothing up there but barrels. Empty, most of them."

"Still, I imagine the view is splendid."

"That's true. From the topmost level one may see almost the entire estate, perhaps even a bit of the sea."

He led the way up the narrow stair along one side of the barn. Close behind him, watching the play of muscles under the snug buckskin breeches, Brendan observed, "I was correct. From where I stand, the view *is* absolutely splendid."

"*Mister* Townsend!"

"You said this would be a private place," Brendan protested as they stepped out onto the next level.

"It is," Philip said. "Still…"

There was, as Philip had informed him, nothing up here but rows of empty barrels, laid on their sides. He walked along the rows, assuring himself that they were indeed empty. "May we go all the way to the top?"

"I suppose so. But you go first, this time!"

"Oh, gladly!" He really had not intended to tease his lover, but Major Carlisle was so very serious that the temptation was almost irresistible. He climbed as slowly as he dared, until at last a sharp swat on the arse sent him skipping up the last two steps like a naughty boy. He put his gun on the floor, and Philip did likewise. Brendan saw that he had guessed the purpose of this climb, and read both excitement and apprehension in the shaded depths of his hazel eyes.

The topmost floor was entirely empty, and he stood in the center of the floor, gazing around him. Two of the windows Philip had spoken of were boarded up, no doubt to keep out the rain, but from the other two he could see nothing but blue sky. "No prying eyes here, I think," he said, taking Philip's arm in a companionable way. "We can see if anyone approaches, and certainly hear them, if anyone opens that excellent door. And if we were to step over to this corner, so... I think that even a spy with a telescope could not see me do this."

He took Philip's face in his hands, reached up just a little to kiss his lips. He felt Philip shiver after nothing more than the merest touch, and drew back, gazing at Philip's flushed face. "Should I say the coast is clear?"

"Smugglers say 'the coast is clear,'" Philip corrected. "I would say that we must take any chance that presents itself. I've wanted to do this—" He caught Brendan in his arms and returned the kiss with such fervor that Brendan was taken off guard, pressed back against the heavy oaken wall. He was thrilled at the power of Philip's response, and when he felt those strong, competent hands slip beneath the shooting jacket and slide it from his shoulders, he let his own arms drop to his sides. The jacket fell to the floor with a rush of cool air; the hands slid over his shoulders and down his back, heat replacing the chill.

Was it possible to want something so badly and not know what it was until one had it? The strength of the hands now gripping his waist, the tenderness of the mouth exploring his own, the hard, hot length of Philip's cock rubbing against his through their clothing—the sense of being completely overpowered even though he knew that he was, paradoxically, perfectly safe—he could not have articulated all this even if he'd known he wanted it.

But he knew now. As Philip's hands slid down to cup his arse and pull him closer, Brendan did the same, grinding against his lover even as a whimper was forced from him.

"Too much?" Philip mumbled, pausing.

"No, never. Don't stop!"

"What shall I do?"

"Anything!" Brendan thrust forward, suddenly so desperate for continued contact that he was half-mad with desire. He captured Philip's mouth again, scrabbling with the laces at the back of Philip's breeches. His lover, seeming to understand, pushed Brendan's shoulders back against the beam and held him there, frantic with frustration, for the few seconds it took to undo the buttons, first of Brendan's fly and then his own.

Their breeches fell around their knees as he was able to pull Philip close once more, all his awareness focused in his cock. He had not even the ability to continue the kiss; he found his face pressed against the side of Philip's collar and he did not care. He felt the breath pushed out of him with every thrust, felt Philip's sobbing breaths—and suddenly he was up and over, spilling his seed against his lover's belly. A moment later, Philip did the same, then leaned against him once more, not with passion but with passion utterly spent.

Brendan turned his head slightly, and brushed a kiss against the side of his face. "Amazing," he breathed.

Philip nodded, and they slid to their knees, still holding one another. Brendan let go long enough to locate the shooting jacket with one hand and spread it out upon the floor. They slipped further down and lay together for a little while, as their breathing went back to normal.

"That was…" Philip shook his head as though dumbfounded. "I needn't hold back with you."

"No," Brendan said. "Why would you? That was …" He shook his head, rendered nearly speechless with bliss. "Glorious!"

"With Lillian…" Philip said, and fell silent. "A woman is so much smaller," he said after a time. "Weaker… only a brute would use his full strength. But you're as strong as I am, maybe stronger."

"Probably not," Brendan admitted, "but I love your strength. Last time… I loved being in control, and this time … *not* being in control."

Philip nodded, and held him close. "What you said earlier today…with regard to trust… I understand that, now."

Brendan smiled foolishly, and kissed him again.

◖ CHAPTER 18 ◗

The days were getting longer, but it was still dark enough by ten that night that Carlisle's operatives could get into position without much fear of being seen. Carlisle, Brendan, and Matthews were joined by half a dozen Customs riders, "Preventives" ready to take the weight of Carlisle's unofficial assignment from his shoulders when there was an actual arrest to be made. Another force of some twenty troopers was stationed a few miles off, awaiting the signal to move in and surround the smugglers if they happened to outnumber the Customs officers.

At the moment, due to the good offices of Sir Thomas Livingstone and the weight of his own military experience, Carlisle was in command of the smaller group until Bowker was actually in custody. Carlisle himself would have been content to allow Lieutenant Berry, the Preventive officer, full rein, but he could well understand the military's point of view: if a civilian botched the job, it would be no reflection on their performance.

Sitting in the dark storage shed beside the oast house, the matter now out of his hands, Carlisle wondered whether the arrival of his team had been noted by the lookout the smugglers must inevitably have posted at the oast-house. He had made as much fuss as he possibly could while riding up, and his horse was tethered outside. He intended the smugglers to know he was waiting for them.

The others, poor souls, were distributed at various key points. Two of them, Lieutenant Berry and his aide-de-camp, were up on the lowest drying floor, perching along the joists at the edge of the floor's framework. Carlisle hoped they managed to stay awake, because if either dropped off to sleep the experience was likely to become literal, and they would not land on anything soft. Two of the other four government Riders were deployed about the shrubbery outside the oast-house, and the last two were hiding behind the stacks of jute sacks used to ship the dried, compressed hops to market.

Matthews and Brendan were the rear-guard, concealed in the upper drying floor. Both had objected strenuously to being stationed in a position of greater safety, but Carlisle had been adamant: the Customs men must be nearest, where they could hear what was being said, and the men he could trust had to be in a position to move in if the government men failed.

Once they were all in position, the time crawled. For a little while they had conversed, but as the night grew deeper and the hour later, as the moon rose, they had fallen silent. After all, no one suggested that the smugglers were stupid—they had proved themselves quite clever thus far, and they had more to lose from being caught red-handed than if they were to be deprived of the profit to be made from the hundred or so barrels in the oast-house. The slightest hint of anything wrong would likely frighten them off.

It might have been two in the morning when the faint creak of hinges reached Carlisle's ears, and he checked to be sure his pistol was within easy reach in his pocket. He heard voices, pitched low, and guessed that at least three men, maybe as many as six, were crossing the storage shed to the oast-house itself. Carlisle made no move toward it; he wanted a confession, not a shooting match. He simply waited until his visitors discovered his presence, which occurred when the flap of a dark-lantern was opened and shone directly on him where he sat, upon one of the barrels of contraband spirits.

He held his hands out, saying, "Don't shoot, gentlemen! I merely wish to talk."

Much to his relief they held their fire, though they swore a great deal. Apparently they had not been watching the building—at least not closely enough to know that its owner was waiting for them. Finally one of them said, "I know who you are, Major. Would you mind telling me what the devil you think you're doing here?"

"This building is part of my estate," Carlisle said reasonably. "Why should I not be here? I am attempting to determine what is going on in the independent brotherhood of Free Traders, insofar as it affects my land and my people. I have had a reasonable working arrangement with you gentlemen for many years, as did my father before me. If you are changing the rules, I have a right to know what the new rules may be. And would you be so good as to take that light out of my eyes?"

The lantern shifted slightly, and the same voice said, "Fair enough. What do you want to know?"

"Who—No, you may not wish to answer that question… how shall I put this? Can you tell me whether the man now running the free trade is the one who has been in command these past ten years or so?"

After a moment's pause, the voice in the darkness said, "Well, now, that's being discussed among us, as you might say. What difference does it make to you?"

"It makes a difference in a number of ways. The first is, I have had an understanding with the organization that, though certain livestock of mine might be available for evening duty, I was not willing to have contraband stored on my property. There have been any number of occasions on which I might have summoned the authorities; I chose not to do so, in exchange for an absence of incriminating property on my premises. If you are new to this enterprise, I suppose we must renegotiate the terms."

"Now, then, I had no idea you had that arrangement," the man replied. "I suppose we might continue with that, should I take over the organization."

"Very good," Carlisle said. "My other question is far more serious. I can only guess that the death of Tom Jenkins is in some way involved with the changes in the group. As far as I know, young Jenkins was a reasonable young man, a good candidate to step into his father's shoes. I would like to know if you are willing to turn in the man who killed him."

"Now, *that,*" said the speaker, "that would present certain difficulties, as a gentleman like yourself might say, seeing as I have an interest in protecting that man."

"Or because you *are* that man," Carlisle said evenly.

"Since you put it that way—yes. But you should know, Major, that what that crazy old man Jenkins is saying is only his side of the story. What happened was, young Jenkins attacked me, and all I meant to do was defend myself."

Carlisle said nothing more for a moment. Then he asked, "From *behind?*"

The crack of a pistol preempted a reply; Carlisle had been waiting for that signal from Lieutenant Berry, and he flipped open the flaps on his own dark-lantern, diving to one side in the seconds while Bowker's eyes would be dazzled. He rolled into a space he had cleared behind the rows of barrels, but not before he caught a bullet that sent searing pain through his left arm. That was not too bad, but in the scramble to get away, he knocked over one of the stacked barrels and it caught him a glancing blow on the side of the head.

When he came to himself he was cold, and realized that was because his jacket was off while Matthews, muttering imprecations under his breath, was bandaging his left arm, which hurt like the very devil. He held still for the ministrations until Matthews buttoned his arm inside his coat as a makeshift sling. Brendan hovered on his other side, holding a vinaigrette, of all things, under his nose. He pushed it away and growled, "Where did you get that damned stink-bottle?"

"Lieutenant Berry, sir. He says it often comes in useful in his line of work."

"Well, I'm not a swooning Excise man. Take it away!"

"Yes sir." Brendan sounded very subdued. "You were shot, Major."

"Is it serious?" He fumbled in his coat pocket and found the flask he'd brought in case of emergencies.

"Just a graze, Major," Matthews said. "You've had worse falling from your horse."

"I never fall!" Carlisle protested. He realized belatedly that he could not open the flask one-handed. Brendan took it, and poured a tot into the cap. The heat of brandy did nothing for the pain, but it did make him feel a little less battered.

"You'll be fine, sir. Mr. Townsend and I will—"

"Major Carlisle?" It was Berry, now apparently aware that Carlisle had rejoined the ranks of the conscious.

"Yes?" Brendan poured a second dose and Carlisle sent it after the first. If this kept on he would soon be feeling no pain at all.

"We've got them, sir—eight men, including their two lookouts, plus that admission of murder by the ringleader. We're only waiting for our military escort to take them off to the Tower; we know there are more than eight involved in the free-trade, and we do not intend to lose these lads to an ambush. Your man here tells me your injury is not serious, but the rest of our work will be strictly routine, and I will be happy to come to your home in the morning to take your statement. I had your gig driven over from where it was hidden in the woods, and I would ..."

Carlisle saved him the trouble. "You would like me to remove my slightly damaged person before I acquire any more damage that could be construed as being your fault."

Berry laughed. "Indeed, sir, you put the words into my mouth. I am very grateful for your part in this, but there is nothing more you need do here and I would prefer to know that you had been seen safely home."

"That will be a consummation devoutly to be wished, Lieutenant," Carlisle agreed. "If Mr. Townsend will drive me—

Matthews, I tied Sailor at the west side of the building, would you fetch him back to the stable?"

"Yes, sir." Matthews would probably have been a more reliable escort in the gig, but although Brendan had been quiet, Carlisle could feel the waves of anxiety coming off his young lover. He wanted to be alone with Brendan for a few minutes, even though he could do no more than hold his hand.

Brendan and the Lieutenant helped Carlisle climb into the gig. He was annoyed by the attention, but as soon as he rose to his feet he realized that the blow on the head, not to mention the generous doses of brandy, had left him slightly unsteady. Swallowing his pride, he permitted Brendan to cosset him… discreetly. He needed that arm around his waist, the strong shoulder under his own good arm. And though he could have managed without it, he was warmed by the knowledge that someone cared for him so much.

Certain that the man he loved was settled securely in the seat beside him and wrapped in the carriage-robe, Brendan snapped the whip and the well-trained Reverie stepped out, shifting the cart into smooth motion.

"I heard that gunshot," Brendan said as soon as they were safely on the road back to the house. He checked himself to keep from pouring out the fear that still tightened his throat, adding only, "I thought you'd been killed."

Philip chuckled. "My dear—my *very* dear boy—it would take more than that to do me in."

Brendan sighed, knowing he must have sounded like a lily-livered civilian. "I suppose the thing that matters is that it did not. What happened? We could barely hear, so far above."

"I maneuvered Bowker into admitting he had killed Jenkins' son. Lieutenant Berry chose that moment to announce his presence. If I had been a trifle more agile in avoiding the bullet, I'd have had no problems. This—" he lifted his left arm—but not, Brendan noticed, very much. "This is nothing."

He guessed there would be no arguing with Philip on this; he could only be glad that the matter was settled, and hope that they would be able to find a way to spend some time together, soon. "Whatever became of Mr. Jenkins?"

"He used his common sense, thank God. I wasn't sure he would. After he'd let me know the cargo was on my land, I told him I'd be calling in the troops and advised him to stow his personal vengeance and let the law handle it. It would have done him no good to be caught in the net tonight."

"If he's as clever as he must be to have escaped all this time," Brendan said, "he is probably meeting a ship somewhere along the coast."

"You are beginning to sound like a Kentish man."

"The place has become surprisingly close to my heart." With only Reverie in harness, Brendan was able to manage the reins with one hand and slip his other into his lover's. "But with all the people you have here… I wonder how we shall ever be able to find some privacy."

"Well, we do have the apple barn. In the spring and summer, you might set up your studio there."

Their fingers laced together, a perfect fit. "Are you certain you'll want me underfoot?" Brendan asked, feeling suddenly reluctant. "This must all be very sudden for you."

"It is, somewhat. But truly… in a way I am but returning to something I left a long time ago. And I do admire your talent, you know. In fact, I hardly expect you will wish to stay rusticated here in Kent when the world begins to recognize your ability."

"Which I might never have thought of developing, if not for you. And you cannot be certain—I may not have the knack for painting."

"Then you will draw. You can do that much, I know. In fact, now that I know what you can do, I would like to commission you to do a series of drawings of my horses. It will give me good reason to keep you close, and I would like to have accurate pen-and-ink records in any case."

"You needn't commission them," Brendan said. "I would gladly do them as a gift." The mental picture was irresistibly alluring. To have nothing to do all day but draw, and exercise Galahad, and study art in a serious way? That would be heaven.

"My boy, you will never have a career if you give away your talent, and a commission is what will give you reason to stay with me," Philip said. "You shall have a room in the house. Perhaps a studio as well; there's an upper room with a northern exposure that would work quite well for that, and the barn is too cold most of the year. Neither of us is an elder son with heirs to worry about—in fact, I am quite devoid of family—and all you will be required to do is what you want to do anyway."

Brendan was uneasy about actually moving into the same house, even out in the country. "What if someone were to find out about us?" he asked, as the cart left the dirt track where it joined the gravel drive to the house. The pale gravel reflected enough light from moon and stars to see by, even between the shadows of beech trees that lined the path.

"Rumor is one thing; established fact is another. Society loves gossip, but it shies away from scandal, and open scandal is what we must avoid. If rumors fly, we may be shunned by the more particular members of polite Society, and I confess I see few disadvantages in that. Never to spend another evening at Almack's, paying off social obligations and disappointing the young ladies desperate to escape their mamas' clutches ... would you find that so painful?"

For all he had wanted this, Brendan was now struck by conscience. "It's not Society that concerns me, Philip. Are you no longer afraid of the law?"

"I am mindful of the law, yes. But this is my own home. If we exercise strictest discretion, there is no reason anyone need ever learn our secret."

"Do you think we can?" Brendan had an uneasy feeling as they neared the house, as though they were being watched; he looked around, but saw no sign of movement.

"To involve the law would require a plaintiff to bring charges," Philip answered, apparently unconcerned. "If we are reasonable and discreet, the chances are slight that anyone would have cause to do so, and I know few men who would call attention to themselves in such a distasteful manner. People would wonder where they got such particular information."

Brendan nodded, feeling foolish. "I must seem a timid creature. Perhaps it is just the memory of the Arbor affair."

"Not at all. Caution is necessary. We shall have to be extremely circumspect. Still, if worse comes to worst, we might move to the Continent."

"And leave this land, and your horses? You would do that for me?"

"Yes… and for myself." Philip smiled. "Horses can travel, you know. Don't look so worried. We are both cautious by nature, I think, and we both realize what is at risk."

"Yes, but—it seems you are giving me everything, and all I can do is say 'thank you.' I wish I were able to give you something in return."

Philip looked at him as though not understanding what he'd said. "Mr. Townsend, if you count youth, beauty and joy as nothing, I can only say I strongly disagree."

Brendan looked away. "That's not the same."

"True enough. One is material security, the other is much rarer, and of immeasurable worth." His thumb stroked the side of Brendan's wrist, a curiously sensual touch. "My father and grandfather gave me the means to enjoy a comfortable life. But it has been a very long time since I was able to share anything more than friendship with another human being. I only hope that when you become famous and spread your wings, I will have the grace to let you go."

Brendan's fingers closed on Philip's without thought. "Never. No, don't shake your head; I've seen what the world holds for men like me—fear, and risk, and stolen moments with strangers. Do you think me fool enough to go back into that world, when I am honored with the regard of such a splendid man?" He could hardly bear to continue, but forced the words out. "It seems far more likely that you will one day tire of my foolish prattle and ask me to leave."

"If you speak that way, I might. My dear boy, you must remember that I am nearly twenty years older than yourself. When you are a man in your full powers, I will be growing old."

"Do you think I *care*? That I am so shallow?"

"No. The loyalty you showed to that reckless young hound tells me you are not." Philip seemed to sense that he was near tears, and changed the subject.

"I think there is one thing you must do when you are established as an artist—develop a reputation for eccentricity. When you are working, you will tolerate no interruption! You will lock your door even to the servants."

"I could do that," Brendan said, slowly seeing the usefulness of such an affectation. "And I might get a small dog, as well—a terrier, perhaps, that would bark if anyone came near, to sound the alarm."

"Or a large dog, to prevent unwelcome intruders."

"Or a bullmastiff, to knock intruders down and sit on them!" Brendan felt almost giddy with relief and happiness. "Or perhaps—"

"*Stop!*"

The warning was unnecessary; Reverie had shied violently as a figure stepped out from behind the last beech in the avenue, a pistol in his hand. Brendan had both hands full keeping the horse from bolting.

The shadow of his hat hid the man's face. "Who are you?" Philip demanded. "What do you want?"

"You know who I am. And I know who you're *not*—you're no relation of young Hillyard's. Not his father, I'm sure, unless his mother was as big a slut as her son. And what I want is what you stole from me, you silk-lined weasel."

Brendan's blood froze. Dobson, of all people. *How did he ever—*

And then he realized how. *That letter from Tony. Of course.* Dobson had gone after Tony, who ran off to hide behind marriage and respectability, after throwing his rescuers to the dogs. He could not even find it in him to be surprised.

"The book was burned," Philip said, his voice perfectly even. "Mr. Hillyard must have told you that."

"He told me that's what you told him," Dobson said. "That's not the same thing, is it?" He sounded drunk, and that worried Brendan more than the pistol. He didn't know the man well enough to anticipate what he might do.

"Perhaps it is not, among your friends. I do what I say I will do. We burned it that same night."

"You *bastard!*" Dobson brought the pistol up, waving it toward Philip, and Brendan wondered for one wild second if he should just urge Reverie to run. But that would do no good; the man was beside the gig now, and at this range he could hardly miss.

"Do you know what you've done? That club was my livelihood!"

"Yes, of course I know. I let your customers see that the trust they placed in you was false, that you might sell them out for a whim. Wasn't it enough that you were well-paid to provide a safe meeting place for men who needed one?"

"A gang of damned sodomites," Dobson spat. "What difference does that make?"

Brendan felt the shred of pity he'd had for the man dissolve to nothingness, and anger let him find his voice. "So your word is good to some men, but not others? I would say that means it's no good at all."

"And what would you know? Not that I meant to blackmail anyone, if Hillyard had only been more sociable about— *Never mind that!* I demand satisfaction!"

"You—" Philip gave a short laugh. "Then ask it of yourself, sir, because you've no one else to blame! Were you not doing well enough without trying to coerce that young fool into risking his reputation and life?"

"Reputation? He has none. He's a merchant's son, same as I am—and it was one of you swells was pushing me—a man who wouldn't take no. But he's above my reach, Mr. Carlisle—*you* are not!"

He aimed the gun, his intention obvious, and Brendan realized the man was paying no attention to him at all. He flicked the carriage whip sideways, sending the weighted tip around Dobson's gun-hand. He heard the man cry out and launched himself out of the carriage and onto the blackmailer. They collided with a surprisingly painful thud and fell to the ground together.

Brendan had never been much of a fighter, but he didn't care. That didn't matter. Philip was hurt; he could not defend himself. The only thing Brendan knew to do was get hold of the gun, or at least Dobson's gun hand, and the only advantage he had was surprise. He got both hands around Dobson's wrist, trying to shake it hard enough to make the pistol fly clear.

No good. He wasn't weak and he wasn't stupid, but his boxing teacher had never taught him gutter-fighting. A head-butt slammed him into brief oblivion; the next thing he knew, steely thumbs were pressing into his windpipe. He couldn't breathe, he could hear the blood throbbing in his head—and then a tremendous sound, a weight fell upon his body—but the pressure on his throat went away. He dropped back, gratefully filling his lungs with huge breaths of air.

"Brendan!"

Philip sounded worried. He tried to answer, made a strange croaking noise, and swallowed painfully. On the second try, he managed, "Yes... one moment…"

He shoved Dobson's lax weight away, rolled to hands and knees and sat back on his heels just in time to see Philip haul himself awkwardly out of the cart. Philip fell to his knees beside him, wrapping his good arm around Brendan's shoulders. "Oh, my boy. Are you all right?"

His throat ached and his head was pounding, but Brendan said, "Yes. Nearly. And you?"

"Well enough. What ever possessed you to take such a chance?"

"He was going to shoot, and you—"

"Had my hand on my pistol." Philip held him close, then released him. "But I'd never have had it out in time. Thank you."

"Is he dead?"

Philip reached over, checking Dobson's throat. "It seems so. And just as well, I think."

"I'm certainly not going to miss him." Brendan heard hoof-beats, approaching fast. "Are you expecting company?"

"They must have heard the shots." Philip darted a look down the drive and spoke quickly. "Listen: neither of us has ever seen this man before. Until someone tells me otherwise, I shall assume that he is another smuggler intending revenge for tonight's arrest."

"I understand."

Philip's smile was bright even in the shadows. "We're even now, you know. I may give you a place to paint, but you've given me my life—if you can endure the company of such a feeble, decrepit old man."

Brendan ran a fleeting hand along the back of the hard thigh conveniently within his reach. "I hope this is an example of your feebleness, sir. I hope to test your stamina… and soon."

They had no time for further speech; Lieutenant Berry and two of his men arrived at a gallop, sorely disappointed to have missed the excitement.

◖e Chapter 19 ◗

The next few days were full of official goings-on, and no time to be alone. Their testimony at the inquest, perfectly truthful in that the dead man had indeed accused Major Carlisle of ruining his business, convinced the coroner's jury that the stranger must have had something to do with the smuggling incident. His London clothes gave rise to speculation that he had been in the area to receive the goods, a notion that the witnesses could neither confirm nor deny.

The smugglers arrested that same night denied any knowledge of him, but, as one of the villagers remarked, what sort of fool would make the case blacker for himself by claiming acquaintance with a would-be murderer? The bruises on Brendan's throat were evidence enough that Carlisle, wounded himself and in no condition for a fistfight, had good and sufficient cause to fire at their attacker. The coroner's jury brought in a verdict of self-defense on the night's second shooting.

In Bowker's case, the man's own confession was enough to have him bound over to the Assizes on a charge of murder, above and beyond the charges of being caught with illicit goods and assault on a gentleman temporarily in His Majesty's service.

When the inquest concluded, Carlisle accepted thanks and a mug of ale from Ezra Jenkins, who had thrown open the Owl's bar after the inquest to celebrate the bittersweet victory. Carlisle got away as quickly as he was able, pleading his obligation as a host; Mr. Townsend had to be sent safely back to London as soon as possible.

Brendan drove the gig out of earshot of the village before asking, "Do you really mean to send me back this afternoon, or did you just wish to get out of the crowd? Is the arm troubling you?"

"It could be better," Philip admitted. "But I do think you should give some thought to going back, at least for a little while. You will need to begin inquiries, find a teacher... obtain books and art supplies, if nothing else."

"You're right, of course." He cast a sidelong glance at his lover. They'd had nothing but a few stolen kisses these past three days, and he was at the point of wondering whether unrequited love had not been better than this ache of longing. "How long would I need to stay away?

Philip met his look. "Until you are ready to come back, of course." His expression softened, and he put his hand on Brendan's thigh. "I know, this is difficult."

"Unbearable," Brendan said. "And you needn't tell me—it is necessary."

"You know it is. I shall follow you to London as soon as I may. It will be easier for us to be private there, with only two servants in residence."

"Their rooms are at some distance from the main bedrooms, then?" Brendan asked. "Though I should have asked that the last time I was there!"

"Oh, they're some distance away." Philip smiled ruefully. "And yes, I do want to be with you there—if for no other reason than to make up for my infamous behavior the last time."

"I apologize for such a clumsy seduction," Brendan said. "I wonder, now, that you did not call me out."

"I wonder that you did not ride out here and shoot me where I stood, after what I did."

"If I could have been so stupid, I'd have needed a second pistol for myself. I would not want to live without you."

"Don't say such things. It makes me want to kiss you here and now, and we dare not."

Brendan thought he could fall into those mutable eyes and

never come out. "Could you not come back to London with me? That long journey, in a closed carriage…"

Philip frowned for a moment, thinking, then nodded. "I believe that might be managed. Now that the inquest is over, I think our official obligations have been met. When we get home I shall send a note to Sir Thomas, just to be certain."

The note explained that Mr. Townsend suggested Major Carlisle return with him to London so that a proper doctor could examine the Major's arm; Major Carlisle omitted mention of the two stitches Matthews had already put in it, as well as the fact that it was healing cleanly.

Sir Thomas Livingstone sent a note back with the stableboy. He confirmed that their presence in Kent was no longer required, and begged the favor of a ride to London so that he might to confer with the court in the matter of the smuggling and murder investigation.

Mr. Townsend exercised true gentlemanly restraint by uttering no more than a single "Damn him!" when privately informed of the change in plans.

Major Carlisle sent a reply that he would be more than happy to offer Sir Thomas a seat in his carriage. The three of them enjoyed an uneventful trip to London, although one of the party was unaware that his presence was regretted by his host and sorely resented by the youngest of the group.

"I have arranged to stay at my club," Sir Thomas said as they began to approach the heart of London. "Would you do me the honor of being my guests at dinner?"

Brendan would have preferred to decline, but knew it was not his decision. "Of course," Philip said. "And I thank you. My cook will have gone home for the day."

"Home?" Livingstone asked.

"Yes." He shrugged deprecatingly. "The arrangements in my town home are slightly unusual. I spend so little time there that I have only my butler and a footman in residence. The cook comes in and prepares meals, then goes back to her own home."

Sir Thomas smiled. "I'll wager the cook is another of your charity projects," he said. "Let me guess—woman of good family in reduced circumstances?"

Philip looked away as if embarrassed at being caught out. "I had an excellent bootmaker," he said. "When he died, yes, his widow was left with several children, including a son who is not yet a master of his trade. They live above the shop, there is no need for me to house them—so you see, the arrangement is not so much charity as it is good value. Mrs. Massie cooks well enough for ordinary purposes, and her two daughters handle the housework under Goodbody's iron rule. If I were to entertain here in town—which I have not done in years—I would try to persuade Mr. Townsend's mother to let me hire her French chef for the occasion. And so, rather than hope for a little cold meat in my own home, I hasten to accept your hospitable offer."

"And you, Mr. Townsend?"

"Certainly, sir, thank you. My family does not expect me at any particular time." Brendan was intrigued at the further glimpse into Philip's character and wondered how his own measured in comparison. He knew that his mother occasionally made arrangements to have the doctor in when a servant was ill, but beyond that he knew little about them—only as much as was useful to himself. That was all that was required, but he thought Philip's active humanity was more admirable.

He wondered if, as an indigent artist, he would be considered one of Philip's charity projects. Not a bad notion, actually, and far better than the truth.

Although Sir Thomas was an agreeable host and the meal far better than a plate of cold meat, Brendan had never found it more difficult to give the appearance of carefree enthusiasm. All he wanted was to be alone with his lover. Such a simple wish—and so apparently impossible to achieve.

Night had fallen by the time they left the club. They were scarcely in the carriage, and the shades drawn, before Brendan was in Philip's arms. "How long must we wait, do you think?" he asked between kisses.

"It is nearly ten now." He slapped Brendan's exploring hand away from his trouser buttons. "*No*, you may not—not here in London! If we ask for hot water for bathing—and you may not need to bathe, but I certainly do—we should be finished by midnight. One in the morning, or perhaps half-past, should be safe enough."

Brendan sighed happily, and let his head rest against Philip's shoulder—the one attached to the uninjured arm. "I do want to bathe. I mean to give you everything tonight, and I should hate to be dirty."

Philip was suddenly still in the darkness. "Everything?" he asked. "Whatever do you mean?"

"You'll see." Brendan slipped his hand behind his lover's head, and pulled him down for another kiss.

After their baths, after a final glass of sherry, Carlisle went to his bedroom and lay on the covers, still wrapped in his dressing gown. Too keyed up to sleep, he watched the moonlight shadows move along the wall until he heard the faint boom of the eight-day clock that stood at the foot of the stair. One a.m. He waited for the quarter-chime, then rose silently, and on cold bare feet left his own room and traversed the silent hall to Brendan's bedroom. He opened the door carefully, soundlessly, and passed into the chamber, closing and bolting the door behind him. The room was dark and silent, and for a moment he thought his lover had fallen asleep.

He turned to leave, and heard a movement from the bed. "Philip?"

"Of course."

There was no answer, only a flurry of movement, and Brendan was in his arms, young and eager and enticingly naked. The touch of his warm skin through the silk sent a thrill through the older man, not all of it physical. To be desired again, so ardently… it was something he had never even hoped for.

But he had no time for reflection; Brendan captured his lips in a slow, teasing kiss that left him gasping. "I thought you'd decided not to come."

"I told you I would," he said, stroking Brendan's slim, muscular back as he might soothe a nervous colt. That intention lasted only as long as it took to reach the smooth curve of his arse. With a gasp, Brendan thrust against him, already fully erect, and captured his mouth again. *Ah, youth!*

He pulled back long enough to catch a breath and say, "Did you think I was so old and feeble that I would fall asleep, with all this waiting for me?"

"Please stop calling yourself old," Brendan said between greedy kisses. "You are perfect."

Carlisle realized that his age was no obstacle to arousal; he was not sure what Brendan had intended in his whispered promise after dinner. *"I mean to give you everything tonight,"* could have any number of interpretations, but he was willing to take whatever he was offered. He shivered as hands slipped up the back of his thighs, kneading and exploring. The belt of his robe was coming undone, and he groaned as his own erect, naked flesh touched its counterpart.

But he did not want this to be another hurried encounter, as their tryst in the apple barn had been. "Let me draw the curtain," he said. "I want to see you."

Brendan obligingly stepped back, and as Carlisle moved the curtain aside his body showed clear and beautiful as a statue even in the half-light of a waxing moon. He was not quite Michaelangelo's David; unlike the statue's, his hands were slender and graceful, and his face far more beautiful. But there was something of the sculptor's art in his stance, relaxed and unselfconscious and innately beautiful. The marks on his throat, covered by his neckcloth in daytime, faded to invisibility in the moonlight.

Then Brendan moved, breaking that illusion of immobility. "Fair's fair," he said, and stepped forward to slide Carlisle's robe from his body. "What, no nightshirt?" he teased, tossing the garment onto a nearby chair. He skimmed a hand down Carlisle's chest, sending a tingle in its wake. "You are so beautiful." Another step, and he was within Carlisle's embrace, rubbing against him like a cat.

Every time they were together, Carlisle was aware of something new. This time it was Brendan's height; he was struck with how pleasant it was to have a lover's body so nearly the same size as his own. And yet... the skin beneath his hands, warm and smooth as raw silk, was strangely not so different from what he remembered from years past—or what he thought he remembered. Strange that it would be so. But the hands exploring his back were far surer and bolder than Lillian's had ever been; this boldness in a lover was very different, and very exciting.

As if reading his mind, Brendan whispered, "I love to touch you," in his ear, and followed the declaration by a line of gentle, biting kisses down the side of his neck.

Carlisle caught his shoulders, pushing him away a tiny bit. "Not so fast, you randy youngster. Tonight it's my turn." He made Brendan turn around, so he could admire his back, running a single finger down his spine and smiling as he felt the shiver that followed. He explored the line and angle of shoulder blade, drawing both hands down his sides from shoulder to hips.

Carlisle could not restrain himself any longer, and pulled Brendan against him, letting his cock ride in the cleft of the young man's arse. *Everything?* He had begun to wonder how it would feel to bury himself in that firm, beautiful flesh. It seemed to him that such a thing must be uncomfortable, and he did not mean to ask for that privilege unless it was offered.

Brendan pushed back against him, and Carlisle reached around, cupping Brendan's hot, rigid cock with his right hand while his left explored his lover's chest. When he found and tweaked a nipple, Brendan trembled and leaned back even harder. "Shall we go to bed?" Carlisle suggested.

"But then we should have to move," Brendan murmured, leaning back to nuzzle Carlisle's ear, "and I am already in Paradise."

"Well, you'll be in Paradise on the floor if you are not careful," Carlisle warned. "My right arm is as strong as I'd like, but the left one is not."

He regretted speaking the moment the words left his lips; Brendan turned from an amorous wanton to a remorseful faun, chivvying his lover over to the bed as though collapse were imminent. "I'm sorry! Would it be better to stop—are you in pain? Shall I—"

Carlisle dammed the torrent with a kiss, pulling him into an embrace that left no doubt of his intentions. He thought of picking Brendan up to demonstrate his fitness, but knew that such a performance was more likely to cause problems than resolve them. If he were twenty years younger he'd have done it… except that if he were twenty again, he'd never have dared this.

The moonlight was bright in the room, and Carlisle considered the risk of someone peeping through the keyhole. Unlikely, but why take the chance? With the bed-curtains drawn on the side visible from the door, they would have perfect privacy. "Let's go to bed," he said.

Once there, with the curtains drawn and only a little moonlight to see by, Carlisle lay back against the pillows with a tremor of uncertainty. This was no spur of the moment decision, abetted by drink; he had brought this young man to his home with serious intent. What they were doing here had meaning; it might be as close as they would ever get to a wedding night "What would you like to do?" he asked. "As we did before, in the barn?"

Brendan reclined beside him, propping his head on one hand. "Yes. Or we might do… I might do what I did that first night." He broke the strangeness of the moment by touching—only a hand on Carlisle's chest, but suddenly the anxiety was gone. He leaned over for another kiss, bringing a leg over Carlisle's thigh. "I want this to be good for you," he said earnestly.

Carlisle laughed and pulled Brendan over to lie upon him. "No fear of that." He leaned back, accepting a deep kiss, stroking down until he could just hold the curve of that lovely arse. The heat and pressure all along his body was wonderful. "I have much to learn. What would you do if I did—*this?* " He squeezed, pulling Brendan's hips close and thrusting up, and Brendan threw his head back with a gasp of pleasure.

The experimentation became much less considered for a time, touch and taste and scent mingling. When Carlisle felt himself on the edge of climax, Brendan pulled back, straddling Carlisle's legs, his cock rising out before him like the prow of a ship. "I want you to take me," Brendan said. "As—as a man takes a woman. Inside me." He ran his hands across Carlisle's chest, leaned down for another kiss.

Carlisle felt his sex stir in agreement with the proposition, but he had to ask, "Have you done this before?"

"No, not—only the other way, with…"

"My dear boy, you can say the name."

"I would rather not. He…found it most pleasant if I was—was the—" He shrugged and sought another kiss, as though for encouragement.

"The active member, as it were?" Carlisle offered. "I think the words may be more difficult than the deed. And I would be honored, so long as it does not cause you pain." In fact he was so hard, and so eager, that it took all his self-discipline not to simply roll the boy over and find release in simple friction, as they had done before. But that would never do. He reached out and took Brendan's cock in his hand. "We needn't jump all the fences tonight. This will do for now."

Brendan's face had gone soft and focused, his body following the movements of Philip's hand. "Oh… But please—I want to give that to you… something important. I've been practicing."

With his other hand, Carlisle reached up to tweak a nipple. This position, this free access to a lover's body, was something entirely new. "How could you do that?" He leaned forward and took the nipple into his mouth, and Brendan thrust forward so suddenly he almost tipped backward.

"It's stupid, you'll laugh."

"No." Carlisle's cock was riding smoothly between Brendan's cheeks, the tip of his cock nudging his lover's balls with every thrust. He was very near to climax, and did not need anything more.

"A candle."

He did laugh, but caught himself immediately. "I'm sorry. But that seems… inadequate, surely?"

"Not a good candle, Philip! One of those big ones, that burn for hours. Bigger than you, so I would know."

"Did you like it?"

"It was … not bad. I put salve in, before you came. Please, Philip. I want to try."

His eyes were very dark, and very sincere, and much as Carlisle loathed the idea of hurting Brendan's body, he knew that for a very young man like Brendan, an injury to the pride would be even worse.

And Carlisle's own cock was so hard that if he did not get some relief soon, he would burst.

"Very well. Raise up."

Brendan rose on his knees, the muscles of his thighs suddenly standing out in relief. A born rider… well, perhaps this was a fence they both needed to take. Carlisle reached between his legs and held his own cock upright. Strange, that his own touch was so much less exciting than his lover's. "Now lower yourself… here, you put it where it needs to go. Slowly, now."

As the tip of Carlisle's cock nudged the hidden opening, Brendan held his breath, tensing. Then he began to breathe again, and slid slowly down, impaling himself.

Carlisle held as still as he could, sliding his hands up Brendan's body until his thumbs caressed the hard little nubs of his nipples. He forced himself to think of his lover's body, rather than his own; the surge of desire was nearly overwhelming and it took all his strength not to throw Brendan down and fuck him with all his strength. This slow, tentative enveloping was torment—sweet as it was, it tested his will as nothing ever had, until at last he was fully inside that hot, tight channel.

Carlisle opened his eyes; he could not remember closing them. The look on Brendan's face resembled an angel or saint enthralled by a mystic vision. "My boy, are you all right?"

"So *hot!*" Brendan whispered. He clutched Carlisle's shoulders. "Philip, please—*touch me!*"

Carlisle took that to mean his cock, and took it in hand again, his left hand resting on Brendan's thigh. He began slowly, feeling that quick pulse and squeeze around his own cock as he pumped Brendan's eager organ. He did his best not to thrust, but the small, intense movements of his lover's body did all that was needed, and as Brendan gave a muted cry and came across his belly, Carlisle felt his own body surge upward in release.

Brendan fell onto his chest, limp and panting, and kissed the side of Carlisle's neck. For a little while, neither of them spoke, and Carlisle began to wonder if Brendan had dozed off.

"Well?" he asked, finally. "Was that…agreeable?"

"Oh. Oh, yes." Brendan rolled to one side, leaving a sudden coldness where he had lain. "I… I think the next time will be better, it was such an unusual sensation."

"Indeed it was, but you please me beyond words when you say 'next time.'"

Brendan smiled. "I know you must go back to your own bed," he said, "but do you think we might rest a little while, and try again?"

"You greedy brat," Carlisle teased. He slid down on the pillow, and pulled the coverlet up over them both. "I think we might. And I promise you—I must indeed go back to my own bed soon, but I will still be here in the morning."

"I never even thought to doubt it," Brendan said.

When Brendan went to the family home the next day, he found his grandmother still ensconced in his room and showing no signs of budging. His mother was delighted that Major Carlisle was so generous with his hospitality, and thought it a good sign that after being in mourning for so long, he was finally coming out of himself a bit. Brendan advised her not to start looking for a wife for the Major, as he was so preoccupied with his horse-breeding that he seemed to have no inclination in a matrimonial direction.

They had a few more nights together, a clandestine honeymoon of sorts. But Philip was not able to stay on in London; there were matters out at Twin Oaks that required his supervision, and he had never intended to be away from the land at this time of year.

"It's for the best," Philip said, closeted with Brendan once more, in his study. "You must begin to find yourself a teacher, and learn what sort of preparation you need to make. I would only be a distraction. And I have work to do, from which you would be a distraction."

"I know," Brendan said. He sighed. "I understand... but right now I would rather be distracted than anything else in the world."

"So would I." Philip put a hand to Brendan's face, tipping it up. "And it will always be this way, my boy. It's the price we must pay."

"You are worth any price," Brendan promised, and opened his lips for a kiss that turned into a long, wistful embrace. "Take care. I shall be back as soon as I possibly can."

"Am I respectable?" Philip asked, straightening his clothing.

"Not a hair out of place. And I?"

Philip regarded him fondly. "A scruffy, charming brat. But you'll pass muster in polite company."

"That's good to hear. I must lunch with Grandmama today."

"Brave lad."

Viscountess Townsend sent for her eldest son after her youngest son set out for Kent. She could see that Brendan was enjoying high spirits, but found it difficult to believe that a box of paints and a few lessons had elevated him to that degree.

James understood her concern, but he was able to set her straight. "Of course he's in high gig, Mama! I don't believe Brendan ever spoke of it to you, but he has been fretting over what to do with himself ever since he came down from Oxford."

"But, really, dear—*painting?* He seems quite taken with the notion, but he never showed the slightest interest when Miss Dennis was instructing the girls."

James laughed. "Of course not. Brendan was never the sort of boy to stay cooped up in the schoolroom. You must remember he was always out in the stable. And what sort of half-hearted boy would condescend to paint pretty pictures of flower-gardens with his sister and her governess? I'd have worried if he'd showed that inclination. He showed me some of his sketches, though, and I have to say they're better than most."

"You think he would succeed, then?"

"Oh, no doubt, Mama—if he applies himself. I can't say I would find any pleasure in spending my days drawing pictures of a bunch of oat-eating brutes, but my brother's been horse-mad since he was big enough to sit astride. And I suppose we must all admit that if a Townsend has to make a career of horses, it's better that he be painting their pictures than currying them or mucking out the stables."

"Nonsense, my dear. Brendan is going to be a *proper* artist. I intend to persuade him to paint a family portrait. Or at least a portrait of your children. I think that would persuade their grandpapa that his son was embarking on a *respectable* career."

James stifled a grin, knowing that it was not his father who required persuading. "Poor Brendan. You'll be lucky if he doesn't put ears and a tail on the infantry."

His mother narrowed her eyes. "I am quite sure that Brendan will see the wisdom in impressing his father with the seriousness of his intentions."

"*Poor* Brendan," James said again.

Some thirty-five miles away, Poor Brendan was stepping out of Major Philip Carlisle's traveling carriage, a fresh supply of pens, ink, and high-quality drawing paper in the case in his hand. By the end of that summer at Twin Oaks, he planned to have a portfolio that would show the range of his abilities. Sketches and pen-and-ink drawings of horses, humans, design details of several cathedrals in London, and the vast panorama of the estate visible from the upper levels of the apple-barn. He was beginning from a point of absolute ignorance; he had much to learn. But now he had someone who believed in him, and that made all the difference. With luck, he would assemble a portfolio that would gain him the attention and instruction of a reputable artist who would take him on as a student.

And if not… If not, then, he'd buy set of paints and teach himself.

Brendan stood at the front entryway as Edward drove the carriage off to the stable. He was about to knock at the door when it opened, and Major Philip Carlisle walked out and smiled at him, and he knew that life could never hold a greater joy.

"Welcome home," Philip said.

ABOUT THE AUTHOR

Lee Rowan has been writing fiction since a first grade teacher explained that made-up stories did not constitute lying. In the intervening decades she has read several thousand books, climbed trees, raised many cats and dogs, married, divorced, worked in a number of boring office jobs, walked on fire, run a business, planted gardens, found and married the love of her life, helped rehab an old house, seen four of the five Great Lakes and both sides of the Atlantic, moved to a foreign country, and is now writing romantic adventures while learning bits of French from the bilingual labels in the grocery store. Visit her website at *www.lee-rowan.net*